CHILDREN OF THE DEAD
A ZOMBIE ANTHOLOGY

EDITED BY
ANTHONY GIANGREGORIO

OTHER LIVING DEAD PRESS BOOKS

MONSTER PARTY
THE TURNING: A STORY OF THE LIVING DEAD
THE DEAD OF SPACE BOOK 1 AND 2
PLAYING GOD: A ZOMBIE NOVEL * THE JUNKYARD
PLANET OF THE DEAD * THE HAUNTED THEATRE
ZOMBIES IN OUR HOMETOWN
NIGHT OF THE WOLF: A WEREWOLF ANTHOLOGY
JUST BEFORE NIGHT: A ZOMBIE ANTHOLOGY
THE BOOK OF HORROR* KNIGHT SYNDROME
THE WAR AGAINST THEM: A ZOMBIE NOVEL
CHILDREN OF THE VOID * DARK DREAMS
BLOOD RAGE & DEAD RAGE (BOOK 1& 2 OF THE RAGE VIRUS SERIES)
DEAD MOURNING: A ZOMBIE HORROR STORY
BOOK OF THE DEAD: A ZOMBIE ANTHOLOGY VOLUME 1-6
LOVE IS DEAD: A ZOMBIE ANTHOLOGY
ETERNAL NIGHT: A VAMPIRE ANTHOLOGY
END OF DAYS: AN APOCALYPTIC ANTHOLOGY VOLUME 1-5
DEAD HOUSE: A ZOMBIE GHOST STORY
THE ZOMBIE IN THE BASEMENT (FOR ALL AGES)
THE LAZARUS CULTURE: A ZOMBIE NOVEL
DEAD WORLDS: UNDEAD STORIES VOLUMES 1-7
FAMILY OF THE DEAD, REVOLUTION OF THE DEAD
RANDY AND WALTER: PORTRAIT OF TWO KILLERS
KINGDOM OF THE DEAD * DEAD HISTORY
THE MONSTER UNDER THE BED * DEAD THINGS
DEAD TALES: SHORT STORIES TO DIE FOR
ROAD KILL: A ZOMBIE TALE * DEADFREEZE * DEADFALL
SOUL EATER * THE DARK * RISE OF THE DEAD
DEAD END: A ZOMBIE NOVEL * VISIONS OF THE DEAD
THE CHRONICLES OF JACK PRIMUS
INSIDE THE PERIMETER: SCAVENGERS OF THE DEAD
BOOK OF CANNIBALS VOLUME 2 * CHRISTMAS IS DEAD…AGAIN
EMAILS OF THE DEAD * BOOK OF CANNIBALS 2: THE HUNGER

THE DEADWATER SERIES

DEADWATER * DEADWATER: Expanded Edition
DEADRAIN * DEADCITY * DEADWAVE * DEAD HARVEST
DEAD UNION * DEAD VALLEY * DEAD TOWN * DEAD GRAVE
DEAD SALVATION * DEAD ARMY (Deadwater series book 10)

CHILDREN OF THE DEAD: A ZOMBIE ANTHOLOGY

Copyright © 2011 Living Dead Press
ISBN Softcover ISBN 13: 978-1-935458-90-6   ISBN 10: 1-935458-90-6
All stories contained in this book have been published with permission from the authors.
All rights reserved. No part of this book may be reproduced or transmitted in any form or by any means, electronic or mechanical, including photocopying, recording, or by any information storage and retrieval system, without permission in writing from the copyright owner.
This is a work of fiction. Names, characters, places and incidents either are the product of the author's imagination or are used fictitiously, and any resemblance to any actual persons, living or dead, events, or locales is entirely coincidental. This book was printed in the United States of America.
For more info on obtaining additional copies of this book, contact: **www.livingdeadpress.com**

Table of Contents

BULLY

KELLY M. HUDSON

Timmy's Dad always told him you had to stand up to bullies. Once you showed them you meant business, they'd more than likely run off. But Timmy reckoned his daddy had never had to stand up to Curtis McGrath and his gang of rejects.

They were the local bad guys, all of whom had failed fourth grade only to have to repeat it, putting them right in the same class as Timmy, and as it turned out, on the very same field trip when the world turned upside down and the dead started living again.

But before that, before the corpses got up and walked again with ravenous hunger, Timmy was standing out by a park bench, his tiny fists balled, his blonde hair mussed, with dirt on his face and tears in his eyes, daring Curtis to take another step towards him.

"Come on, fatso," Timmy said. Behind him, Timmy's best friend Daniel gasped. He and Timmy were small for their age, commonly referred to as runts, but Daniel was the tinier of the two and the more frequently picked-upon by Curtis. So when Timmy made a crack about Curtis being fat—not hefty, not big-boned, but fat—Daniel surely must have thought they were going to be beaten to death.

Not today. Not if Timmy could help it.

"The runt's got a big mouth," Curtis said with a greasy smile to match his greasy hair. "The only big thing on him." He was a large boy, no doubt about it, standing nearly five and a half feet tall and weighing at least a hundred and seventy pounds, and not all of it fat. To Timmy, his fists seemed the size of concrete blocks and the arms backing them up were like pistons. Timmy had been on the receiving end of those fists a couple of times; nothing serious, just punched in the arms and stomach. Curtis was smart enough not to hit any of the kids he picked on in the face because he knew doing so would bring in the adults. And as tough as Curtis thought he was, he certainly didn't think he could measure up to grown-ups. Not yet, at least.

"Why don't you shut it for him?" said Steve, Curtis' right hand man in all matters of bullying. This was the problem with the whole deal: Timmy thought maybe he could take Curtis in a fight, maybe, but that also meant brawling with Steve—another bigger kid with bright red hair and freckles covering his face like leprosy— and the other members of Curtis' gang, namely Tom, Arnold, and Ben. They were all big in their own right. He might be able to get Curtis, but the others would surely whip him good.

"Just maybe I will," Curtis said.

They were in the picnic area just outside of Fort Boonesbor- ough where their field trip had taken them for the day. Most of the kids were over in the sheltered area with the concrete floor and sturdy wooden tables, but some of the more adventurous ones had gone out into the sun and ate at the more rickety, weather-worn tables. They were on their way back to the school, stopping off to eat their sack lunches after a morning spent touring around the

Fort, going into log cabins, seeing the battlements, staring at employees dressed as frontiersmen as they reenacted some of the famous events in the history of the Fort, and getting to run around as much as they could get away with under the watchful eye of Mrs. Anderson, their teacher.

Mrs. Anderson was in her thirties, still young enough to care and think she could make a difference, but old enough and experienced enough to know when the kids were trying to pull a fast one. As it turned out, she was the only one who could step between Timmy and Curtis and possibly save Timmy's rear end.

"You boys stop it right now," Mrs. Anderson called. She got up from the table she was sitting at with some of the students from the third grade and pointed her finger at Curtis. "I've had about enough of your bullying, Curtis Stigers."

"Shove it," Curtis said, apparently having had enough of Mrs. Anderson and her teaching.

Mrs. Anderson's face fell and she was shocked for a moment, just long enough for Curtis to lunge at Timmy and take a swing. Timmy, momentarily stunned by Curtis sassing his teacher, caught the blow full on the chin. Curtis had broken his own rule about punching in the face and Timmy was suffering for it. He fell hard, whacking his head on the side of the picnic table and knocking himself silly. He landed and rolled in the grass a moment, the entire world spinning. He felt like he did when he got on the small spinning ride they had at the park where you could make yourself as dizzy as you wanted. He lay there and watched as the ground tipped up to his right and then back down again to his left. Curtis took the opportunity to kick Timmy a couple of times before Mrs. Anderson reached them and she grabbed Curtis by the scruff of his neck.

"Curtis Stigers! You are in so much trouble right now!" she shrieked.

"Blow it out your ass," Curtis said. Today was the day Curtis thought he was a man, apparently.

Timmy lay on the ground, watching and listening to the events unfold around him, unable to move because of the braining he'd taken. It was all kind of funny, in a weird way, because the ground kept flipping and Timmy was beginning to feel like he was in a movie, watching stuff happen to a character on the big screen.

A shabby man in torn clothing stumbled from the woods, his face ash-gray and his eyes glazed over. A long spool of drool dripped from the corner of his open mouth, one continuous string that ran from the bottom lip to the top of his knee. He seemed to come from nowhere and nobody noticed him except for Timmy, who in his current condition, wasn't sure if the man was real or not.

The man staggered over behind Mrs. Anderson, and before Timmy could cry out and warn her, the man bit her on the neck, like a vampire from the movies. Mrs. Anderson screamed and pulled free, but not before the man tore off a chunk of skin, bright red on one side and pink on the other. Blood squirted through the air from Mrs. Anderson's wound, spraying Tom and Arnold directly in the face. They screeched, the blood pouring into their open mouths, but didn't move as Mrs. Anderson fell to the ground, her left hand clutching her gash, as blood kept jetting between her fingers, the woman bleeding out—she would be dead in less than a minute.

The man grinned and gobbled down the wad from Mrs. Anderson's neck, moaning with pleasure as blood dripped down his chin.

Curtis turned to see this new addition to his day and backed up slowly. Next to him, Tom and Arnold fell to the ground, grabbing their throats as they gagged on the blood they'd swallowed from Mrs. Anderson's.

The man fell on Tom and Arnold, biting them both on the arm, one on the left and the other on the right. They kicked and screamed until they pushed him off and he tumbled to the grass. The shabby man got up and staggered in place for a moment.

"It burns," Arnold managed, before he stopped speaking altogether. He and Tom writhed, their bodies curling up like ants under a magnifying glass, contorting in unnatural positions.

Daniel bent down and helped Timmy to his feet as Steve jumped forward, coming between the man from the woods and Curtis, just as the man was reaching out greedy fingers for Curtis' face.

Steve punched him in the gut twice, both sterling blows, both ineffectual. The man pushed forward, his hands grabbing Steve by the face now instead of reaching for Curtis. His fingers tore into Steve's cheeks, ripping the flesh clean and exposing both cheekbones. Steve screamed and fought hard, kicking and punching, but the man was unrelenting. He had no sooner gobbled down the two clumps of skin before snapping his teeth together and clamping down on Steve's nose. The man gnawed and wrenched his head to the left and the right, tearing Steve's nose off completely. Steve crumpled to the ground, passing out from shock, as blood poured out of his face, pooling at first on the stiff grass and then soaking slowly into the hard ground.

Curtis staggered back a couple of steps, his fists raised, his face disbelieving. Ben, his last friend still standing, took off running in a blind panic. He ran straight into a picnic table, the surface of the wood slamming into his stomach and knocking the wind from him. Ben fell to the side and rolled into a ball, trying desperately to breathe.

The man from the woods dropped on Ben, digging his fingers deep into the boy's stomach, the dead fingers scrabbling at his shirt and the soft flesh beneath until he tore and revealed the treasure beneath. Ben almost immediately stopped squirming when the man yanked out his intestines and stuck a long rope of it into his mouth and started chewing.

The kids over the in sheltered picnic area screamed and ran, heading for the surrounding woods. Daniel, in the meanwhile, had gotten Timmy to his feet but that's about all he could do because Timmy was swerving in place, unable to get his perception back the way it belonged. For him, the world was still turning, although not quite as severe as before. He felt slightly disconnected.

That disconnect shattered when the dead body of Mrs. Anderson suddenly rose from the ground and she hissed loudly. She stumbled to her feet and cast her dead gaze towards the three remaining boys, namely Daniel, Curtis, and Timmy. Next to her, Tom and Arnold had stopped their own thrashing and sat up, dead as road kill but still ambulatory.

Timmy looked around, desperate for a place to hide. His first thought was to run after the other kids, but when he saw them turn from the direction they were headed and back towards the picnic area again, he reckoned something was really wrong.

He was right.

Four adult zombies, in various states of disrepair, shuffled after the children, catching a few at a time and biting their arms, legs, and whatever else they could lay their teeth or hands on. In that briefest of moments, Timmy watched at least ten kids fall to the zombies, with the others close to death as well. Mrs. Anderson, Tom, and Arnold stumbled over after the remaining kids, pinning them between the advancing zombies and those newly reborn. Some kids got away, managing to squirt through the holes of the encroaching creatures, but not many.

Over to the right of Curtis—who still standing stunned—Ben sat up, the man from the woods no longer interested in him. As Ben stood, the contents of his midsection spilled to the ground, splattering wet and thick. The man from the woods stood next to Ben, his face smeared with blood, his throat gagging; he couldn't swallow Ben's intestines. In fact, the greasy red rope sat in the creature's mouth, one open end sticking from between its teeth and dribbling out bits of digested bologna, white bread stained blood red, and potato chips, all parts of Ben's bag lunch.

Timmy watched everything unfold and quickly came up with a plan. He pointed at the table next to the covered picnic area and screamed at Daniel to run for it. They both dashed, hard and fast, leaping up onto the table while dodging between attacking zombies. They jumped up on top and Timmy told Daniel the rest of the plan.

"Let me boost you up so you can climb onto the roof and then you can help me up," he said. Daniel nodded and Timmy noticed his friend was crying. He wasn't gasping and huffing, but tears streamed down his face. Timmy couldn't blame him one bit. Their world had suddenly turned upside down and now it seemed that the fear of being bullied was the last thing on the planet they needed to worry about.

That is, until Curtis caught up with them, jumping on the table to join them. He pushed forward and tried to shove Timmy out of his way. Timmy quickly grabbed Daniel and hoisted him high into the air until the smaller boy could reach the edge of the roof and grab hold. He scrambled up top and looked down at Curtis, who was glowering at Timmy.

"I'm next, asshole," Curtis said. Timmy stepped back. Curtis jumped, grabbed the edge of the roof, and couldn't haul himself up. He landed and shook the table, puffing for breath. "Dammit," he huffed.

Around them, the newly risen dead were shuffling towards their table. Mrs. Anderson was only twenty feet away, with Ben, Steve, Tom and Arnold right behind her. The man from the woods was busy snacking on another fallen child. Mrs. Anderson pointed to the boys on the table and a loud moan rose in her dead throat, rattling like death itself.

Timmy shuddered. They didn't have much time.

He turned to face Curtis and said, "Let me help boost you."

Curtis stared at him, unsure. "Why would you help me?" he asked.

"Because we're going to die if I don't," Timmy said quickly.

Curtis thought it over for a moment and nodded. "Okay," he said. He moved to the side as Timmy knelt next to him and meshed his fingers together.

"On three," Timmy said.

They counted and on three Curtis stepped into Timmy's hands and Timmy simultaneously rose and lifted as Curtis leapt into the air. The bigger boy's fingers found the edge of the roof and then scrabbled over until he was as high as his shoulders. He grunted and kicked at the open air as he tried to pull himself up.

Timmy looked around. Mrs. Anderson and the other kids were only ten feet away now. They moved slow but methodical, honing in on their target and eager to feast. Timmy stared; he couldn't believe what was happening. Somehow the dead were rising, and killing and eating people. The people they killed got up and joined them. It was all like some kind of video game, only he didn't have any guns with unlimited bullets and he only had one life to spare— and it was his.

Up on the roof, Daniel sat down and cried. He buried his face in his hands and shook, his tiny body quivering. Timmy wanted to do the same, but he was stuck on the table, about to be food for his teacher and classmates.

He spun and screamed at Curtis. "Stop kicking!"

Curtis stopped. Timmy slid under Curtis and put his hands on the bottom of his feet then shoved up as hard as he could. Curtis strained and grunted. With one more push, Curtis slid onto the roof.

Mrs. Anderson swiped at Timmy's left leg. He jumped and dodged her but Ben was right next to her, his empty midsection hanging open like a cavity left by a pulled tooth. Ben grabbed his arm but Timmy yanked it away, freeing himself for a brief moment. He looked up at Curtis who was on the roof, staring down at him.

"Help me up!" Timmy yelled.

Curtis turned and crawled away.

Timmy's eyes flickered over to Daniel, but he was no good; the little boy was curled into a ball and sucking his thumb. His eyes were closed and pouring tears.

Dead fingers scratched Timmy's leg. He kicked out, striking Tom in the face. He felt Tom's nose crack from the blow but the boy only stumbled back a step and came lurching towards him again.

Hands fell on Timmy's back and he whirled around to face Arnold, who had somehow managed to climb onto the table. Timmy shoved Arnold in the chest, pushing him back, even as the dead boy tried to bite his hands. Timmy punched Arnold and kept shoving until the small zombie was at the edge of the table. Arnold's teeth snapped open and shut as he leaned forward and tried to bite him again. Timmy hooked one leg behind Arnold's right ankle and shoved. The dead boy tumbled over the end of the picnic table, falling headfirst to the ground. A loud *pop* cracked the air and Timmy watched Arnold's neck and head snap to the side at a ninety-degree angle. The boy thrashed on the ground, only his torso moving; his legs had gone dead forever beneath him.

Timmy turned and saw Mrs. Anderson climb up onto the table between him and the roof of the picnic area.

"Please, Mrs. Anderson," Timmy begged.

The thing in front of him looked like Mrs. Anderson, as if she was really sick, but the only resemblance was on the surface. She bared her bloody teeth and growled. Timmy could see flecks of bloody skin stuck between her once pearl-white teeth. Her eyes were glassy and dead, with no spark of life or awareness other than something a wild, dying animal would show. This was Mrs. Anderson blocking his path, but it really *wasn't* Mrs. Anderson at all.

In a strange way, this realization gave Timmy the strength he wouldn't have had otherwise. He charged her, dipping his head as he ran. He slipped inside her outstretched arms and rammed her with his full weight. He wasn't a big kid, but he was just heavy enough to knock Mrs. Anderson off the table and send her sprawling onto the grass.

The other zombies closed in, climbing up on the picnic table bench-seats and reaching for him.

Timmy looked up. Curtis was gone from sight and Daniel was still curled into a fetal ball, whimpering and slobbering over the thumb in his mouth. Timmy knew he was on his own, there would be no one to save him unless he did it himself.

He backed up to the opposite end of the table, as far as he could manage to go because there was Steve, his hands clawing the wood at Timmy's feet. And next to Steve was Tom and next to Tom was Ben and next to him...

Timmy's lower jaw fell open and he froze with despair. Looking out over the park, he saw the other prone children in his class sit up and stand. Those that couldn't stand or sit rolled onto their bellies and clawed the earth in front of them, crawling towards him. There were at least a dozen of them and they were all bent on killing him and eating his flesh.

Steve groaned and bit Timmy's pants leg, gnashing his teeth but catching only the material of his jeans. It was enough to snap Timmy from his stupor. He kicked Steve in the forehead, jerked his leg free, spun, measured the height of the jump he needed to make, and leaped.

He ran and jumped, and for the briefest of seconds, he was floating in the air. Then he crashed chest-first into the edge of the roof and knocked the wind from his lungs. His hands smacked on the rough shingles and scratched for some kind of hold, but it was for nothing. He slid back, scraping his fingertips and drawing blood. He came to a stop at the edge of the roof, finally managing to get a grip.

Down below, he felt dead fingers and hands grab his legs.

Another set of hands landed on his and Timmy almost screamed until he realized they were warm and full of life, if a bit gross because they were covered with slobber and snot. It was Daniel.

Timmy kicked his legs free of the zombies and used his friend's strength to get up onto the roof. He rolled onto his back, safe for the moment, panting heavily. He looked up at the sky and saw the clouds had turned gray, obscuring the blue and casting a hazy pall over the immediate area. It was a sad sky and it perfectly mirrored the feelings in his heart.

If this was happening here, was it happening everywhere else, too? And if so, were his mom and dad safe? What about his sister, Peggy? She was in daycare while his parents were at work. Was she okay?

The whole thing was overwhelming and he understood now how Daniel felt. He wanted to curl up in a ball and suck his thumb, too.

"Get up, pussy," Curtis said. He was looming over Timmy, staring down at him with a look of utter contempt. "We need to talk."

Despite himself, Timmy clambered to his feet. Curtis put his arm around Timmy's shoulders and guided him to the far side of the roof, away from Daniel. When he spoke, he did so in hushed tones so Daniel couldn't hear him.

"I always thought you had vinegar in your nuts," Curtis said. "You're a wimp, but you stood up to me, which means you got guts. And right now, only guts are gonna get us through this."

Timmy stared at Curtis, unable to say a word.

"These things want to eat us and they're not going away until they do," Curtis said, pointing out over the park area.

He was right. The dozen children had been joined by some straggling adult zombies and they were all looking up at Curtis and Timmy as they spoke.

"What we need to do is create a distraction and then make a run for it. If we get them focused on something else, we can make it to the woods and get away," Curtis said.

Timmy looked around. It was a solid plan. If they could get the zombies to the right side of the roof to gather there, they could jump off the left side and the treeline was only forty yards away. And once they were in the woods, they could lose the zombies, no problem.

"What kind of distraction?" Timmy asked.

Curtis pointed at Daniel.

"We shove him off the side and run for it," Curtis said.

Timmy's heart fell into his stomach. "But he's my friend."

"He's a little baby," Curtis said.

Timmy stared at Curtis, not believing the bully was actually considering it, but one look into his piggish eyes and he could see he was wrong. Not only was Curtis thinking about doing it, he was going to, regardless of what Timmy thought or said.

Curtis, not getting the reaction he wanted, tried a different tact.

"I tell you what," he whispered. "You just go over there and keep him busy and I'll do it. That way, 'cause he's your friend, he won't ever have to know."

Timmy kept staring.

Curtis sighed and his face changed from placid to livid, his skin fiery red and his nostrils flaring as he leaned forward into Timmy. "You do this or I'll beat your ass and throw you over, too," Curtis steamed.

Timmy thought of his dad and his advice on bullying.

"Just stand up to him, son," his dad had told him. "Bullies, they're tough on the surface, but you fight back and you earn their respect. Then they'll leave you alone."

But his father hadn't known anyone like Curtis, and frankly, neither had Timmy until this very moment. Curtis was willing to kill anyone who got in his way and there was no way to stop him or beat him.

Timmy's shoulders slumped. His heart sank. He couldn't see any other way out of this. Daniel was going to have to die. Curtis, not yet sensing he'd won, seized Timmy by the scruff of his shirt and hauled the smaller boy in close.

"I guess it's gonna be you then, huh?" Curtis said, his breath hot and repulsive, like a slaughterhouse in the summer.

Timmy shook his head, finally finding his voice. "No, it's okay. I'll go over and distract him and then you can push him off."

Curtis grinned. "I knew you had stones." He slapped Timmy on the back. "You give me the signal when you're ready."

Timmy nodded.

Daniel called over to them. He was near where they'd crawled up and was looking out over the zombies in the park. "Guys, you better see this," he said.

Timmy trotted over. Curtis hung back, turning to watch in the opposite direction, plotting the escape.

Daniel pointed at the ground when Timmy came over, and what he saw nearly made him throw up. Apparently, a group of their classmates, four boys and two girls, who had made their escape earlier, had stumbled back into the picnic area and fallen victim to the zombies. It must have been quick because Timmy couldn't recall hearing any screams. He wanted to scream right then, but his open mouth only squeaked like a rusty door hinge as he gazed out on the vista of slaughter before his eyes.

The kids had been torn apart. There was an arm here, a leg there. Half of a face was sitting on one of the tables before a zombie scooped it up and slobbered it down. Bloody organs were strewn all about, hanging from the tables and tangled in the grass like bizarre yard ornaments. Timmy saw a set of toes, sitting in the grass as if the foot they belonged to were invisible and still there. Ben staggered over to the digits, kicking them. They rolled through the grass like bloody marbles.

All told, there were close to thirty zombies in the picnic area, all feasting, munching on limbs and other gobs of flesh.

"Good Lord," Timmy gasped.

Curtis coughed and Timmy turned.

"It looks good over here," Curtis said, not so subtly hinting that the coast was clear if they were ready to make a run for it.

Timmy gazed at Daniel, staring at the boy's wispy hair and delicate features. He'd known Daniel for close to a year now. Their family had moved into Timmy's neighborhood in Lexington just two houses down the summer before and it wasn't long before the two found each other. They liked to ride bikes and play card games, which was peculiar because most kids their age were playing video games or watching TV. But they both had strict, old-fashioned parents who kept them away from such things. So they bonded; and later, when the bullying began, it cemented their friendship.

And now here he was, thinking betrayal on his friend. How could he do it? Timmy wondered.

Turning around slow to face Curtis, Timmy felt his arm rise. It was mechanical, as if it was a robot acting out some pre-programmed action. He waved to Curtis and the bully smiled. He came running, full-bore, his fat jiggling and his jowls wiggling.

Curtis moved fast for a big kid and he was on them before Timmy blinked. The bully was only a foot away from Daniel, about to plow into him when Timmy shoved Daniel to the side.

Daniel fell and skidded on the roof, scraping his arm. He cried out and looked up, betrayed, but he fell nowhere close to the edge of the roof.

Curtis tried to slow down. He slid on the roof and his arms flailed but he'd been going too fast for too long and his momentum was sure to carry him over.

Timmy stuck out a foot and tripped the big bully, just to make sure.

Curtis plummeted over the side, head-first. He fell into the crowd of zombies below, screaming bloody murder.

"Good riddance," Timmy said, leaning over the side and spitting on Curtis' thrashing body. "You fat turd."

He watched only for a second as Steve dug his fingers into the bully's face, tearing off a fat cheek and an ear. Curtis squealed as Ben joined the fray, biting his left flabby breast. Tom and Arnold were there, too, and they tore themselves a piece of the big boy to munch on. As did Mrs. Anderson, who apparently found Curtis' hairless testicles quite the treat.

Timmy turned away. He stuck a hand out and helped Daniel up.

"Come on, buddy. We gotta go," Timmy said.

They ran to the opposite end of the roof, saw the way to the woods was clear, and lowered themselves down by hanging off the edge and dropping to the ground. They made a run for it and cleared the distance in no time flat.

Soon they were wandering through the woods, away from the zombies, heading God only knew where, safe at last from the bullies.

A MOTHER'S LOVE

WILLIAM TODD ROSE

The monsters came into the house like a stream of ants attacking a picnic. They shambled through the splintered remains of the door, crowding and pushing, their hands reaching out with fingers that clutched and grasped at empty air. For the most part, the creatures looked like people, like the friends and neighbors Davie Stapleton had known his entire life.

The one in front, for example, could have been Mr. Shockley from the butcher shop. It had the same round belly bulging out against a stained, white apron. The same bushy sideburns and crop of curly, gray hair above eyebrows that looked like two albino wooly worms had made a home on the furrows of his brow.

Only this couldn't be Mr. Shockley.

The monster's face was torn and shredded, the waxen skin flapping in loose ribbons that revealed dark seams of glistening flesh below. Where lips should have been, there was nothing more than a jagged hole that exposed the teeth and gums in an expressionless sneer. Plus, Mr. Shockley would have said something, would have made some little joke about girls which Davie never really understood.

No, that *couldn't* be the neighborhood butcher shouldering his way past something that was shaped like a woman, but looked more like a marshmallow that had been held in the flames of the campfire for too long.

Davie's mother pressed his small face into the side of her yellow dress and cupped her hand over his ears as if she could somehow muffle the screams, explosions, and shots filtering in from the streets outside. But even through her hands, even through Daddy's shouts and the sound of his own heartbeat thudding in Davie's head, the wail of sirens and cries for help invaded their home as thoroughly as the creatures at the door.

"Don't look, Davie, don't look, don't look..." His mother's voice quivered and her face glistened with tears streaming from the corners of her eyes. His arms were wrapped around her and he pressed his face against her thigh so tightly that he could feel the trembling in her legs. It was like an electrical current that coursed into his wet cheeks and it made him want to throw up, almost like that time he'd ridden the merry-go-round after eating half a bag of candy.

Davie's stomach churned and the back of his throat stung as sharply as his eyes and he wanted to listen to Mommy, to simply disappear into the fabric of her dress and be safely hidden within the folds and creases. But somehow, he couldn't turn away. Not entirely. There was something about the monsters that seemed to make it almost impossible to look anywhere else. Maybe it was some sort of magic or evil spell. Whatever the cause, he glanced at them continually from the corner of his eye, watching as they shimmied through a veil of tears, like blurry nightmares emerging from a waterfall.

They had stumbled into the front hall now and Davie's Daddy was running down the stairs, the fire poker raised over his head like a samurai sword, and his voice cracking with a wordless battle cry rattling through his throat. His Daddy looked different, however. His face somehow seemed older and more like the pictures of Davie's Grandpa that hung over the mantle in the living room. His cheeks and forehead were etched with deep wrinkles and his yell pulled his cheeks and chin downward, making them appear to be longer and more angular than what they normally were. But then Davie could only see the back of his Daddy's head as he charged at the crowd of monsters that had burst into their house.

Davie's Mommy screamed Daddy's name as her hands pressed tightly against the sides of his head. It felt like she were crushing his skull and he was sure she wasn't meaning to hurt him, that she didn't realize her clenched fists were pulling his hair or that the sound of terror in her own voice had caused a warm, wet stain to blossom across the front of her little boy's pajamas and trickle down his thighs.

"Charles!"

Davie saw that Daddy was halfway down the steps, when a monster with a ragged stump where the left arm should be, pounced like a cat. It flew through the air with its tattered and ripped clothes, arms stretching out with fingers that were as stained as if the thing had been picking raspberries earlier in the day. At the same time, his daddy swung the fire poker and the metal rod cracked into the thing's head. The little hook on the end of the tool tore a craggy gash across the monster's brow and it thudded to the floor.

"Sons of bitches! Sons of bitches!"

Davie heard Daddy screaming bad words again and again as he swung the poker in an attempt to beat back the creatures that thronged through the door. The metal thudded and whacked against bone and flesh, but they just kept coming. Even the one he'd knocked to the floor had sprung back to its feet, as if it didn't feel any pain from the bloodless slash across its forehead.

Snot bubbled from Davie's nose and he tried to pull away from his mommy as he yelled for his daddy, but she grabbed onto him and pressed his body against her own as he squirmed to be free.

"Daddy!"

The creatures were closing in. They'd formed a ring around his father now and darted forward as he whirled and spun.

"Kathy! The attic!" Davie heard Daddy yelled. He swung the fire poker in wide arcs, and kicked monsters away as their fingers clutched and pulled at his red shirt. *"Now, Kathy!"*

But, for some reason, Davie's Mommy didn't move. It was almost as if she was as much a part of the stairway as the wooden banisters and scarred handrail. All she could do was hold her little boy and scream her husband's name in a shrill screech.

Davie saw that Daddy had started backing away, as if he were making a retreat for the stairs, when one of the monsters leapt in a blur of movement. He scrambled backward as he thrust the poker like a spear into the monster. The sharpened end plunged into the thing's right eye, but even that didn't stop it. It continued clawing at Daddy's clothes until he grimaced and rammed the tool even further into a socket that now leaked a thick goo down the monster's face. For a moment, the thing twitched like Davie's friend from school, Sally Peterson, when she was having one of her epileptic fits, but then its body slumped to the floor as if whatever magic that had possessed it was suddenly and inexplicably gone.

As the thing fell, Davie saw Daddy try to pull the fire poker back out, but the little hook must have got caught on something within the creature's skull. He yanked with both hands and cussed so loudly that the word turned into a meaningless sound of frustration and rage. But his weapon was firmly embedded into the monster and, as it fell, the weight of its body yanked the iron rod from his hands. It jutted out of the fallen creature's eye like a dark flagpole and Davie saw Daddy was swinging his fists now, punching and kicking and head-butting as the ring of monsters closed in around him.

And then all Davie could see was a glimpse of his father's arm jutting through the wall of bodies engulfing him. His screams caused Davie's Mommy to fall to her knees and bright spurts of blood splattered against the family portrait by the bookshelf. Davie could feel Mommy shivering and trembling and he could feel the hitches of her sobs against his body; but he felt numb now, kind of like when he'd sit in front of the TV for too long and his legs would fall asleep. Only this tingling sensation seemed to burrow deep down inside him, into the bones and organs of his body, into the dark and secret places that no other living soul would know existed. Davie's tears were cool against his hot face and everything taking place at the bottom of the stairs seemed like something from one of the movies he wasn't allowed to watch, not something that was really happening, not something real. There was too much blood. People didn't really have that much blood in them, *couldn't* have; it had to be a nightmare, something he'd awake from in the darkness of his room. His daddy would always bring him a glass of water and tell him how monsters were nothing more than shadows and imagination, that there was nothing to be afraid of under the bed or in the closet or...

Davie realized his mother was shaking him by the shoulders so roughly that his teeth clacked against one another. He blinked several times and tried to focus on her blue eyes, the round and dark pupils, on the words tumbling out of her quivering lips.

"Run, Davie! *Run*!" she shouted.

His father had stopped screaming at some point and the monsters' heads had all snapped toward the stairs, as if noticing the woman and little boy crouched upon them for the first time. For one moment in time, that instant seemed to stretch into eternity. Davie watched the creatures hunker over Daddy's torn and motionless body with blood-streaked faces and unblinking eyes. They peered at Davie as if they could somehow see all the plump and juicy guts hidden within his too frail flesh. But there faces were blank; they didn't look hungry or even angry, they were simply as expressionless as the carpet beneath their feet.

"*Now! The attic*!" She yelled.

He felt his mommy's hands shove him toward the top of the stairs as she pulled him to his feet at the same time. The flurry of movement seemed to break through whatever paralysis had momentarily possessed the monsters and they rushed toward the staircase, scrambling over one another in a tangled cluster of arms and legs.

Davie took the stairs as fast as his legs could carry him, but his muscles felt like cooked spaghetti and he kept hoping to hear his father's voice boom out, "*Leave them alone*!" But there was nothing but his mother's labored sobs, the creak and pop of wood, and the thudding of feet against steps.

Davie's Mommy kept shoving his back, as if she could somehow make him run faster, and the top of the stairs seemed further away than it had ever been. It was as if it were somehow growing longer, expanding five steps for every two that he covered, and he was crying again.

"*Go, go, go!*" she yelled.

The staircase wobbled and shook and he knew the monsters were almost there, that the things had almost caught them, and that what happened to his father would happen to him and Mommy, too.

"Run, baby, run!" she begged.

Davie finally reached the top of the stairs and spun around to make sure his mommy was still with him, that she was still there, still safe.

He saw her pale face inches away and her hair was all messed up and stringy, as if she'd just gotten out of bed. Her face looked longer than it normally did, kind of like when his father first started to attack the monsters. Her nostrils flared wide with each snort of breath that gusted through them.

Just over her shoulder, a face appeared. It was like something that had been clawed by a large and viscous animal, criss-crossed by scratches and gouges with one eyelid dangling from its brow by thin strands of tissue. A hole in the side of its face revealed a glimpse of a pink and swollen tongue. Ribbons of flesh flapped from the wound and dangled over the corner of lips that were pale and wrinkled. The thing's teeth gnashed and chewed at these strands of flesh, pulling them away from its face with a sound resembling the ripping of wet fabric.

Davie screamed and his mother whirled around, pushing out with her hands at the same time. The thing tumbled backward and fell into the crowd pressing in at its back, toppling all of them over like pins at the bowling alley. The ones furthest away tried to climb over the writhing knot of bodies, but they were already grasping at the railing. Then they were pulling themselves back up, scrambling and crawling up the stairs, dragging their twisted, broken bodies closer and closer to the little boy and his mother.

"*Damn it, Davie!*" she screamed. Then his mommy was running toward the top of the stairs again and Davie knew he had to run, too. They had to make it to the attic and lock themselves inside, where the monsters wouldn't be able to get to them, just like his daddy had told them to do just before the creatures had broken through the front door. But just as he was about to dart down the hall, he saw his mommy fall. Her chin hit the top step and he felt the thud travel through the floor and up into the soles of his feet.

"*Save yourself, baby, run,*" she said through a mouthful of blood.

One of the monsters had its hand wrapped around her ankle and she kicked with her feet like Davie's Cousin Brittany did when throwing a tantrum. He saw Mommy's sandals pound into the creature's face as her fingers clawed at the hallway carpet, as if she were trying to pull her way toward the yellow umbrella Daddy had told him again and again to get out of the hall and put in his room.

The other creatures almost seemed to be fighting with each other and for a second Davie felt hope flutter within his stomach. Maybe they were turning on each other, maybe they would fight it out until none of them were left and he and Mommy would be safe and all the monsters would be gone. They would all rip one another apart and then he and Mommy could call 9-1-1 and the ambulance would come and they would save Daddy just like they always did on television.

But then it dawned on him. They weren't wrestling each other; they were struggling to get to Mommy, to reach her before she could free herself. They would swarm over her just like they'd done with Daddy and then...

Davie found himself moving across the hall and it almost seemed as if he were sitting in the back of his head somewhere, watching as someone else controlled his body. He saw his small hand wrap around the handle of the umbrella, felt his feet carrying him toward his mother's thrashing body. Her screams sounded muffled and distant, almost like he had cotton stuffed in his ears, and an image of his father flitted through his mind; it was right before the monsters had gotten him, when he'd killed one of them with the fire poker.

The creature that gripped his mommy's ankle had its face buried into her calf and it jerked its head away, revealing a large chunk of what looked like pink rubber clenched in its teeth. And Davie saw there was a hole on Mommy's leg that hadn't been there before. Blood pooled up within the ravaged flesh, pulsed and throbbed as it streamed down the sides and spurted with each kick.

Davie jabbed the metal tip of the umbrella forward, just like his daddy had done with the poker, and it sank into the creature's eye. If it felt any pain, it didn't show it, but simply continued chewing on the flesh within its mouth even as Davie threw himself forward with all of his weight.

The umbrella sank further into the creature's head and there was a squish and pop that Davie could feel more than hear. The creature fell backward, thumping down the stairs and tripping the ones that had made it back to their feet. It was like a line of dominoes falling as each monster crashed into the one behind it.

Davie's Mommy was on her feet and she wrapped her arms around him, continuing to push him forward as she limped down the hallway. Blood oozed from the wound on her leg, weaving a trail of bright crimson splotches against the beige carpet, and a small line leaked down her chin. She'd bitten her lip upon falling.

"We won't make it. The bathroom, baby! Get to the *bathroom!*"

Davie darted into the bathroom as his mother hobbled behind him. Though he couldn't see them, Davie could hear the monsters in the hallway now, their feet padding against the carpet as they charged toward him and his mother.

She slammed the door closed just as something thumped heavily against the other side with enough force to shove his mommy backward. For a moment it seemed as if the door were about to fly open. He could see clothing through the gap between it and the wall: the torn sleeve of a flannel shirt, and a blood-spattered apron. But then he saw Mommy drive her shoulder into the door and it slammed shut.

As her hands fumbled with the lock, the things on the other side began pounding and scratching. They hit the wood hard enough to make it look as though the door were bulging inward, as if it were only seconds away from exploding amid a shower of wooden shards and splinters.

Davie sank to the floor and pressed his face against the cool tiles as his mommy ran to his side. She dropped to her knees and scooped him into her arms, pressing his face into her shoulder, allowing his tears and snot to seep into her dress. Stroking his hair, she rocked back and forth and whispered to her little boy.

"Shhhh, it's okay, honey. Everything's going to be okay."

He didn't want to look at the wound on her leg. In fact, he wanted nothing more than to squeeze his eyes closed until everything went away, until the hammering on the bathroom door stopped and his daddy came in with a smile and told him it was time for dinner. And after dinner, he would go outside and play. Maybe he would see if his friend Tommy Gibson—who lived across the street—wanted to go to the playground and he would get so dirty that he'd be forced to take another bath before he was tucked in for the night. But for some reason, he couldn't tear his eyes from the blood that gurgled out of Mommy's wound. It looked so dark against her pale skin and there was so much; it just seemed to keep coming and coming. It flowed down the side of her leg and spread across the white tiles, the puddle growing larger with each passing second.

"Shhhh, it's all right." His mommy trembled as if she'd gone outside and forgot her jacket, and even though she kept telling him that everything was going to be fine, he knew it wasn't. He could hear the strain in her voice, the fear and pain that made her stutter, and feel the way her muscles tensed when the bite flared in agony.

The door shook and rattled and he saw fingers reach in through the one inch crack between the door and the floor, as if one of the monsters were lying down and trying to flatten itself to the point it could slip under the door like a sheet of paper.

He saw his Mommy look at the bite on her leg and choke back a sob. Her eyes then flittered to the bathroom door. Sharp snaps filled the room, cutting through even the sound of Davie's crying, and the wood on the door was beginning to look as if long cracks were beginning to appear, like fault lines in the crust of the earth.

"Oh, my baby, my sweet baby boy."

She was looking at the stand across from the toilet now, taking in the stacked rolls of toilet paper, the hairspray and bars of soap.

Something about the plastic shopping bag on the bottom shelf seemed to catch her attention, almost as if she were wondering exactly what it was doing there. But then she shook her head like a dog flinging off water and hugged Davie so tightly he had to squirm in her arms just to take a breath.

And still the things kept throwing themselves against the door.

Why didn't they just go away and leave them alone? Why couldn't things go back to the way they had been before?

Mommy's eyes flitted between the bathroom stand and the hinges on the door. The little pins were shaking so badly that while he and his mommy watched, they were inching their way out of the slots holding them. At the same time, the wood around the frame had begun to bow. This was just how the front door had looked before the monsters had broken it down and Davie knew what would happen once the creatures battered it in.

His mommy placed her hands on his cheeks and made him look into her eyes.

"Do...do you trust me, baby?" she asked.

He nodded his head so vigorously that snot flung from his nose and splattered against the side of her face. She didn't seem to mind, and started caressing his face as tears streamed down her cheeks.

"I love you so very, *very* much. You were the best thing to ever happen to me, you know that? You changed my life, honey."

She was crying so hard that Davie could barely make out the words and he had to bite his bottom lip to keep himself from crying even harder, too.

"I...I got bit, sweetie. That's not good, not good at all. Even if those things don't get in here, it's only a matter of time be-fore...before I...before..." She collapsed against his chest, pressing her face against his t-shirt as sobs overtook her words.

"Trust me, okay, Davie? I never want to hurt you. I never want..."

Loud pops resounded from the door and the pounding was so loud now that it nearly drowned out his mommy's whisper.

"I'm sorry, sweetie. I'm so, so sorry..."

She pulled herself away from him and took a deep breath through her nose. Turning, her hand reached toward the bathroom stand but stopped halfway, as if unsure of whether or not she had the necessary strength within her quivering arm. But then, with a low moan, she continued and snatched away her prize.

"I'm gonna send you somewhere safe, okay, sweetie? Somewhere they'll never be able to get you, okay? A place where I'll never be able to hurt you..." She broke down into sobs again, then wiped the tears away from her face with the back of her hand. "I love you, Davie. Don't you ever forget that."

The thumping on the door and the cracking of wood masked the rattling sound within the bathroom. Davie's heart raced within his chest and he wanted to ask his mommy what she was doing, why she was tying the plastic bag so tightly on his head and to let her know that it hurt his neck as she squeezed, but another part of him knew he had to trust her.

She cradled him in her lap and held his wrists as she rocked back and forth. Her strained voice tried to sing *You Are My Sunshine*, but the words blurted out in spurts that were punctuated by moans and sobbing.

"Just go to sleep, honey. Go to sleep, now."

With the plastic bag tied around his head, Davie could barely hear the shattering of wood from the holes that were beginning to appear in the bathroom door and his mommy's voice was nothing more than a low murmur.

"I love you, honey. Be safe. Be safe, be safe. Be safe..."

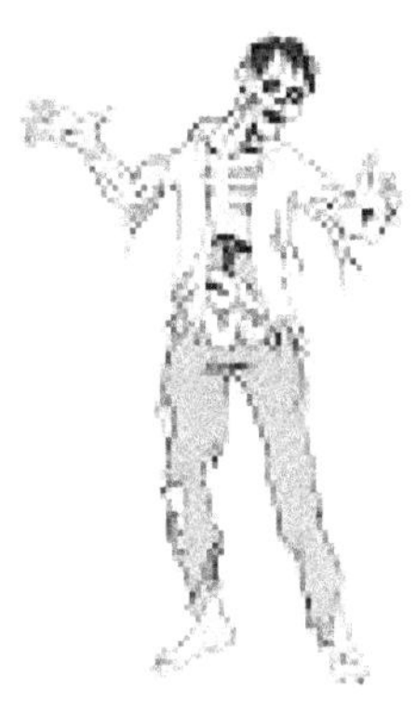

THE HOLE

ANTHONY GIANGREGORIO

"You wanna see something really gross?"

When Timmy heard those words, two things went through his mind. One, Josh was fucking with him again or two, he was in one of his rare moods when he considered Timmy a friend.

Those six words could either bode extremely well, or could end up with Timmy's sneakers hanging on the telephone line by their laces; the clean white-only two week old- sneakers swinging back and forth lazily, never to be returned to the earth again.

Timmy weighed his reply to Josh, knowing the simple words he could say would result in the former event.

Then with a sigh and a breath, both similar to how a cliff diver looks before taking that leap, he said, "Sure, I guess."

Three simple words spoken quickly and succinctly; three words weighed carefully and then phrased with a slight shrug to the shoulders.

Josh grinned. It wasn't an evil grin, like the one he flashed Timmy before he yanked his shorts down last month in gym class. There, Timmy had stood in his tighty-whities, for the entire fifth grade class to see. He just thanked God he had been *wearing* underwear at all.

Timmy looked at that grin, the not so evil grin that was more *malicious*—no, wait—malevolent was the better word to describe the visage of Josh the Bully, Josh the Torturer and Josh the Punisher. But despite being all these things, Timmy still idolized Josh.

See, Josh was in the seventh grade. He had stayed back twice, so he was the oldest kid in his class. He had wavy brown hair that all the girls loved and he wore a wallet—black leather—with a chain on it.

Timmy thought that was the coolest thing ever. An actual chain hung from the back of Josh's pocket and trailed up to his belt loop on his hip. Add that to his all black wardrobe, a t-shirt with some heavy metal rock band on the front, and Josh was the poster child for an American bad boy.

"Good," Josh grinned so wide his teeth peered through his lips. "I knew you weren't that big of a pussy. Come on, follow me." He turned and began walking, Timmy following like an obedient lap dog.

The two boys walked down the street of their neighborhood, past the gas station, a 7-11, and a Laundromat until Josh reached the end of the street. The dead end sign with its dents from rocks, leered over them like a cross adult. Josh entered the woods lining the road.

He glanced over his shoulder just once to make sure Timmy was still behind him. Timmy was, though the deeper they penetrated the thick forest, Timmy began to have second thoughts. Was

Josh going to do something to him once they were so deep in the woods no one would hear him scream?

To make matters worse, Josh glanced over his shoulder as he climbed over a fallen tree and the look in the older boy's eyes gave Timmy the chills.

"Come on, it's not much further," Josh said and continued on.

Timmy scurried over the fallen tree and picked up his pace to keep up. Glancing over his shoulder, he found he was so deep in the woods he could no longer see the dead end sign. All around him the trees leaned inward, their branches stretching outward to pull him close, holding him tightly so he could never escape.

It's a trap! his inner voice screamed. *Get out of there*!

He was about to do that—turn and run—when Josh crested a slight incline and stopped walking.

"We're here," he said, huffing and puffing from the exertion. Timmy wondered if his shortness of breath was due to all the cigarettes he smoked. If Timmy was correct, Josh sucked in a pack a day at least.

"Come here, take a look at this shit," Josh said.

Hesitantly, he ascended the slight incline and stood next to Josh. Timmy looked down where Josh was pointing, the bully's legs spread wide to prevent him from falling. Timmy's mouth fell open and he let out a silent gasp of shock and surprise.

There was a large hole at the bottom of the incline. It reminded Timmy of a bear trap. He could see the branches and leaves on the sides of the hole, residue from when *something* had fallen through and into the camouflaged trap beneath.

Timmy thought the word *something* was the best description to describe the occupant of the hole. It had once been a woman—he was sure of it—but that was only because of the tattered, muck encrusted skirt the occupant of the hole wore. Her lips were gone, leaving her visage a rictus grin that would never fade. The meat on her left cheek was missing, maggots squirming about the jagged wound, some losing purchase to fall to the ground. Her left eye was punctured, looking for all purposes like a deflated condom, the milky white pus dripping from the socket nothing more than expelled semen.

As Timmy stepped up to the hole, the zombie howled, the dead woman's moan filled with—what Timmy believed—was sorrow, loss and pain.

"Who is she?" Timmy asked as he stared at the walking corpse.

"Don't know," Josh replied. "But she's the first zombie I've seen since all the shit began to happen."

Timmy nodded, understanding completely.

The dead recently had begun to walk a little more than a week ago. Morgues, hospitals and nursing homes were the major hot spots for this bizarre phenomenon. No one knew why and so far the walking corpses had been easy to contain. But Timmy's dad said things were going to get worse real soon. As the news reports kept filtering in. It was clear to most people that whatever was happening was growing each day.

"What are you gonna do with her?" Timmy asked as he stared at the grisly face. Even though the face was filled with rot, Timmy could still see that when the woman was alive, she had been pretty.

"It's not what I'm going to do with her," Josh said, his voice cold and cruel. "It's what you're gonna do with her."

And with the words barely out of his mouth, Josh leaned forward until he was right behind Timmy and he pushed him into the hole.

Timmy let out a cry of surprise to find himself tumbling forward. He went head first, tucking his head in at the last second, and landing more on his shoulders and back. With the breath whooshing from his lungs like a spent balloon, he fell to his side, laying still, his vision flashing white from the impact.

"Let's see if she's hungry!" Josh laughed as he knelt down to look into the hole.

Slowly, Timmy came back to his senses. The first thing he saw were the dirt walls of the hole. Earthworms were squirming out of the walls, and twigs and rocks dotted the surface. The smell of garbage that had been left out in the sun for too long assaulted his olfactory senses, the aroma hanging on his tongue, causing him to gag.

The zombie had soiled herself at some point, the dry rivulets of shit, looking like streaks of mud, ran down her legs. Timmy could see small holes in her legs, and tiny white maggots crawling out.

The zombie's skin undulated as the maggots wiggled beneath the surface, as if they were miniscule prisoners trying to break free.

He craned his neck back to look at her—this dead woman, this *abomination*–and his mouth fell open in terror. He'd heard the stories of what his dad had said.

"The dead were eating the living…"

He knew he was dead, that there was no way to escape. The hole was six feet deep, the walls of soft dirt and clay. There was no way he could climb out. And even if there was, as he struggled to break free, the zombie would be on him, tearing at his flesh, consuming him.

But despite this, Timmy still tried to climb out. His hands dug into the soft earth, the soil falling to the bottom of the hole, some spraying into his face. He spit out what went in his mouth and blinked to clear his vision.

Frantic and panicking, his breath came in short gasps and his hair stood up on the back of his neck as he anticipated feeling the cold hands grasping him, followed by the feel of teeth sinking into his tender flesh.

Minutes passed, and as he scraped at the wall like a dog digging up a bone, he slowed his actions, realizing if he was going to be attacked and eaten, it should have happened by now.

Finally, he stopped trying to climb out. The dirt was piled at his feet, covering them, and he slowly turned around. The zombie was still there, but the dead woman was immobile. She was just standing there, looking at him. No more than a foot away, she could kill him instantly if she wanted to.

Timmy waited for the end, closing his eyes so he didn't have to see it coming.

Seconds passed then…

"Come on, you stupid fuck! Kill him already!"

Timmy opened his eyes and looked up to see Josh standing right at the edge of the hole. The tips of his sneakers were an inch over the edge and he was leaning over with a five foot stick in his hands.

As he poked the zombie, he yelled at it.

"What the fuck are you waiting for? Eat him!"

Josh poked the dead woman in the right shoulder, the tip of the stick penetrating the soft, rancid flesh. Black, congealed blood oozed out. A few maggots were set free and they fell to the churned earth to wiggle and squirm.

Timmy said nothing as he watched Josh beat the zombie. He was still too scared to move, but though frightened, deep down inside, he realized Josh was doing something far worse to him than the other times.

This time Josh was trying to kill him.

Josh whacked the zombie in the head, causing one of her ears to fall off. She moaned loudly and Josh raised the stick again.

"Come on. What the hell are you doing?" Josh yelled, the stick raised above his head, ready to plop the dead woman on the top of her mop of a hairdo.

Before Josh could bring the stick down—all the way down—the zombie did something both Josh and Timmy never expected.

The dead woman raised her left arm and with her hand open wide, she caught the stick as it careened toward her head. The bones in her hand snapped and cracked as the weight and force of the stick destroyed brittle bones.

"What the fuck?" Josh grunted as the stick struck dry flesh.

But the dead woman wasn't finished, and she walked across the few feet to reach Josh rather quickly and stretched out her right hand and wrapped her fingers around Josh's right ankle. She was missing her pinky finger above the knuckle, but it didn't seem to matter.

"Hey!" Josh screamed as the cold hand contacted the warm skin of his ankle.

With a jerk of her arm, the zombie yanked Josh's leg out from under him and he found himself in the air. He landed on the ground hard, knocking the air from his lungs, and as he tried to focus and clear his head, he found himself being dragged into the hole.

He landed heavily, dirt cascading over his face and chest, and as he tried to blink the dirt clear of his eyes, he waved his hands in the air.

As his vision cleared, he spit dirt, and the first thing he saw was the zombie as she leaned over and sank her teeth into his neck, just below his chin. His jugular was severed in an instant and he felt warm blood splashing onto his chest—his blood! The zombie began to slurp and chew and Josh found himself trapped beneath her.

Timmy stared in horror, feeling a trickle of urine seep down his leg, he was so scared.

And as Josh's arms waved and he yelled for help, his screams quickly becoming a gurgle, Timmy snapped out of his fear and saw his chance to escape.

With a yell of his own to gather his courage, he ran at the zombie and Josh, then jumped up. Using Josh's left shoulder as a step, he was now able to reach the edge of the hole, and he leaped up, catching the edge and then kicking his legs to push himself out. There was a moment when he didn't think he was going to make it, but then his right sneaker found purchase and he was scooting over the edge.

He spun around and peered down into the hole. Josh wasn't moving anymore, the zombie feeding on his neck, chewing and tearing, the skin stretching like elastic before it would snap off in a spray of blood. Timmy stared down with an impassive face as he looked into Josh's glazed-over eyes. He'd never seen a dead kid before and he didn't know exactly how to feel about it.

Not knowing what to do, and realizing he was now safe, Timmy sat down at the edge of the hole. The zombie continued feeding for the next three minutes and then stopped. Timmy leaned forward, expecting something to happen. If the news had been correct, he knew exactly what would happen next and he was curious to see if it was true.

Timmy didn't move, didn't breathe, as he watched Josh's corpse. The dead woman, still chewing on a piece of flesh, seemed not to care about Josh anymore, as if as soon as he was dead, he wasn't appetizing.

And then it happened, just like the news said.

The fingers on Josh's right hand began to twitch and soon the entire arm was moving. Timmy watched Josh as he moved his head, trying to turn it left and right. But with half his neck missing, this wasn't all but impossible.

With a gurgle-like moan, Josh tried to stand up. At first he couldn't do it but after a few more tries he managed it.

"Whoa," Timmy said, his voice cracked and dry.

Josh heard him and his body turned to face Timmy who stood up and backed away from the edge. He felt his stomach turning upside down in fear once more. If Josh was bad before, as a zombie he would be ten times worse.

Josh's eyes locked on Timmy and the newly revived ghoul tried to get at him. But as Timmy had done before, Josh couldn't escape the hole. As he tried to climb, all he did was pull dirt onto him.

As Timmy watched, he realized he was safe and he scooted closer.

The dead woman did nothing, just stood in the corner and stared at the bottom of the hole, while chewing on the last remnant of flesh in her mouth.

Timmy moved as close as he dared and gazed down at Josh. Then he looked at the woman zombie and said, "Thank you."

The dead woman looked up at him but didn't respond. How could she? She was dead.

Timmy watched Josh as he tried to escape the hole, the same one he'd thrown Timmy in only minutes before, and Timmy's face grew hard, his eyes taking on a coldness never seen before.

His mouth went up into a slight smile and he spit into the hole, the wad of saliva landing on Josh's upturned face. Timmy kicked at the edge, splattering dirt into Josh's face. Particles went into Josh's eyes but the dead bully didn't care. He opened his mouth and groaned and Timmy kicked dirt into it.

Timmy stopped kicking and merely stood there, watching the dead boy, understanding Josh had wanted the same fate to happen to him.

But it hadn't.

For some reason, the woman zombie hadn't wanted him, she had wanted Josh. Could it be that there had been some small memory inside her dead brain? Maybe she wanted the person who had thrown her into the hole, some sort of revenge?

Timmy didn't care. It was over.

Turning, he walked away from the hole, leaving the two zombies there forever as far as he was concerned.

He was going home.

He needed a shower.

NIGHT OF THE BABYSITTER

BILLY BURGESS

"They're all asleep," Julia Pearson said into the cell phone. "You can come over now, but don't use the front door. I do not want the neighbors seeing you. Use the backdoor. I left it unlocked."

"No problem. I only live a couple of streets over. I'll be over as soon as my Aunt shows up to baby-sit my sister. She's been sick all afternoon," Dean said.

"What's wrong with her?"

"She's caught the flu or something. It is nothing to worry about. I'll be over soon." He hung up.

Julia turned off the phone. Her mouth dropped open when she saw what was on the television screen, besides the glowing, green word MUTE.

Emergency Alert System
This is not a test.
Please take shelter in a basement or safe house.
Do not go outside for any reason.

Julia grabbed the remote and scanned the other channels. There was nothing else on except for the alert.

A loud siren blared from outside.

"What is that? A tornado warning?" a nine-year-old boy said from behind her.

"Brian, what are you doing up at this time of night?" Julia asked.

"I couldn't sleep. Is there a tornado?" Brian asked.

Julia pointed the remote and the television clicked off. She turned her attention to the boy.

"I don't think so." She moved from the sofa to the window and pulled back the curtains. She was shocked to see that the August sky had a fuzzy orange tint to it. *Maybe it is from the storm earlier today*, she thought.

Her heart pounded, as seven army trucks drove down the street. Dozens of soldiers followed on foot. They all carried automatic rifles.

"Go wake your sister."

"Is something wrong? Is it a tornado?" Brian asked.

"Just go get your sister, now." Julia raised her voice.

Brian's eyes became wide and he ran upstairs. Julia walked to the front door and locked it. She turned her cell on and dialed John's number. It rang six times. There was no answer.

She pulled out a note from her pocket.

Written at the top of the note in red ink was, *Emergency Numbers*.

She dialed another number. It rang and rang. There was no answer. She waited for the voice mail and left a message.

"Mr. and Mrs. Bailey, the emergency sirens are blasting outside. I'm taking the kids to the basement."

She turned off the phone as Brian and Heather came down the stairs.

Heather was five and clutched her Hannah Montana doll.

"Let's go to the basement," she told them.

"Is it a tornado?" Brian asked.

"No."

"Has aliens invaded?" Heather asked.

"Don't be silly. There are no such things as aliens. Now, let's go."

Julia led the way into the kitchen. To the right was a red door. She flipped on a light switch and pulled it open.

"Great, "Julia said. There was almost two feet of water in the basement.

"It fills up with water when it rains, and it's been raining all week," Brian informed her.

"Thanks for the update, Brian."

"Let's go over to the neighbors, maybe they'll let us stay in their basement till this is all over." Julia grabbed their hands, and they walked outside into the humid evening air. It was completely dark, except for the streetlights shining down onto the street.

Three men and four women staggered down the street in a loose group. They grunted and turned their pale faces towards Julia and the kids, eliciting loud moans.

"What are they doing?" Brian asked as he moved behind Julia.

Heather covered her face with the doll. "Make them stop," she cried.

"Excuse me, but what are you all doing? You're scaring them," Julia said to the group.

As they walked closer, Julia noticed that their clothes were torn and dirty and in some places were bloody. Blood dripped down from their lips. They stepped closer and moaned louder.

Julia let out a horrifying scream followed by Heather and Brian. She picked Heather up, looked at Brian and said, "Get back to the house!"

They ran back inside, and Julia locked the kitchen door.

She put Heather down onto a kitchen chair.

"I'm scared. I want Mom and Dad!" Heather cried.

"Me too." Brian sat down in the chair next to his sister.

"Everything's going to be fine. I'm calling the police and then I'm calling your parents."

She pulled out her cell phone, flipped it open and saw that the battery low message. "Great. I'll just use the house phone."

She picked up the cordless phone from the wall and pushed the 'on' button. There was no dial tone. Her heartbeat went up as she started to panic. She looked at the kids. "There's nothing to worry about. We'll just stay inside until your parents come home."

The front door bell chimed.

"Brian, stay here and watch your sister. It's probably the police checking up on people. I'll be right back." She smiled before leaving the room.

The doorbell ranged again.

Julia glanced through the peep hole on the door. A tall muscular blond teenager stood there, looking impatient.

"Dean," she said aloud as she swung the door open.

He stood there with a frightening expression on his face. His left hand was bleeding from what looked like teeth marks.

"You're bleeding. Are you okay? What happened?" she asked, holding the door open for him.

"I'll be fine. Before I left home my sister was feeling better and she bit me."

"She bit you?"

"Yeah, she likes to roughhouse." He briefly glanced back at several men and women staggering down the street, groaning. He stepped inside, then shut and locked the door. "There's something weird going on. I heard the tornado alarm go off, and while I rode my bike over here, I saw dozens of people with weird skin walking around like zombies. It was really freaky," Dean said.

Brian and Heather entered into the room. "Who's this?" Brian asked.

"He's my boyfriend. He came to check up on us." She went to the kids and hugged them. "Everything's going to be fine."

"I need to sit down." Dean began to sweat and took a seat on the sofa. His face became pale.

"You look sick," Heather said.

"You do look a little clammy, Dean." Julia touched his forehead. "You're burning up."

"I feel like my head's spinning. I need to lie down." He stretched out on the sofa and shut his eyes.

Julia turned to Brian. "I'm going to get help. I want you to stay here and watch your sister."

"Okay," Brian said.

"No, I want to go with you," Heather pleaded.

Julia knelt down to her level and said, "You'll be safe inside the house. I'm going across the street and get Ms. Rosenberg. She's a nurse and she'll know what to do." Julia kissed Heather's forehead.

Julia stood up and headed for the door.

"Wait." Brian ran to his room and came back with a blue baseball bat made of hard plastic. "Take this with you for protection."

"Thanks." She took the bat, unlocked the door, and pulled it open. She looked back one last time. "Make sure you lock the door behind me."

"I promise," Brian said with tears rolling down his face.

Julia shut the door as she stepped onto the porch. She could hear the door click from the other side. She took a deep breath and looked at the zombie-infested street. Dozens of them were everywhere. A few screams and gunshots echoed in the night. She shook her head, wondering how this all had happened so fast.

"It's now or never," she said aloud to psych herself up.

She moved off the porch, tripped on her shoelace and smacked into the sidewalk.

"Ooh!" she screamed and grabbed her twisted ankle.

The zombies all turned to face her, their mouths open wide in hunger. Julia looked up and saw the zombies moving toward her. She stood up and hobbled her away onto the street.

When the first zombie approached, she swung the blue plastic bat as hard as she could. With a loud *clunk*, the bat hammered into the zombie's face.

The zombie stumbled back.

She shoved away the next two before they could snap their teeth at her. She hobbled to Ms. Rosenberg's front yard. Lights shined through all of the windows.

Julia knocked on the front door but there was no answer.

She headed down the side of the yard and peeked into the kitchen window and her eyes almost buldged out when she saw the terrifying sight that greeted her.

Ms. Rosenberg wore a white t-shirt with the words ***Haddonfield Hospital's 20th Celebration*** printed on the front. Smeared on the shirt, as well as her face, were dark red stains. Her sharp teeth ripped the meat away from a bone she held in her pale hands. It looked like an arm and as the meat was turned, Julia saw there was a wristwatch on the end! Her husband was nowhere in sight and she was pretty sure she knew what happened to him.

"Oh no, she's a zombie," Julia gulped. She turned away from the window, crying, and began to make her way back across the street. She hit four zombies with the bat, and then the bat broke in half. She tossed the remains to the ground and limped her way back to the porch.

"Brian! Open the door!" she yelled while pounding on it.

The door swung open.

Julia closed and locked the door behind her and Brian and Heather embraced her. She closed her eyes and caught her breath.

"Where's Ms. Rosenberg?" Brian asked.

Julia opened her eyes. "She wasn't home," she lied and glanced at the empty sofa.

"Where's Dean?" she asked.

"His throat was getting sore. He went into the kitchen to get a drink of water."

"Okay. Stay in the living room." She limped her way into the kitchen.

Dean walked toward her. "There you are." His face was getting paler.

When he stepped in front of the wide open basement doorway, Julia pushed him down into it. He rolled down the stairs and landed in the water with a large splash.

"Hey, what did you do that for?" he yelled as he struggled to get up.

Julia closed the basement door. There was no lock on it so she grabbed a kitchen chair and propped it under the doorknob.

She sat down on the floor against the refrigerator and wept aloud.

Brian and Heather came into the room, crying. They sat down beside her.

"I'm not feeling well!" Dean yelled from the basement. "And I think I might have broken my arm in the fall!"

Then, there was complete silence.

Heather fell asleep on the floor next to Brian. Julia carefully picked her up, not wanting to wake her. Ignoring the pain from her ankle, she carried Heather to bed and covered her up.

She looked at Brian and whispered, "Time for bed."

"But I'm not tired," Brian yawned.

"Now."

"Okay." He went into his room and climbed into bed.

"Goodnight," Julia said before she returned to the living room, fell onto the sofa, and cried softly.

Then, she noticed tonight's newspaper sitting on the coffee table. She read the main headline, ***Army to Conduct Emergency Drills For Three Nights.***

She smiled when she read the next headline.

Haddonfield's Hospital Celebrating Twenty Years with a Barbeque.

She busted out laughing after she read the next article titled, ***Zombie Walk Tonight****. Our own Haddonfield Theatre will be showing the 1968 classic Night of the Living Dead. The drama club will be having a zombie walk down Main Street after the movie ends.*

Julia tossed the newspaper back onto the coffee table and went into the kitchen. She removed the chair from the door and opened it. Dean was lying on the stairs, asleep.

She checked the phone.

There was a dial tone, so she called 9-1-1.

Mr. and Mrs. Bailey pulled into the driveway just as the ambulance left. Julia sat on the porch with a brace on her ankle.

"Are Brian and Heather all right?" Mrs. Bailey asked.

"They're fine. I just checked on them. They're both sleeping."

"I could have sworn the ambulance came from our house," Mrs. Bailey said.

"It did. I had a friend over. Dean Grayson. He was ill, so I called the ambulance."

"Oh, yes. We saw his parents at the party tonight. His sister has the flu. It's been going around lately," Mr. Bailey said.

Mrs. Bailey looked at Julia's ankle, "Oh, my. What happen to your ankle?"

"It's a long, long story," she laughed.

"Well, I hope you're well enough to baby-sit again next weekend," Mr. Bailey said.

"I'm sorry, but my babysitting days are over," Julia sighed.

KENTUCKY FRIED ZOMBIE

GARY WEDLUND

"You're just a girl. Aren't you scared of the zombies no more?"

"Nope. Don't like their stink. You're scared, I betcha." I lean over and spray half the can of lighter fluid into the curbside storm drain, being careful not to get any on my mother's wedding dress. It still flares out, even though I've cut it off at my knees. The built-in bra part has underwires in it, making it rigid. I have to be careful, bending over, or the lacy top of the cups hits my chin.

I kick in a wad of newspaper before adding more lighter fluid. The wrinkled-up headline reads, ***Riots at Mercy Hospital—Governor Calls Guard.***

There are stacks and stacks of newspapers with the same head-line, all yellowing in the warehouse where I'd hid in the middle of all that stinky paper. Forever, seems like. That was before the government came last spring, and I got to move back to my old house.

"Sure, I'm scared a little," Timmy says, "but I got the shot when the Guard chased me down—before I knew who they were. Besides, nobody's seen a..." He puts his hands out in front of him, gums his mouth while moaning, and shifts side to side, "...since Christmas." He wipes his nose with his short sleeve, smearing half his upper-arm with snot.

"Oh, it was just a little in-oc-ula-tion! Weren't nothin'. And just because you can't see 'em, don't mean none are out there hiding like we used to." I put both hands on my hips and tilt my head, scolding him for his snotty arm with my eyebrows and eyeballs like I remember adults did, back when we had some. In fact, I put a face on me like my mother used to put on her when I'd done something accidental, like when I was six and spilled that whole can of yellow paint on the carpet.

"You look stupid," Timmy says, but he goes over to the grass and takes off his pull-over shirt, cleaning the sleeve off by rubbing grass and dandelion stains into it instead.

I light a big wooden match and toss it in. The sewer goes up with a whoosh, tonguing flames out the curb grate. Good thing I'd scooted back, knowing it might happen. Two seconds later—and a block down—a manhole cover pops up, spewing white fire as tall as a house. The lid launches a hundred feet in the air. It lands on a big Mercedes, or something else black, which is the same thing as a Mercedes. I fall to the ground and nearly bust myself laughing while kicking my legs.

Timmy laughs a little too. He looks funny doing that while try-ing to put on his shirt. "Whadja put that on fire for?" he says into a clump of cotton before pulling it the rest of the way over his little round tummy. Timmy is all bones, except for where his belly button sticks out. He looks pregnant, but I know he can't be pregnant 'cause he's only eight, like me.

"It was P U. I think there's somethin' down there."

Somethin' is our way of saying dead people. Last year that might have meant zombies, but the Nash-no Guard and our new government wiped them out. Now it's only us.

The zombies mostly just wore out a few months after running out of food, and things started falling off—or they got shot in the head. Now, *somethin'* means rotten meat in general, like arms and torsos and whatever—sometimes a whole, puss-filled body, all crusted over, sunken eyed and teeth. Somethin's everywhere now, and I mean to burn it up.

The government gets all prissy if I burn down whole houses, 'cause it might burn up the entire town, and I'm too little to know when it might or might not. But they don't say nothin' about burning other things up as long as it's somewhere safe, like in the street or in those big green trashcans. It's a public service, even if nobody in the government asks. Still, I itch to burn down houses, 'cause half of them smell to heaven.

I love matches, too. And lighter fluid. They have lots of matches and lighter fluid down at the Wal-mart. I got in trouble there once, burning up the rotten meat displays 'cause they were pee-utrid. At night, Big Henry falls asleep holding the chain on his Rottweiler while watching the pitch-dark Wal-mart. Once I figure out where he is, I can go in and get all the matches and fluid I want and they don't even know. Big Henry's the oldest, almost sixteen, and one out of three of the government. Otherwise, I'd steal his Rottweiler. But, before the Nash-no Guard left, they said we had to mind the government.

"You coming, scaredy-cat?" I ask.

"Don't call me that. I ain't afraid of nothin'."

"Uh-huh, says you. Watch out, you don't trip on your shadow. Look, there it is. Don't step there. Not there. Not there. You're gonna trip for sure."

"Shut up. Stop being stupid."

I take off running in my light-up-when-you-step-on-'em shoes, heading toward the edge of town, past the mold and ink smelling newspaper building. Now that I don't live there anymore, I hold my nose whenever I pass.

"We goin' to your secret place, where you live?" Timmy asks.

I turn around backwards, still nearly running. "So you can kiss me?" I turn back around. My feet are lightning, going pink, yellow, pink, yellow. "If you can catch me."

He runs faster a second, then I hear his shoes slow. "What if I don't want to kiss you? You're a girl!"

I walk, letting him catch up, but don't look at him. "Then you won't know my secret hiding place, will you, dummy? Then if you turn into a zombie, you won't know where to get me."

"I'm never going to be a zombie. I got the shot. Did you get the shot?"

"Uh-huh. Said so already. They didn't have to make me. I didn't need it though, 'cause I'm not scared, like you."

"I ain't afraid of nothin'!"

"Says you. You're afraid to kiss me."

"I ain't afraid of that."

"You're afraid of girls."

"Well, just 'cause they're icky."

I stick my tongue out at him, then I hear a screen door bang.

It's old Mrs. Wilson, coming out of her big, white house. That house used to have a kitty in the window. It would look out at the crows that landed on her lawn.

Mrs. Wilson falls over and crawls down the three wooden steps while mouthing something. She doesn't look all eaten. She still has her arms and legs and everything. Still, the wind shifts, and she smells like she hasn't had a trip to the creek in a hundred years. I don't like that much, and it's one reason I don't hold Timmy's hand either, 'cause he needs a bath, too.

"See. The Nash-no Guard didn't get 'em all." Timmy backs up, pointing.

"You gonna run away again?"

"Why not? The government says that's why we made it, and my ma and pa died. Zombies are slow, don't you know. You just gotta run away and hide." But he stays in the middle of the street and doesn't back up any more.

In the meantime, Mrs. Wilson keeps crawling through her yard gnomes. She makes it way past the foot tall frog, and if I don't do something, she's sure to clear the jockey-boy holding the lantern that doesn't work because there's no place to put the kerosene.

"It's only one zombie, and it's really old. I'm gotta fix it."

Timmy grabs my shoulder. "No, wait, what if…"

I shake him off. "Run away if you wanna. She makes my nose hurt."

I spray her real good with the last half of the can, mostly on the head so her ratty gray hair drips and droops.

"But, what if she's not…"

"Can'tcha see she's slow and makes me wanna retch?"

Mrs. Wilson looks up with bloodshot eyes. I can see down the filthy top of her dress, see her boobies all thin and wrinkled up and hanging like two of those summer sausages at Wal-mart, which is the only meat I didn't burn up in there 'cause they last way long and have pee-servatives.

"Ohhh, she's pretty bad wrinkled," I say.

"She's maybe a hundred," Timmy says. "Maybe you shouldn't put her on fire. The government might want to keep her for an experiment, seeing she lasted so long."

I look back at him. "Stupid. Our government don't know experiments. We don't have to go to school and do science class no more." Then I go back to looking.

Leaning over and glancing past the sausages, I count her ribs, which reminded me I'm standing too close. I back up a step and light a match. I can do it in one strike with just my fingernail 'cause I bite my nails instead of cut 'em, so the ends stay rough.

Mrs. Wilson is mouthing stuff, like a whispered secret, seeming to say, "Help me, please." Zombies are tricky. They can't really talk, so I know she's only pretending to say, "Help, me please."

"Maybe she ain't a zombie. What's she saying?" Gullible Timmy steps beside me and asks. He's trying to be brave, but I can see his knobby knees knocking.

I grow antsy and toss the match in the old woman's hair. "She's saying…"

Mrs. Wilson fills in the rest by croaking, "Ahhhh! Ahhh! Ahhhhhhh!" after standing up and batting her head. She's bent over, but still manages to stumble around, knocking half those gnomes over like she's some kind of drunk bowling ball. After a while she just spins under the cherry tree. It's near the end of summer, and nobody's watered anything in two years, so the tree catches on fire about the time she falls down and starts rocking from side to side. Flames catch all the way to her toes. Nylons…they catch fire like crazy. I love it.

Flaming leaves keep floating by, but she stops burning after only a few minutes, which is disappointing, making me want to burn down her big house because I got cheated. I'm not allowed because the government says so. She still stinks, but she's out in the open, so I know the birds will eat her. Maybe even the crow that says meow. I shrug. When the tree finishes burning all its leaves, the show's over. I hope it still gets cherries next year, 'cause I love 'em.

Timmy's puking, so I kick him almost as high as his butt and start us toward the edge of town. We head down the weed-grown path leading to my old house. I have chickens I've chased down in back, all fixed up in a long wire cage leading to a little coop. They squawk as soon as they hear me. Chickens love me—and grass seed from Wal-mart. Except the kind with fart-lizer in it.

Timmy follows, probably because I live on the only farm right next to town. I'm farming, too, with real animals!

"You got a cow!" Timmy runs up to Betsy and pats her on the upper part of her backside that I've magic-markered RUMP ROAST. Betsy glances back, probably thinking about kicking him, but decides to moo instead. She takes a step and lets a cow-pie the size of a soup can drop on Timmy's shoe.

After what seems like a hundred minutes, I get up and stop laughing. Timmy has wandered off to wash his shoe clean in the pond. "What you need with a farm? The government's got cans. Sarah and John both made a rule, says we get three cans a day for ten years."

I roll my eyes. "Yes, I know, and the government can't lie, 'cause they're teenagers."

"Yep, I know that. The government can't lie. It's a rule. The Nash-no Guard said so when they came through, and they killed the zombies for us."

"I knew that before you said what you did, but cans aren't the same as farm food. And cans aren't forever either—only ten years worth," I say. "I'm practicin' for when we need corn, and there's already no chickens in cans. And I want a watermelon."

Timmy shuts up. He looks through the wire at my chickens. He licks his lips.

"Do you see that?" I point to my planted field. Timmy looks out at the green stems on brown dirt and cow poop. Ten rows of corn, carrots and watermelon are sprouting almost as tall as the weeds. The furrows cross each other, all over the place, but I'm only eight and I did my best. "The only way I could get Betsy to move was to hang a can of spinach in front of her nose. Then she wouldn't turn or stop. It took me all day just to get the old plow out of the creek. She dragged it in three times. I almost ate her for that."

"My old man drank. You plow like he used to drive before his head got chewed up." Timmy kicks a chicken through my wire.

"Hey, stop that."

"Are these Kentucky Fried chickens? I ain't had Kentucky Fried since two years," he says.

I only have nine chickens and don't know how to do Kentucky Fried. I just cook them on the fire because there's no gas or electric.

"Sure," I say, "but you got to play cowboys and Indians with me. Then I'll ring one's neck and do Kentucky Fried."

"Oh, all right. I get to be the cowboy." Timmy puts his forefingers in his pockets and draws, going, "Bang! Bang!" before he blows imaginary smoke off his fingernails.

"Good. Then I get to tie you up."

"No way."

"It's my chicken, and I showed you where I live." I poke him in the chest. "If you get to be a zombie, you'll know where I live, and I'll have to know how to tie you up."

"What if I don't wanna be tied up?" He squints hard, pretending his brain is actually working.

"You don't want to be no zombie. If you was a zombie, you'd want me to tie you up. Nobody wants to be a zombie, unless someone takes care of 'em and ties 'em up."

He still looks at me hard, but finally sighs. "You sure you can make Kentucky Fried?"

"I got all eleven spices: salt, flour, coffee, onions, eggs and brown gravy mix."

"Fine then, but you gotta stand guard in case of more zombies."

"Didn't I say I was?" The ropes are right there on the rain barrel.

I lasso him like he's the cow. The rope drops over his skinny chest, and I start running around and around, pinning his arms to his sides before tying him off. I do the same to his knees. He falls down and I prop him back up next to a clothesline pole, where I tie him so he can't waddle away.

Timmy makes a palms-up, *what's up*, expression with the parts of his arms that are still free. "I can go home and get my gun. Then I can put a blanket on Betsy like a saddle and ride you down and shoot you, you wagon train scalping squaw." He makes more finger guns, and says, "Bang, bang. I got you. Fall over."

"Nope. Don't wanna."

"You got to. It's a rule for playing cowboys and Indians."

I put some firewood around his feet, go inside and come right back out with a new can of lighter fluid.

"What're you doin'?" Timmy has that 'running away' look on his face again.

"I could burn you up."

"I'm done playing cowboys and Indians."

"I ain't gonna. I'm just pretending. I might let you go, soon as you kiss me." After squeezing the can, making clinking can noises, I close my eyes and shuffle toward his face.

He wiggles against me some, and turns his head back and forth, but I open my eyes, grab his face, and smooch against his hard-pressed lips.

"Yyyuuuck!"

"Stupid, even Big Henry's Rottweiler kisses better than that."

I go over and snatch some feathers by reaching through the chicken wire. The slow chicken runs off clucking like nobody has ever yanked any of her feathers out before, like they weren't all around under her feet. I put one in my hair, and another one in Timmy's. "Since you kissed me, you're family now."

"No way." He pulled at the rope and tried to get his hands around.

"Yep. That makes you an Indian, too. You got to wear a feather and armbands."

"Arm what?"

"Look. I'll show you." I go to the back porch and reach into my box of arm and headbands. They're made out of a leaf printed sheet I stole from a trailer house that didn't smell bad enough to have a double-dead zombie in it. One fits loosely about my left arm. I tie another around my head, which is how Indians look.

"Now you get two, too. Two-to, two-ti-to ...." I start tooting a made-up song. His body is tied, so I have to push his sleeve way up and poke one of the armbands between his arm and body near his pit. Then I tie his armbands on, super tight.

"Ouch. Careful. Hey, not so tight. Hey, that's too tight! Stop, it's pinching! Hey, I mean it. It's pinching bad."

"Big baby!" The other arm gets the same treatment. "Your arm-pit smells. PU." Soon veins are sticking out, and up above where I tied, it's red. The fingers start getting really white.

"Whatcha doin'?" Timmy's asked. "Untie me. It's pinching, it's pinching so bad I can't see it for skin. I can feel my heart beating in my arms!"

I'm waiting for, *I can't feel my hands*, but that's probably going to take a while.

"I got a secret to trade you."

He bites his lip. "Aren't you hungry for Kentucky Fried? I can make the fire if you want. Untie me and I'll make a teepee fire like Indians do."

My eyes roll, like they did it all by themselves and I had nothing to do with it. "Later. And I *always* get to make the fire. Now, tell me a secret. I showed you where I live already, but I got another secret I wanna tell you soon as you tell me one."

"All right. I'm afraid of night."

"Oh, that's not nothin'."

"And I'm a little afraid of fire at night. I near burnt up when I put a house floor on fire when I was hiding."

"Why're you afraid of fire? That don't make good sense." I shake my head and put both hands on my knees, looking up at his face. Doing that, I almost drop my lighter fluid and instead put the can down on a rock.

"Aren't you gonna tell me your other secret."

I stand up and bite my lip. "Oh, all right. You know I hate how much dead zombies smell." He nods his head, so I go on. "They don't stink so bad if they get to eat once a month or so."

"What's that got to do with a secret?"

"I'm just telling you…before we get to play zombie Indian dancing. Besides, it's a secret to me, like an experiment. How's your arms doing? Can you bend your elbows any?"

"A little. Why?" He looks at his arms. His little fingers are blue on both hands.

"'Cause before we eat chicken, we got to play zombie dancing Indians. You got to have zombie arms to zombie dance." I bend over a little while walking around in front of him. My arms dangle down like I don't even have bones in 'em.

"See. Like this. You try it."

He moves his bound arms around some, mostly by moving his shoulders. A finger or two twitches, but not much.

While he's trying to get loose, I start dancing around the pole, letting my arms flop. Getting tired of that, I put my hands up under my cheeks and around my face, framing myself and dancing to the hum of *Lady Gaga's Poker Face* that's playing in my head.

"Hey, don't zombies reach right out, like they want to get you?" Timmy interrupts. "You know, like Frankenstein arms?"

"Only some, like those who didn't get their arms ate on, which most of 'em did." I smile. "Dummy. Don't you know nothin'?"

"Well, I know that already."

"Do not."

"Do too."

"Okay, then you understand why it's important we do our zombie dance."

"I do?"

"Well, didn't you just say, like you know everything?"

"Uh, I forgot what I was saying, but I know lots of stuff."

"Then I can untie you and we can play zombie around the shed, and then people can eat around here."

"That's a good idea. I'm tired of being tied up. I don't like playing cowboys and Indians now. I can't even feel my hands no more."

I smile at him while I untie his chest from the clothesline pole. Unraveling all the turns around his body and knees is easy. I grab both ropes and run real fast. Timmy ends up falling-down dizzy from spinning. That only leaves the rope armbands.

After putting lighter fluid on the wood under the clothesline pole, I light it up with a match.

"There. Now I got a fire to make Kentucky Fried with."

"Good. I love Kentucky Fried chickens," Timmy says.

"You got to get the eggs for the batter while I catch a chicken so I can wring its neck."

The best way to do that is to crawl into the end where the long tunnel of chicken wire's loose, and grab one when they get all bunched up next to the little coop. I come out holding a squawking white one's feet.

"Look at this." I grip the head and twirl the chicken around in the air a bunch of times. It looks like a Nash-no Guard helicopter until the body spins all the way off, plops down in the dirt, and starts running around and even on top of my shoes. Its wings are flapping, and the feet seem to work perfect for a half minute until I almost think it's a zombie chicken, but it finally topples over and only twitches a little.

I jump up and swing on the arm of the clothesline pole opposite the fire and laugh at the chicken. "Zombie chicken!" I call it, over and over, like I'm doing a rap song.

Even Timmy finds that funny. "Where's the zombie chicken eggs? In that little coop?" he asks.

"No way. That's the cardboard daytime coop and it's only big enough for two chickens. Chickens lay eggs in the big shed near the barn during the night— where it's private."

"Well, I suppose I can go in there."

"But first, we gotta do Indian dancing around the egg laying shed to wake up the chickens inside and tell 'em we're coming to steal their eggs right out from under their butts."

Timmy says the word butts about ten times, like it's funny, which it is. "There's more chickens in there? Are they Kentucky Fried chickens in there?"

"Uh-huh. Big ones, like giant ones, so you only need one wing and you can save the rest of the chicken for breakfast." I take off around the shed, going, "Woo, woo, woo," and making popping sounds with my palm smacking my lips. I've got the dead chicken by the feet, and every four steps or so I yank another handful of feathers, tossing them in the air.

Each couple times around, I divert to the fire and spray more lighter fluid on it because I didn't start it with newspaper.

Timmy's following, running into the floating feathers. He's going around, saying, "Woo, woo, woo." His arms are flopping around like they're not even his. "When you gonna untie my arms? I can't feel nothing, and I can't untie myself 'cause I can't feel nothing. And my fingers are getting fat."

"Soon as we've gone around enough and are pooped, and you get the eggs. Oh look, your hands are blue. Look at 'em. Blue's a boy color, so that's perfect."

I keep going around, sometimes banging on the sides of the shed, sometimes jogging backwards, looking at Timmy. By about twenty times around, the chicken's only got half her feathers. I'm almost embarrassed for it too because hens are girls, and toss it beside the fire.

"Okay, I'm ready for you to get the eggs. After that we can eat Kentucky Fried."

Timmy's stops going around when he hears that and looks like he really wants to.

"Can you open the door for me, 'cause I can't do it until you untie my armbands, which I guess is after I get the eggs 'cause you're being extra weird today."

"I've got it fixed so you don't have to." We walk over by the side of the shed. Two hatchet-made holes are cut in the faded wood siding about knee level.

"What's that?"

"You got to get on your knees and reach in those little holes with both arms. You feel around. I got a slide, like at school. It lets all the eggs roll down under the chickens, so I don't have to go in. Coops are stinky and full of poop, don't you know."

"I'd rather go in, I think."

"Can't, 'cause it's full of poop and big chickens…that'll get out…and peck you." Something inside the shed starts banging against stuff. "See. That's a big, Kentucky Fried chicken."

Timmy bends his head, putting an ear next to one of the holes. "But I…"

"You want Kentucky Fried, you gotta do it. Don't let them big chickens scare you, chicken. Chicken. Chicken. Bawk, bawk, bawk. You want Kentucky Fried, don't you?"

"Ohhh, all right." Timmy gets on his knees with his nose nearly touching the shed. "Now I can't put 'em in. See." He bangs has shoulders against the shed, showing me his arms don't work.

"Here, let me help." I go behind him and grab both of his wrists, then slide them into the holes.

"I can't feel nothin'."

"Them eggs are in there. You'll feel 'em in a minute." Shoving Timmy on the shoulders gets the arms in there nice and far.

The shed nearly rocks on its foundation. There's some more banging, and then Timmy's whole body shakes as he slams face first into the shed.

"Now you're really part of the family, Timmy. Now I gotta feed you. Here, have some more Kentucky Fried."

Timmy gives me the evil eye. I've got a rope around his chest, holding him in the seat, 'cause he sometimes gets a fever and wants to fall off. He's pretty good today, though he smells from that stinging red stuff you gotta put on booboos. He should be better. It's been over two weeks since he fed my momma.

I know Momma's not going to last much longer. Her ears and nose are just holes and a hand fell off wrestling Timmy for his arm meat. Maybe she'll only last until after I have to feed her Timmy's legs, but in the meantime she smells a whole lot better. Zombies smell better after they eat.

So, what does not-in-a-good-mood Timmy say to my offer to keep him fed and happy?

"This ain't Kentucky Fried."

"Stupid," I say. "I only have six spices, not eleven: Salt, flour, onions, coffee, eggs and brown gravy, remember?" My head shakes, almost like I don't have to make it do it. "You can't count. Besides, barbeques are way better than old, yucky pan fried. My mommy says pans make you fat."

Timmy frowns down at his newly-sunken stomach and wiggles his arms. Momma ate most the meat off the arm bones, and I could only chop loose the bones past his elbows 'cause he still has meat clinging below his shoulders. I still have him tied near his pits and had to singe his wounds up some. So, Timmy has half as long bone arms now, which are kind of funny. Sometimes he reaches for stuff with his stubby arm bones instead of asks. His reach always comes up short, like he's a numbskull and doesn't know he can't grab anything.

I should probably add that I'm glad the Nash-no Guard chased him down and gave him the shot. If not—*I flick a match, lighting a candle*—I'd have to burn him up after Momma eats his legs.

IN THE MIND SNOW GLISTENS

MARC SHEMMANS

It was two weeks before Christmas when the dead started walking. It began with the first fall of snow. A small dusting at first—with the dusting came a few deaths. But then the dusting became a blizzard and the deaths became harder.

Gerard gazed at the empty bed, thinking about how it all began. He thought of the horrendous things he'd seen on the around-the-clock news. Things no one should ever see. He still wasn't sure what was worse, all the horrors they'd watched on the news, or sitting around without any TV or radio, waiting for the madness to find it's way to their doorstep.

Not many believed the reports when word of the snowstorm first made the news. The fact it was snowing a bit more than usual was hardly worth worrying about—especially when the world offered so many other more immediate concerns. It's hard to worry yourself with inclement weather when you were living in fear that some lowlife might knife you on the street.

The severe weather didn't let up, and when it crawled across the UK, the news coverage ramped up a bit. Then unseasonable cold and snow was reported in the Midlands. People reported lakes frozen far earlier than had ever been recorded, and although scientists predicted doom and gloom to anyone who would listen, their cries were buried by feel-good media reports, commercials for Ford trucks, reality television shows, and a general unwillingness to believe anything so mundane as snow could truly endanger such a modern society. It was, after all, the twenty-first century.

However, in the coming weeks it became infinitely worse. The snow continued to fall and then there were reports of things out there in the snow. Nobody knew who or what they were, at first. There were just random sightings of them.

Then the first of the bodies was found. Mutilated and eaten. At first it was just a journalist's dream—dark, morbid and sensational. But then the other bodies were discovered—in masses. But that wasn't the worst. Victims of the creatures seemed to be rising from the dead, only to become monsters themselves. Parts of the media thought they were part of an alien invasion; they believed the earth was being colonized by an alien race. Others labeled them zombies. It didn't matter. Regardless of what you called them, they were the undead. And if they got hold of you, you became one, too.

It took the storm over a month to make its way down to Birmingham, but it finally arrived. Gerard remembered the first snowflake. He was at school and it had been a difficult day. As soon as he saw the snow, he told his teacher he was feeling sick and went home. He spent the rest of the day building snowmen and snowball fighting with his best friend, John. It had been such a beautiful day. Who would have thought it would end so badly. Gerard could hear him now. His giggle, his laugh, his happiness.

Who would have thought that his best friend would be dead just a few weeks later?

The human race had become complacent, arrogant and because of this, it had to suffer. Mother Nature had decided she'd had enough and was obliterating those who had destroyed the planet. Only a handful would be allowed to survive, to evolve once more. Gerard hoped he would be one of those lucky few. But if his parents were gone he was no longer sure if he wanted to survive. After all, what if he was the only person left alive? Other than his parents, he hadn't seen another living being for over a week.

And now, he stared at his parent's bed. It sat empty, layers of blankets tossed aside, the sheets still warm. It took a few seconds for him to defrost his mind and come to grips with the enormity of the situation. It hit him like a cricket bat to the chest.

The zombies had gotten them. Somehow they got into the house and took them.

Gerard began a furious wrestling match with the duvet, unable to accept that they weren't somewhere within the voluminous folds. After several moments, though, he gave up. He tried to control the rising panic welling up inside of him.

He padded out of the room and called their names.

No answer.

He tried to pull himself together. He wasn't about to lose his parents, not on Christmas Eve. Not a chance.

He searched the bathroom. No one. Then headed downstairs.

The front door was open, like an invitation to a world of frozen death. Snow blew in through the opening, and a thick snowdrift had already formed in the hallway.

He searched downstairs and all he found were stacks of canned food looming in the corners, surrounded by gallon after gallon of water in plastic jugs.

When all this started, his parents had intended to survive it, one way or another. His father told them he was the man of the family, and by God it was a father's job to provide, to keep his family safe. Before the dead even crossed in from Scotland, he'd emptied most of his savings; bought everything he thought they would need to weather the storm. His father had spent some time in the army, back before he met Gerard's mother, Margaret, and he knew a thing or two about survival.

Gerard called out their names once more.

Nothing.

The ugly teeth of defeat gnawed at his brain like a starving pit bull. Gerard grabbed his ski jacket from the rack by the door. The pockets were heavy with bullets. He zipped up the jacket to his chin, pulled on the hood, and took a gun from his pocket. It felt warm in his hand. He'd been carrying the pistol around for at least a month now, always loaded. His father had shown him how to use it. He had told him that Gerard would eventually need it. He even gave Gerard shooting lessons. But Gerard had never, ever thought he would really need it.

He guessed he was wrong.

Gerard wore a pair of long johns beneath his jeans, and a pair of heavy gray jogging bottoms over them. With three shirts layered beneath his jacket, he judged himself ready for winter combat.

He thought about taking along some food and water, but how would he carry it? Better to just go, before his parents traveled too far, and hope they were still close. The last thing he did before he left was go into the living room. He gazed around the room, his eyes stopping at the Christmas tree. It had three presents resting at its base and was adorned with chocolate candy and tinsel. He stood there for almost a minute, just gazing at its sparse decorations. He took off a chocolate from a middle branch and ate it. He pulled off another and popped that one into his mouth, too. After all, his mother wasn't here to tell him off for eating more than one today.

He strolled over to the mantelpiece and picked up the Christmas card his parents had given him. As he read their message, a single tear trickled down his cheek. He wiped it away with the back of his hand and put the card back.

Resting on a nearby table was a hunting knife. He padded over to it, picked it up and placed it in his coat pocket. He prayed with every frigid shard of his shattered faith that he wouldn't have to use it. He'd seen what his father had done with it and he didn't know if he could do it himself.

He wrapped a scarf around his face and threw himself into the maelstrom. It was difficult to stand against the cruel wind and driving snow. His layers of clothing did little to protect him from the ungodly cold, and his bones felt like they might shatter before he made it to the end of the driveway.

Gerard shook his head to clear it. No way could he let this happen. How had he missed them slinking through the house? Taking his parents without even waking him. He was to blame. He should have heard them. He should have helped them. If they were dead, if they were one of those *things*, then it was all his fault! He'd failed them.

No! Arguing with himself and wallowing in self ¬pity wasn't going to bring them back.

A quickly disappearing path lay before him. Not footprints, but a slithery trail through the snow, leading up the street. The snow and wind would wipe it away fast.

Gerard trudged up the street, past dark houses filled with people too afraid to leave. Or worse, empty, the occupants now part of the undead horde. The path cut between two houses, one of them being Charles Dawkins', his neighbor. Gerard passed by the curtained windows, wondering if he was inside. He listened for the incessant bark of their big German Sheppard but the home stood silent. Either the zombies had taken them, or they'd somehow taught the dog to keep quiet.

Charles' house backed up to a low, forested area, and the trail led directly into the trees. Gerard raised the gun and willed himself into the trees, grateful for the temporary reprieve they provided from the snow. The stuff was falling hard, erasing the earth like television static, the kind they'd seen when the networks finally stopped broadcasting. But he could hear the zombies—their high, mournful song—singing in the snow, just like the reports said. They seemed to worship the stuff, and Gerard gripped his gun a bit tighter. The sound wasn't far ahead.

He stood there as the snow fell, looking all around at the houses which were decorated in lights, tinsel and Christmas trees.

He couldn't believe how this had happened. This was a simple, friendly village. A good village. A village where everyone got along, where everyone spoke to each other and helped each other out—until now. Now Gerard no longer lived in a nice, small village—he lived in a frozen Hell.

He heard something and stopped walking, listening.

Nothing.

He continued walking. The snow was deep, and he had to lift his legs in a slow, cumbersome march. He pressed on, keeping an eye on the alleys of tree trunks, anywhere the dead could spring from. Who knew if they could climb? But he wasn't about to get ambushed. One quick bite to his body and it was lights out.

Then laughter, sweet and high carried on the wind. It broke his heart because he recognized the voice—it was his mother's.

Tears froze on his cheeks before they could reach his chin. He wasn't sure when he'd raised the gun, but it was up and ahead of him. He walked through the snow in the direction where the voice had come from. He needed to know if his parents were dead or not. He came to a glade and stopped. He could hear them, eating.

Then the monsters came at him.

The sound of the gun sounded in the storm with a musical moan. He couldn't tell if he hit anyone but one of them sprang out of the darkness. It leapt at him and knocked him to the ground, into the snow, and its eyes were blazing. Its mouth opened in a hungry snarl. It tried to bite, and scratch, and chew but Gerard held it at bay.

He shook with fear and determination and finally found the power to raise the gun up to its head, and in a fluid motion, he fired.

The creature fell to the side, staining the snow red.

He stumbled to his feet, and less than ten feet ahead, he saw her. She broke free from the darkness like an angel, his mother, all blonde hair and smiles, pretty white teeth and fuzzy pajamas.

Behind her were another couple of zombies. Brittle strands of hair masked the monsters' scarred faces, and one of them rested a fingerless hand on his mother's shoulder. She didn't seem to mind.

"Geeraaard!" she cried.

He saw genuine excitement in her eyes. And hunger.

You know what you have to do now! You couldn't help them before so make up for it now! They need peace. They deserve peace. They don't want to be damned like this! he told himself.

The crack of his gun sent shards of ice falling from the sur-rounding trees. The bullet pierced ice and bone. One of the crea-tures fell to the ground.

Gerard pulled the trigger again.

Missed.

Then another gun crack.

Second one down.

Two left.

Then his father appeared.

"C'mon, Gerry," he said. He smiled at him the way dads do when they're thinking how much they love you.

His mother smiled at him, too, and in that smile she said what she wanted to say.

Tears welled Gerard's eyes.

"Isn't it a beautiful night, son?" his father asked.

"It is," Gerard answered.

"Isn't the snow lovely?" his mother laughed.

"Yes, it is."

"Remember when we all went to build that huge snowman by the lake? It was the biggest we'd ever made, wasn't it?"

"I remember."

"We can all go and make another, can't we?"

Gerard began to sob.

"What's wrong?" his mother asked.

"Nothing."

"Come with us, Gerry," his mother said.

"Let's go and make another," his father added.

"It's too late," Gerard said.

"I know it's late, but we can sleep-in in the morning," his father smiled. "There's nothing to get up for."

Gerard lifted the gun and aimed it at his mother's head.

Kill them Gerard, you know you have to! But don't forget to cut off the head, you know what'll happen if you don't.

His mother stood out of arm's reach. He could see the wounds on her arms and shoulders, the places where the zombies had gnawed right through her pajamas. Already the holes were filling with chunks of red ice, frozen death creeping into her veins.

"C'mon, Gerry," she said. She smiled at him.

The other zombies were back up now. The ones he'd shot. He didn't have much time. He had to do it before he completely lost his nerve.

He pulled the trigger, heard the sound of the shot, and watched as his mother fell and sank softly into the snow, half her chest now missing.

He remembered when his dad killed John. How innocent it had been, just a quick trip to the grocery store, maybe the last chance to pick up a few more supplies. He and his father came across John on the way, and John had come lunging at them, all teeth and claws. His father shot him in the head and John collapsed in a heap on the ground.

Gerard had been shocked by the violence and that moment had given him nightmares for a week.

But a week later John came back.

Gerard shook away the memory and raised the gun at his father.

He shot him in the head.

He re-loaded his gun and shot the other zombies in turn.

He stared down at the carnage. He didn't know if he could finish it.

He pulled out his hunting knife. The blade was wide and serrated, ugly and cold.

Images of John, smashing through the window in the living room while Gerard and his parents huddled around the kitchen table, spooning cold beans into their mouths, came into his mind. The way John had come for him was so feral, so void of humanity that his dad never hesitated. He shot John with the same pistol that Gerald would eventually use to shoot his father.

Gerard had watched his dad work on John.

He knew what to do now.

He knelt before the bodies. Gazing on their corpses, he wept for a long time.

Now, holding the blade to his mother's throat, he wondered if the weeping would ever stop. He lifted her head, cradled it, mucus running freely from his nose, and he shook with sobs. Gerard lowered her head back to the frozen ground and dropped the knife.

"*Nnnooooo!*" he screamed at the top of his lungs, vanquishing the voices from his head.

He ran.

Back through the mocking trees, past the eerie silence of the Dawkins' home, up the street to his front door. Inside he would be safe, just for a while, and maybe this would all go away. He thumped down the hallway, tired and sick, and didn't bother to remove his heavy coat before climbing into his parents' bed. There was a fleeting memory of warmth attached to the duvet, and the sweet odor of them. His tears were unstoppable, and he huddled underneath the blankets, ashamed of himself.

What have I damned them to? By now the ice is doing its work, filling up the bullet holes, pulling them up with icicle puppet strings so they can go out and find somebody to eat.

"Geeraaard!" his father's voice floated down the hallway, into his broken sanctuary.

Terror pulsed in his temples, even as a stiff resignation settled in his stomach. He couldn't remember if he'd locked the front door in his grief. It didn't matter. They'd find their way in somehow.

Horror pulsed at his temples. He'd always wanted to be an adult. But not like this. This was murder. This was Hell.

Or was it just a new way of life?

Whatever it was, it was something he'd have to get used to. He decided that in the morning he'd start boarding up the windows. There was wood in the shed, but it was too dangerous out there now to go get it.

He heard them bang on the door and he ignored it, hoping they would go away.

They didn't.

He heard a window smash, then the sound of footsteps on broken glass.

"Geeraaard!" his father called again, the voice closer this time.

They climbed the stairs.

He heard them search his bedroom.

"Come on, son," his father called as his parents walked down the hallway.

"Geeraaard, come and build a snowman with us!" his mother screamed. "Then we can open presents under the Christmas tree!"

The voices moved closer, staggering footsteps striking against the floorboards. Through the blankets, Gerard could see their shadows under the door, sliding closer. They were right outside. "It's cold, Gerard. Let us in," his father said.

Gerard felt a wintry wind lift the blankets. The air in the room was cold enough to freeze his soul. He squeezed the gun tighter in his hand.

"It's freezing," his mother hissed.

He raised the gun, aimed it.

"You don't have to be cold anymore, son," his father said.

Gerard heard the rustle of the door handle. Saw the door open slowly, saw the dark figures just before they lunged for him.

He fired once.

ZOMBIE RAIN

JIM BRONYAUR

One day it started to rain.

It was Tuesday. I knew it was Tuesday because Mom had her weekly meeting with the medical staff and Dad was on one of his twelve hour days at the factory.

That's how it went in my house. Dad worked Monday through Thursday, twelve hour days, and Mom tried to work the normal nine-to-five job.

Most weeks she's in the office by eight and not home until seven. And the weekends? Forget about it. When I was a kid it wasn't so bad. But now, thanks to technology, it never ends. The company bought her one of those fancy smartphones because she refused to spend the money. She accepted it as a sign of doing a good job, but all it did was make it easier for them to call her on weekends.

Dinner for me was pizza, Chinese, or most nights, cereal. My room was my sanctuary, where I lived.

And I miss it.

All because of the rain.

I stomped through the puddles on purpose of course and made my way to school. I live about thirty minutes from school. Mom thought it was too far to walk, but since I was a year short of getting my license, I couldn't drive. So what then? Take the bus? Screw that noise. For whatever reason, the genius people that ran the school—they fit themselves much better now. Trust me, you'll understand what I mean soon enough—decided that where I lived—a small country road hidden from the rest of Pacbell, Pennsylvania—wasn't worth sending a bus to pick me up. They offered to send a van.

Yeah, that's right, a school van. Worse than the 'short bus' if you ask me. Not to mention the lady that drove the van was clinically insane. And if I dared to take the van, I was the only one and the crazy lady talked to me…even if I had head phones on my head. Then I'd feel bad, you know, listening to some tunes while this old bat is talking to me.

Anyway, back to the rain.

Like I said, it started to rain and then I walked to school. Seems simple, right? Well, not so much. You see, it didn't just rain, it *rained*. I'm talking pouring so hard and fast that it hit the windows like pellets. The raindrops were so fat they could have been small water balloons being dropped from the clouds. And if that wasn't bad enough, the rain hit the ground so hard it actually bounced back up at you. It was like getting rained on twice…by the same rain drop!

Now Mom had her 'big meeting,' which from what I gathered consisted of standing in front of twenty people to tell them what they did wrong the previous week while her boss watched. If she said enough things that everyone else did wrong, then she'd have done her job right. Confusing? I know. That's why I'm never growing up. Dad was working one of his long shifts at the factory, and little old me was walking along through the monsoon that had hit Pacbell.

I stayed on the sidewalks, minding my own, trying to avoid being splashed by cars. Which, oh by the way, was impossible. Now don't get me wrong, I'm not some prissy 'oh-don't-get-me-dirty' girl or anything like that. I actually would be one of the kids standing on the sidewalk, waving at cars to splash me. But not on a school day. I'm not sure why, perhaps there's some kind of 'inner-girl' that cares, but I like to look nice for school. But on that day, it didn't matter. I was as close as I could be to the other side of the sidewalk, scraping against fences and bushes, and I was still getting soaked.

The rain was unstoppable.

The streets were flooded in minutes. Cars were stuck. All you could see were headlights bobbing in and out of the water, like one of those light-up bobber's you use for night fishing

What? I'm not a prissy girl. I like to fish...big deal.

People climbed out their windows and onto the roofs of their vehicles to wait for help. People with pickup trucks were stopping and letting other people jump inside so they could get away from the rising waters. Yeah, it was pretty intense. And yes, little old me was just walking along, watching it all happen.

Okay, hold on. I know what you're thinking. Be real, right? How can a car flood but me, four foot eleven Dani, still be walking?

Well, that's because Pacbell is a big valley with lots of hills. What does that mean? I'm no scientist or weather man, but in simple terms, there were streets that would flood and streets that wouldn't. End of discussion. There were streets that all it took was a passing shower to make it impassable. Regardless, the point I'm making is that I was walking along Sanderson Avenue, which is in an upper part of Pacbell. A couple blocks down, literally down, was Eagle Drive, which was flooded.

That's where the cars were floating along, like some crazy vehicle in a James Bond movie or something. So there, that's how Pacbell is set up. But this story isn't about Pacbell per say, or the streets. It kind of isn't about the rain when I think about it, but it's all very important.

Why?

Well, you see, there's a very old cemetery at the edge of the town. Its sign is so old that it's broken in many spots so the only letters you can make out are, **RESTEW CETRY**.

I think it means Restview Cemetery. Or Crestview Cemetery. Or my friends and I joke and say it's Really Good Stew Cemetery or the gross ones Tommy Rohi thought of, Regurgitated Stew Cemetery. He's so gross sometimes, even for me. Anyway, my point is that the cemetery was flooded, too. Bad. Water was rising up to the headstones and everything. They were like rocks in the rapids, something really scary looking if you think about it. The cemetery was on a part in Pacbell that wasn't too high or too low. Like Baby Bears porridge, it was just right. But on that day, it didn't matter. The rain still flooded it.

The good news in this story is that just as quick as the rain started, it stopped. I mean literally stopped. I was standing on the one corner thinking about how I was going to eventually be washed away and never found. I say 'one corner' because I really had no clue where I was. Well, I knew I was in Pacbell and I knew I was somewhere between Sanderson Avenue and Morris Street, because I was on my way to school and because I could see the cemetery. But the rain was so hard, it was impossible to see. Until it stopped.

When it stopped, people started to come out of their houses to survey the scene. I stood quiet for a minute or two, trying to convince myself that what I was seeing was true.

What was I seeing you ask?

Well, this is where this little story takes a turn, a big turn. I'm talking U-turn at top speed while holding a topped-off cup of hot coffee.

As I stood on the corner of what I now knew was Sanderson and Jefferson, I watched as large cement blocks were washing into the streets. The blocks were tombs. Yes, tombs that held dead bodies, those kind of tombs. I've heard stories of how flooded areas would bury their dead above ground so they don't float out of the ground. Well, guess what? The ground had absorbed so much water that it pushed the tombs to the surface.

Now wait, before you 'oh' or 'ah,' I'm not done.

If it wasn't bad enough that the tombs of the dead were littering the street like forgotten rocks, one had tipped over and its old cement top had cracked into pieces.

And that's when I saw the old man, hobbled over, in a worn-out suit with frayed hair and rotten skin. He was sitting up and had worms crawling in and out of his one eye socket like it was a passage way. He tipped his head back and growled. I stepped back in horror as my mind played the 'yes/no' game where one said it was a zombie and the other side said it wasn't.

I took three steps back and hit something. When I turned, I saw that more tombs had tipped over and broken up. Before I saw it, I knew I was going to be face to face with one...with a zombie.

Okay, so here I am standing face to face with a zombie. Like, a real zombie. And it's not like in the movies where they show people doctored up with makeup and fake blood, walking with a limp and their head bouncing off their shoulder. Oh, no. I wish it was that way this morning in Pacbell. Maybe these were super zombies or something, I don't know—like I said, I'm not a scientist, I'm a fourteen-year-old girl just trying to get to school.

This zombie, which I recognized as Mrs. Hartley, was eyeing me up and down. She knew I was there and knew what I was. Her faded blue dress was covered in mud and splotches that I prayed were ketchup stains, but I knew it was blood. Her hands were curled in a permanent attack position, but that could have been because of her bad arthritis. Mrs. Hartley was such a sweetheart. She used to tell us her husband's name was Arthur Itis and then hold up her crooked hands and laugh. Yeah, I guess it is creepy when you describe it, but she meant no harm.

Well, maybe *she* meant no harm, but the zombie version of herself wanted to kill me.

I know this because before I could say a word—in all my time of thinking and planning out life, I never imagined I'd be face to face with a living dead person, so what do you say? —Mrs. Hartley was on the attack. For an old woman with 'Arthur Itis' in her entire body, not to mention being dead, she moved pretty quick. Lucky for me, I sidestepped just far enough away from the initial attack that when she went for my throat, she got my shoulder instead. Her crippled hand clutched it with enough strength that I could feel her rotting nails dig into my skin. Then I wondered, *If she touches my blood, do I turn into a zombie? Or wait, was that vampires? Or something else?*

Whatever, that didn't matter as much as the fact that I had to get away from Mrs. Hartley before I found out what happened. It was kind of sad when you think about it, because I went to Mrs. Hartley's viewing. Not by choice though, I hate that stuff. It's so creepy to sit in a little, wooden folding chair, and stare at a dead body. But I do remember Mrs. Hartley being the first lady to give me money on Halloween. At the time I thought it was terrible, until I went to the candy store and was able to buy more with the money than what she would have given me. It was a great moment for me. Well, those moments are gone now because there really isn't such a thing as a candy store these days. Sad but true.

Anyway, I knew it was wrong, but I also knew it was survival when I punched Mrs. Hartley in the arm. She moaned and let go of me. I apologized—even though I'm a 'tom-boy' I still have manners—and ran. My jeans were soaked and stuck to my legs and my shoes were like heavy sponges strapped to my feet. I was so happy I wasn't a prissy girl wearing some kind of dress—that would have been terrible to run in.

Getting away from Mrs. Hartley wasn't that hard really. She was still old and wobbly. Plus, she found a new interest after I ran away—a squirrel. She plucked that thing from a low branch with the accuracy and speed of one of those cranes that swoop down and grab a fish out of the water. I jogged along with my head turned, watching it unfold. She grabbed the squirrel and shoved the thing in her mouth like it was a piece of popcorn. No lie. Her jaws expanded and the furry little creature was gone.

That's when I started to run faster.

Oh, and if that wasn't bad enough yet, from the corner of my eye I saw more zombies crawling out of their tombs. And it seemed they all had a keen eye for me.

I had one choice, get to school.

In my mind, I remembered those silly drills we had where they would make us sit under our desks—I think that was for terrorists—and then the ones where we sat in the halls with our backs against the lockers. I think that was for tornados. I thought maybe if I could get to school, there would be enough people there to help with the situation at hand. And I didn't mean the flooding.

I feel like there's more twists in this story than a knotted ball of Christmas lights because zombies were starting to appear everywhere. The first set of zombies I understood—they came from the old cemetery. Most of those zombies were really old people, some with skin and some just bones. But now, waiting for me at the end of Sanderson Avenue, was a gathering of more zombies. Only these were people that last time I saw them, had been very much alive.

There was Becky, Tim-Tim, and Frank. Becky was the only other girl in school that could beat the other boys in gym class. We weren't really friends, but we knew each other. Tim-Tim was a big...oh, how should I put it. A doofus. Remember those football movies with the really fat linebacker guy who couldn't spell his own name but could lift a car over his head? Yeah, that was Tim-Tim. Rumor was that he got hit by a car two years ago and the person that hit him knew him and got out of the car and asked if he was okay. All he could respond with while drooling was 'Tim-Tim.' His real name is John Ryder, nothing original, I know, but forever in Pac High—as we call the high school—he's Tim-Tim. Even to the teachers and principal.

And Frank, well, Frank was a moocher. He had rich parents. That meant a big house, lots of entertainment, and a car. So of course Frank was popular. To me, he was a tool. The type of kid that would end up in the background of peoples pictures, but in his mind, thought he was part of it. Creepy.

Yeah, so anyway, I had to walk towards them. I figured once Mrs. Hartley was done with her afternoon snack, she'd come for me.

At first I didn't realize that Becky, Tim-Tim, and Frank were zombies. I mean, sure, they were just standing there with their heads bobbing and looking all ragged, but that's how I always pictured them looking. Then I saw that Frank was missing an eye and Becky was missing an arm. Oh, and Tim-Tim...he was gnawing on Becky's other arm like it was a chicken wing on Rookies' wing night.

I screamed, I'll admit it. I shouldn't have, but I did. When I yelled, Tim-Tim looked up at me with a set of red eyes that made me want to scream again. His skin was all flaky and kind of gray, but yellow at the same time—if that makes sense. Becky stood a few feet from Tim-Tim, unconcerned that her arm was missing. Then I wondered if Tim-Tim took her arm before or after she was dead.

Dead.

Wow. People dead. Rising again.

I was left with little options. If I crossed the street, it was like going into zombie-ville. The cemetery was now flooded with walking corpses. Behind me was Mrs. Hartley and in front of me, blocking my way to school, were people I considered friends. Well, to their faces anyway.

Frank just stared at the ground. He was lost. But he didn't look discolored.

"Frank?" I called out. "Are you...alive?"

Becky moaned and stepped towards me. I stepped back. Tim-Tim went back to chewing on Becky's arm, peeling off pieces of muscle like string cheese.

My stomach flipped, flopped, and if I had eaten that second bowl of cereal that morning, it would have made a gallant return.

Then Frank, such a wise-guy, he winked at me. You know, with his good eye. I actually think he tried to blink, because when he winked, the eye socket missing the eye started to pour out some green stuff, kind of like squishing spinach out of a can.

No Pop-Eye here though. This was real stuff.

Then, if that weren't enough, I made a terrible realization. These guys were alive yesterday. I know I already said that, but that meant they were changed. They were like eaten or bitten or something and then came back.

That meant everything was worse than I'd thought.

Becky took another wobbly step towards me.

"Hey, Becky," I said in a shaky voice. I don't know why I tried talking to her. "How's it going? How about the rain, huh?"

Becky moaned. She stepped towards me again.

Tim-Tim fought with Becky, still not done with his morning snack. Frank looked at me again, with his one eye, and lunged.

Then everything happened so fast that I'm not sure if what I'm going to say is completely true.

Frank was in the air, about seven feet at least. He was like a flying zombie. But his limbs, it was amazing to see, they curled up and positioned as if he were an animal. I stepped back, like yeah, that was going to do anything. I put my hands over my face and started to think about what my last thought should be. And you know what? That's not easy to do. Having your life flash before your eyes and stuff. There's so much to think about. But anyway, back to flyin' Frank. I assumed he was just about to hit me, like I said, my hands were over my face. I heard a popping-squishy sound, something like if you threw a twenty pound tomato against a brick wall.

When I opened my eyes, Frank was on the ground. His head, well, let's just say that was the twenty pound tomato if you catch my meaning.

I looked over and saw Mr. Killborn. He was the redneck, gun nut of the town. He had a big rusted pickup truck with a set of deer antlers duct taped to the half busted grille of the truck. He had three big antennas on the truck and his back windows were littered with stickers—everything from 'A Bad Day of Hunting is Better than a Good Day at Work' to 'Help Control the Deer Population—Have Your Deer Filleted and Pan Fried.' Mr. Killborn had a full on mullet, wore ripped clothes, and had a faded truckers hat, but that son-of-a-gun saved my life.

Before I could say a word to him, he reloaded his gun and then BAM! BAM! There went Tim-Tim and Becky's heads, too.

Gone.

Just like that.

They were nothing but piles of human burger meat. It really didn't bother me so much, like I said, I didn't like those people that much.

"Ya's gotta get to that there high school," Mr. Killborn called out. His speech was messed up because he had a wad of chew buried in both bottom sides of his mouth. He spat and the lump of spit kind of looked like what used to be Becky's head.

Weird.

"Thanks, Mr. Killborn!" I called out.

"Eh, there, Dani-girl?"

I turned back.

"Yer friend jumped like that cuz they's can change the animals, too."

Surprisingly, I understood everything Mr. Killborn said. Not only could the zombies change humans, but they could change animals. Another great twist. Stupid rain.

I turned to run but stopped. Call it having a heavy heart, but I felt bad for Mr. Killborn. Here he was, helping me and yet everyone in town talked behind his back. They actually talked about him to his face but he sometimes didn't understand what they were saying. Or doing.

"Mr. Killborn!" I called out.

He turned around, spat on the ground, and nodded.

"Why don't you come with me? To the school. It's safe there, right?" I said.

"Hell yeah, it's safe there. They's asked me to come out here to, ya know, help out a lil' bit."

Mr. Killborn cocked his gun, then smiled, showing a set of brown teeth.

"Plus, I love me a good killin'." I nodded and ran away. Okay, fine, Mr. Killborn helped me, sure, but he's still creepy as hell.

As I jogged down the street, there were zombies scattered around. Most were from the cemetery, which I'm not sure if that was a good thing or not. I mean, sure, it was good because it meant that maybe not a lot of people had been turned into zombies, but then again, there were still zombies roaming around Pacbell.

A few of the zombies took notice of me and started to move towards me. Only two came close. One was some old guy, probably dead a hundred years or something. Well, actually, that's not true.

He still had some flesh on his bones. Did I not mention that these zombies weren't like the ones in the movies where they're full-formed people? If I didn't, here's the skinny—however they rise is how they are. If they were a pile of bones, they rose as a pile of bones. I know, crazy, right? Not only did I have to see these dead people rising from their graves, but I had to deal with actual skeletons walking around.

Anyways, the almost skeleton zombie was easy to dodge; it had no real strength or speed. The other one though, which I quickly recognized as Stevey Petersman, was coming at me at about a hundred miles an hour. In case you aren't from the Southeast area of Pennsylvania, Stevey Petersman is the fastest runner in the area—and probably the state.

I had no defense and I knew it. I just stood there. I didn't even put my hands to my face this time. I figured screw it, if I'm going, I'm going. Then I'd be walking around chewing on flesh. But hey, it's better than taking a math test I totally forgot to study for, right?

Stevey was coming at me with big, black eyes. They were dead, for sure. But he was moving, for sure. His arms pumped at his sides and his legs were so damn long, he would have gotten two steps to my one if I tried to run.

Then, as if the world was set on repeat, Stevey's head exploded. I'm talking like a quick *whish* sound and then *plop*, head gone. The craziest part was that his body kept running, kind of like when you catch a Daddy long legs spider and tear a leg off and it keeps kicking. Stevey ran right by me and into a parked car before falling. Even while he was on the ground, his arms and legs kept pumping.

Who saved me? None other than Mr. Killborn. I looked up the street and he was sitting on the hood of his truck with the gun resting in his lap and a pair of binoculars in his hand. I waved and he spat his chew. I took it as a sign of 'you're welcome' and then I hauled ass to the school.

No walking.

No jogging.

Full on running.

For a girl who refuses to participate in any sort of athletic event, I made pretty good time to the school. I wasn't attacked again by any zombies, which was a good thing because at the bottom of the hill, the road turned enough so that even if he wanted to, Mr. Killborn wouldn't have been able to help me.

Our school, good old Pac High, was nothing short of a prison. And no, I'm not lying about that. There were high metal fences, the building was a dreaded, dull-looking color, and the windows didn't open. There was a long, iron gate in front of the parking lot, and in front of the school. The sidewalks twisted and winded as if you weren't sure where or how to walk to the building. At one point, after some problems in other schools, they made all the girls carry see-through purses and no book bags were allowed.

None. At all.

Oh, and they had metal detectors and cops. Well, they still had cops there, but everything else cooled down. It kind of pissed me off because I thought high school would be like on television where the kids can wander in and out of the building, eat at picnic tables, and you know, be a little bit free.

But not at Pac High.

Up until the day the zombies came, I hated that school. But when I got to the gate and saw Bambi with his man boobs puffed out like armor and his hand on his mace, I never wanted to be there so bad.

Bambi was the officer who patrolled the halls of Pac High. I think his real name was John or Jerry or something, and to be honest, I have no idea why everyone calls him Bambi. He's a short guy and quite round—I'm trying not to call him fat. He has stubby fingers and his neck rolled over the collar of his police uniform. But no matter how he looked, he's a nice guy. Takes his job seriously... no, I mean *seriously*, like he's guarding the White House or something.

"Dani, that you?" he bellowed out from behind the iron gate at school.

"Yeah, Bambi, it's me."

Bambi lifted the can of mace and put his hands on his handcuffs. He stepped forward in a stance that reminded me of something I used to have to do when I was forced to take those stupid karate classes.

"What are you doing?" I asked him.

"I need to know you're okay," he replied.

"I'm talking, aren't I? Here, look, no wounds." I lifted arms and then showed him my neck.

"How did you get here? Without getting attacked?"

I looked over my shoulder and saw a small gathering of zombies, all bumping into each other, coming towards me.

"Dammit, Bambi, let me in!"

I took a big risk in that moment and I charged the gate. Bambi, oh sweet Bambi, that big man jumped back and crashed to the ground. His little canister of mace hit the pavement and rolled away. He looked up at me with the most terrified yet innocent eyes, I actually felt bad for him. Almost as bad as I feel when I watch one of those commercials with the animals in shelters and they're asking you to donate money so they show the weakest, yet cutest, animals.

"Bambi, come on," I pleaded.

He rolled to his belly and pushed himself up and let me in.

It was a good thing because when he closed the gate, the zombies were a few feet away. They ran into the gate with a loud thud and started to claw and push each other out of the way, hoping to be the one to get in.

"What's happening?" I asked Bambi.

"To the gym! Now," he said.

I did as I was told and found myself in the Pac High gym with about twenty people. Some young, some old. Some I knew from school, some I didn't. I recognized Tommy Rohi sitting at the top of the bleachers, so I joined him.

"Rough morning?" Tommy asked.

"Both Mr. Killborn and Bambi saved my life, so yeah, it's been a rough morning."

"Attention everyone!" a voice called out.

It was our town's Mayor, Mr. Luvies.

"I'm not sure what's happening or how to explain this, but the rain has wreaked havoc to our town. I've made a few calls and there have been a handful of other towns in the state experiencing the same phenomenon. But there's good news! Our neighbors, Lower Valley, they're all fine."

"That's because they're zombies to begin with," Tommy whispered to me.

I chuckled. School rivalries were so stupid. but yes, Pac High had one—with Lower Valley. Everyone joked that Lower Valley meant that all the kids there were lower in brains or something.

Mr. Luvies continued his speech.

"The military is sending in aid to help us but until then, we're to travel to Lower Valley. We'll be safe there until this...this *event* is over."

The dead walking, killing people, killing animals...that's just an event? Sometimes I wish I could be as shallow as politicians so I could live in a fantasy world. But then again, I'm a teenager, and everyone tells me I'm already living in one.

Mr. Luvies started to explain an evacuation route, when Bambi entered through the door of the gym. I figured he was bringing more survivors.

With me, he'd opened the door and led me in, but this time he came head first through the door of the gym. I'm talking his head went literally through the door. And then he kept walking, taking the door with him.

As soon as I saw Bambi's face, my heart sank. He was a zombie. Then I noticed the cracks in his skin and the rough patches on his face. He was a full fledged, flesh-eating creature.

"Bambi's a zombie," Tommy Rohi said.

Bambi charged towards Mr. Luvies, who was about to say something as Bambi took him down. Mr. Luvies crashed to the gym floor with an echoing boom and then Bambi started to growl and chew into Mr. Luvies' neck. Blood sprayed half the gym and those within a ten foot radius were getting soaked.

"Shit," Tommy whispered as the gym started to fill up with screams. "I don't like this at all."

"I know, it's gross," I said. "And Bambi was a cool guy."

"To hell with Bambi," Tommy said. "If he's a zombie, that means..."

Before Tommy could finish, they came in. All of them. All the zombies. They poured into the gym by the dozens; some with flesh, some with half-flesh, some with bones, and some as people that were just regular people, like you and me, just this morning.

I'll admit it. I froze. I was done. Checked out. Ready to just toss myself into the pile and be done with it all. But thankfully, Tommy stayed cool. He grabbed my shoulder and pulled me.

"We have to get to the end of the bleachers and then climb down."

"Then what?" I whispered.

"Get to Lower Valley."

The horde of zombies chewed and howled like a hungry pack of wolves. Those who tried to run slipped in the puddles of blood and when they fell, zombies piled on top of them.

Tommy's plan was brilliant. We were hidden from the zombies. We were able to step down nice and slow and get to the gym floor in no time. He took my hand so I could jump the last few feet and we were golden, ready to get the hell out of Pac High.

Not so fast, though. We turned and there was Mr. Luvies, back from the dead. A good portion of his body was eaten, there were pieces of skin hanging from him like a ripped shirt. One side of his head was flat from where Bambi had tackled him.

"Mayor Luvies," Tommy said. "You look terrible."

Mr. Luvies grunted and charged.

Then, that son-of-a-gun, Tommy, he stepped away! He left me standing there, just a few feet from Mr. Luvies, the zombie-mayor of Pacbell.

Again, like it was becoming a new routine, I put my hands to my face. I peeked between my fingers and to my surprise, Tommy was on the floor with his leg out, swooping it around. He hit Mr. Luvies' ankles.

"Move!" Tommy yelled.

I stepped to the side and the zombie-mayor smashed his face off the grated pieces of the bleachers. It looked like someone was forcing hamburger meat through a meat grinder, if you catch my drift.

Tommy and I didn't waste a second, we ran out the back of gym, down the long corridor, and out the back door of Pac High.

From that very second forward, I felt like I was in a horror movie. I know, it's crazy, why did it take that long? Well, mostly because I was in a bit of denial. I just expected everything to somehow work out, like it always does. Think about it—when there's some kind of disaster or storm or something, the news people make it out to be the worst thing in the world but then a day or two later everything works out just fine. Little damage, lots of hope, blah, blah, blah.

But that day, when I walked out of the back of Pac High, I just knew things were going to always be different.

For one thing, Tommy had grabbed my hand, and as much as I wanted to fight it, I liked it. Ew, boys, right? Well, not so much for me. Mark it down, folks, sweet innocent Dani—the fourteen-year-old girl who was going to rule the world by sixteen—liked a boy.

The second thing was that zombies were everywhere. Worse than before. Worse than in the gym. It was just masses upon masses of undead things. I watched for a few seconds and saw how some people were eaten right down to the bone, like my Uncle Petey does with his chicken wings—practically gnawing on them like a dog. Some people, the zombies took only a few bites. The person would die and then wake up, only changed into a zombie.

"Dani, come on," Tommy whispered to me. He squeezed my hand and my heart fluttered a little. Damn, I really liked Tommy Rohi. What a terrible thing to happen on a terrible day.

"Where are we going?" I asked him.

"To the mountains," a voice crackled from our left.

I turned and there he was, again, Mr. Killborn. Gun and all. But no truck.

"Where's your truck?" Tommy asked.

"Bastards ate it," Mr. Killborn said. He spit his chew and then blessed himself.

"Why the mountains?" I asked.

"Cuz, they's safe. Plus the other valley's there."

Thankfully Mr. Killborn had a sense of direction. Looking at the mountains, I couldn't tell if they would take me to Lower Valley or China.

"I's only gots 'bout ten more shots, then I'm dry." Mr. Killborn spat again. He raised his gun and aimed. I covered my ears, ready for the bang of the gun. It never came.

"Okay, they's look busy. We should be walkin'."

Mr. Killborn turned and started to move with speed. Tommy pulled me along, and for a quick second, I pictured us on the beach and him pulling me to the shoreline right as a wave was crashing. Then he'd pull me in and we'd kiss...okay, quit laughing. I'm a girl. I like chick-flicks. And I have my own little dreams now and then.

"Ah shit!" Mr. Killborn called out.

That broke up my dream fast. We stopped walking and saw a deer. It didn't have any horns or antlers or whatever they're called. I think that meant it was a girl. Only guy deer's are horny, eh? Yeah, my lame attempt at humor.

Anyways, the deer looked at us and its eyes were red and bulging. Half its ribs were missing and blood and organs dangled from it. It was a zombie, too. An animal zombie. A deer zombie.

Mr. Killborn raised his gun and BAM! There went the deer's head. It splattered like the time my Uncle Petey shot a pumpkin.

The sound of the gunshot attracted the attention of the other zombies and once they realized some fresh, living meat was available, they started to charge us. Mr. Killborn headed for the base of the mountain. He threw his gun over his shoulder, and the way it bounced off the ripped and torn bag on his back, I hoped it wouldn't go off by accident. That would suck.

Every step it seemed we took, the zombies took two, maybe three. They were gaining on us and we were running out of breath.

Twenty minutes later, we reached the base of the mountain, all of us exhausted from running.

Trying to climb the mountain was horrible, especially since the rain made the ground all mushy. Water and mud kicked up with each step, and Mr. Killborn kept yelling random orders out at us, like we were an army.

"No dammit, we stay as one. Else we die alone!" he called out.

I had no idea what he meant.

Tommy never let go of my hand and I never let go of my vision of us on the beach.

I could hear the zombies trampling along behind us, breaking sticks, moaning, grunting as they got closer and closer.

"Mr. Killborn!" I called out. "They're going to get us."

"We keep movin', little Dani!" he cried out.

And keep movin' we did. Until a zombie lunged, grabbed my ankle, and pulled me away from Tommy's sweaty grip.

My face crashed into the side of the hill. I tasted wet dirt, dry leaves, and blood. Tommy dove over me and on top of the zombie and started to punch and kick it. The zombie let me go. For a second, I thought we were saved. But no way, there were hundreds more coming. All of them, with their huge black eyes as they wobbly walked and climbed.

Some were flesh, some just bone, and some had pieces of their bodies missing. One dude, I think it was Chet from English—he used to try and cheat off my tests so I'd give him the wrong answers. Yeah, I'm like that sometimes—he was missing an arm, but he kept walking, blood squirting everywhere.

"I didn't want this now, but to hell wit it," Mr. Killborn said. "You's two back up some steps. I'm gonna light the mountain up!"

Mr. Killborn also loved fire. Guns and fire. His two favorite things. He used his last shots to take care of the zombies that were within range of getting to us, then he dropped the gun and his bag. He opened it and pulled out two gas cans. How scary is that? This guy was walking around all this time with gas cans?

"What are you doing?" Tommy asked.

"They're followin' us, kid," Mr. Killborn said, "so we burn 'em. Then we get to the other side and let nature do its thing."

Mr. Killborn tossed the gas around the trees and ground like he was an old pro at setting forest fires. Who knows, maybe he was. The zombies kept moving forward, making noises, ready to attack.

I took Tommy's hand and then Mr. Killborn pulled out a lighter and lit the mountain on fire.

The yellow-orange flames shot up and ate the trees and ground. I'd never seen anything like it before. It was crazy. And the zombies? Those sons-of-guns, they walked through the flames like the fire wasn't there. Mr. Killborn instructed us to run again, which we did, but the zombies followed. They chased us until all their flesh was melted off, and those who were just bones, well, their bones were charred, cracked, and they fell to pieces. Their skin was bubbly and seeped pus, then turned red and white, and then broke open and oozed and goo-ed, as it fell off like melting chunks of butter.

Horrible. Just friggin' horrible.

As the mountain burned, I thought for a second about everyone back in Pacbell. What about Mom and Dad? They were two towns over so I hoped that once it was all said and done I'd see them again. When I got to Lower Valley, I told myself I'd call Mom's office and check in. Tommy looked sick to his stomach. I could only assume that meant his parents worked in Pacbell. Poor guy.

"Ah, look at her go!" Mr. Killborn cried out.

And there it was. Lower Valley. Right down the other side of the mountain and we were home free. The mountain side behind us still burned and any zombies that dared to follow us would be burned to nothing.

Things were pretty good then.

We charged down the mountain in what had to be record time. I don't know how I didn't end up falling and just rolling to the bottom like a damn fool. But either way, we made it.

I jumped from the last piece of dirt and mountain and onto the road, then smiled. "We did it!" I yelled happily.

"Yup, we did," Mr. Killborn said.

"Tommy, are you okay?" I asked gently, squeezing his hand.

He turned towards me. I felt my heart flutter again. I knew this was it—our first kiss. I didn't even care that Mr. Killborn was picking his nose and adjusting his belt a few feet away.

"I'm fine, why?" Tommy asked.

"Oh, just asking," I said.

Then he let my hand go and turned around...and so ended that relationship. What a jerk.

But we were safe. And better than that, a man came out of a house across the street and offered us a drink. He had an enclosed screen porch and he let us watch television so we could see what was happening elsewhere.

"Crazy rain," the man said. "That's what they're calling it. Saying some kind of chemical in the rain made it happen. There was a chemical plant about a hundred miles or so away that exploded. Somehow the chemicals got airborne and fell with the rain."

"Them's asshole in Hampton County," Mr. Killborn said. "They're experimentin' on things that ain't theirs to do so."

The man nodded at Mr. Killborn. I took a sip of my water and it tasted great. Tommy stood in the doorway, staring at the mountain.

"Clean up ain't so bad," the man said. "They have most of it all contained. Even some of the people infected can be cured, they said."

I thought about the infected people, with their gaping wounds and missing body parts. There was no way a zombie was going to be turned back. That was just something the news was saying to make everyone feel better.

I called Mom and she was fine—at work. She had no idea what was going on until I told her. She didn't believe me at first. You know, since I'm a teenager and all we do is lie. She said she'd call Dad and then make arrangements for me to meet in Lower Valley.

Things seemed good—almost normal. Then I heard the man gasp in surprise, Tommy cry out, and Mr. Killborn curse under his breath. When I walked back out to the porch, it was starting to rain.

SCHOOL FOR ZOMBIES

LINDSAY KUPSCO

It didn't take long for them to leave. The teachers were more freaked out than most of the students. They might not have shown it right away, herding us all into the gym and trying to keep us calm, but you could tell by that sheen of sweat on their upper lips and around their hairlines that they weren't okay. But who could blame them?

I was in Honors level science when it happened. Honors was the only science class that got to dissect before high school. I was the only girl to successfully crack a frog's head open and remove the brain without reducing it to mush. You have to crack the little guy's jaw, thumb on one side, forefinger on the other, and press hard. It'll pop more than it'll crack. Like an egg, but violent and a bit sad. Then you have to use a tiny prodding tool to pull the brain out through the gaping jaw. Mrs. Jacobs was at my lab table leaning in very close to examine my masterpiece.

"Excellent work, Ms. Stevens," she'd said. No one looked up at this. No one ever looked up for me though. I was perpetually unnoticed.

She patted me on the back gently and congratulated me, but then her hand rested there for a moment. Mrs. Jacobs was gazing past me, through the windows that looked out at the soccer field next to the school. Her hand jumped, making me twitch in fear, when the gnarled remains of a human being slammed itself into the window.

It bashed harder and harder, ramming into the glass, like if it could only get that one good hit, it would finally make it through the window. The final time it smashed its head against the glass, it successfully cracked open its own jaw, making a terrible egg pop noise, but it didn't remove its brain whole. Instead, deep red and black molasses and grape jelly brain matter and bone fragments stuck sloppily and heavily to the glass. Finally, the entire class was looking up. Finally I shared something with my classmates, but I'm not sure if it was confusion or fear.

While Mrs. Jacobs turned on the TV hanging in the corner of the lab-style classroom, Janie Olsen leaned forward and threw up whatever breakfast sandwich her mom had prepared for her that morning onto Danny Trevors' brand new red Nike high tops, which were ugly anyway. Missy Newburg fainted and hit her head decently hard on the cold tile floor and stayed down. Jeremy Bankerton fell off his stool, and we thought he broke his tailbone for a second, even though later we'd figure out it was only a deep bruise.

"The dead have risen," the news reporter said from the TV. Her hair was bobbed and the kind of red that looked like a three-year-old had colored her in with a simple crayon. She had her news reporter-concerned face on so I couldn't decide if she was serious, even after I'd watched a 'man' bash his own decaying face into a window. The tone in the room finally decided on fear, the silent and watchful kind.

"In a scene reminiscent of a zombie film, a graveyard in Wheaton, Illinois erupted with crawling dead. No one is quite sure what caused the dead to reanimate, but as in all the movies, they are cannibalistic. They are slow moving but vicious, and until the police can decide the best plan of action, they recommend everyone stay indoors. Keep your televisions tuned to MSNBC for the latest on the rising dead in Illinois. In other news, the gun deaths in the United States are still the highest of any industrialized country in the world. How will this affect the upcoming midterm elections?"

Mrs. Jacobs' face drained to a shade of milky bluish white. She turned slowly toward the class, her face twisted up in confusion and desperation. She turned her gold wedding band around and around nervously. Peter Rancowski was kneeling down by Missy Newburg and checking her head as she shook herself awake. There was blood on his fingers, but she was responsive. Mrs. Jacobs couldn't care less about Missy though. Something inside of me wanted to tell the tall, slim woman to pull it together and help us, but watching someone I always saw as a strong woman, start to pull the tight bun out of her hair and let her limp arms fall to her sides, made me speechless.

We all sat in stunned silence for a moment until the principal made an announcement that everyone should report to the gym. All male teachers and eighth grade boys would help board up windows and doors with whatever was around from woodshop or pieces of desks that they'd break.

"I'm sure most of you are terrified," Miss Jenkins, the fifty-something year old principal told us calmly. "But rest assured, the police will handle this." I could barely hear her over the cell phone conversations with mothers and fathers and the crying and the nurse trying to keep the fainters and pukers in a confined corner near the bleachers. I sat alone on the hardwood gym floor, leaning against the wall, feeling the cool, painted brick under my hot cheeks. I wished I had a cell phone so I could call my parents. I wanted to hear them tell me it would be okay, because no matter how old you are, your mother's voice saying to calm down always works, and your father telling you that he'd rather die than let you get hurt is the thing that will calm your bubbling stomach.

It shouldn't have happened here, I thought as I bounced my knee slowly in rhythm with my breathing. Not in a pricy suburb of Chicago. Not in a place where the kids can walk down the street to buy slushies and the high school kids went to big multiplex movie theaters and hung out at the local hot dog place after football games on Friday nights. Not in a place where the moms drove minivans full of retractable TV screens and dads let their sons drive their Jaguars on their first date with a girl.

But there I was, a meek, average-looking girl with too long, unkempt hair and jeans one size too big. I was dropped off at my Blue Ribbon Award junior high school with too much money in my pocket and with sushi in my lunchbox, anxiously biting my nails and watching all the kids I would never get the chance to be friends with, as they cried into cell phones at their parents, who were desperately trying to figure out how to be the heroes their kids needed them to be.

It took about two weeks for most people to realize that no one would be coming to retrieve us and deliver us to safety. The news reports got worse as the reporters stated cases of the same rising dead much further away than just Illinois. Villages in China, cities in Germany, towns in Mexico, all of them were being overrun. Videos of people getting mauled by their decaying loved ones because they saw their faces, however grotesque, and couldn't bear to kill them; those were the worst to watch. And gradually, after the last report on how if you get bitten and chop the limb off within seventy-three seconds you can save yourself, everyone realized just how awful things had gotten.

The power stayed on, which was nice, but we conserved and left the lights on only when necessary because we never knew when that could end. There would be one classroom with the lights on all night, the big study hall room, for the kids and teachers who heard the random thuds against the walls at night and couldn't handle the memories of the first time they saw chunks of brain matter spewed across a window.

I mostly sat in the library, like before this 'Zombie Apocalypse,' and read silently by the dim glow of the emergency lights in the corners, and thought of my brother Jackson at the high school, probably taking a lot more action than I was, doing a lot more to save himself. He was my exact opposite, but we got along well, and he appreciated my quiet behavior and I admired his personality. He had the same golden brown eyes and the same long, boney fingers as me. I never felt jealous of him until the world fell apart, when I wished I had his bravery and excitement for the unknown so I could do something besides sit in the quiet library reading Fitzgerald and trying to learn not to flinch at the sound of crunching bone against brick outside.

Sometimes I'd hide on the roof by myself when the air grew too thick inside. The zombies couldn't climb anything, so I'd watch them stumble around the parking lot and soccer field and track toward the school, desperately searching for the flesh and blood they craved. There weren't a massive amount of them at first, but people didn't see them as that overwhelming of a threat because they didn't run too fast. And even if they got a chunk out of you, but didn't eat you right away, most people either didn't realize the seriousness or freaked out so bad that they couldn't actually calm down enough to cut their own bodies up in seventy-three seconds or less. So I watched the mothers and fathers and siblings stumble toward the school, like they could smell us out or feel us, with their arms and legs and fingers barely holding on by strips of sinewy flesh.

The ones that I didn't like to watch were the ones with broken ankles and knees. Every time they stepped they had no regard for the damage it did, no regard for the awful tearing crack of bone and muscle. Eventually, their feet would drag for too long and they'd rip off. The zombies would resort to crawling at that point, leaving a trail of sticky black slime behind them like a decrepit snail.

The teachers started to get restless after that first realization that we were on our own. While I was hiding in the library or on the roof, they were hiding in the lounge and in other classrooms and whispering, plotting. When they did see us, they were testy and gave up on discipline. They eyed us suspiciously and slept behind locked doors instead of in the gym with all of us. And then one day, Esteban Fuentes woke up to get a granola bar for breakfast and saw the nails had been pried out of the door next to the gym that led straight to the teachers' parking lot.

"Of fucking course!" he'd yelled from the end of the hallway, his voice the first loud noise we'd heard in weeks bouncing off of the sky blue lockers. The two hundred and eleven kids that got locked in this junior high school two weeks earlier slowly marched into the long hallway. They stared at the doors, left open to the danger that none of us could truly understand.

Some dumb kids like Roger Jenning and Phillip Newland knocked out a classroom window and knocked down a trophy case in sheer rage. The girls started to wail and ran to the bathrooms as if we were still junior high students and not abandoned teenagers with no survival skills of our own. I made my way to the door while avoiding screams and thrown punches and helped Peter Rancowski nail the door shut again, fearing that all the noise would only attract more of them.

"They just left us, Carly," Peter remarked to me. "What are we going to do?"

I was in so much shock that this dark skinned boy with blue eyes knew my name that I couldn't answer him. I just stared.

"Are you okay, Carly?" he asked me.

"They weren't helping us anyway," I finally managed. "We'll figure something out." Glass shattered behind us and he held my hand as he led us back up the hallway, dodging spewing window panes and locker doors.

Peter Rancowski started coming up to the roof with me. He'd hold my hand as we watched the walking dead stumble toward us, losing pieces of themselves as they covered the distance to the walls of the school. He'd settle my stomach with warm water and oyster crackers whenever I saw the zombies turn on each other and rip off each other's ears or bite off each other's noses. They seemed unaware that eating each other's decaying carcasses would only bring about their 'real' death faster. The cracking of weakened bones was a terrifying soundtrack to what should have been our eighth grade graduation, but Peter had hummed Eric Clapton and Elton John and pretended we could still have a life for a minute on the roof.

When July came, the heat was blistering and we couldn't go up to the roof often. The food supply ran so low that we were barely allowed one meal a day, and all of us were losing weight off our already thin, adolescent bodies quickly.

We still had running water, and some days it'd come out a cloudy brown color, but most days it would clear up fast and we could keep drinking and taking showers. The soap ran low as well, and the sweat stains that gathered on our rotation of street clothes and gym clothes were getting harder to wash out. With all of the heat and the less than adequate meals, consisting mostly of oatmeal and occasionally a frozen chicken nugget or vegetable, fights started breaking out.

Faith Masterson ripped out Winona Peffer's earring over a chocolate bar they'd found in Mr. Morrison's room. Barbara Jenson had to sew Winona's earlobe back together because she got the highest grade in Home Ec and we nominated her. Winona gave Barbara the chocolate bar as a thank you.

Eric Gutierez punched Manny Lopez in the mouth and Manny lost three teeth, all because he drew the longest straw and got the last bit of Trix cereal we had left.

Peter Rancowski got hit in the stomach and he puked up the sorry excuse for the breakfast he'd eaten that morning. He got hit because he tried to tell Ben Loman to stop screaming at his girl-friend, Alexis Bontie. I gave him my breakfast to eat. We walked up to the roof to share it.

We hadn't been up there in days and didn't realize just how aw-ful the heat was going to be. The sun had rotted the zombies' flesh even faster and the odor kicked me in the throat so hard my eyes watered. The death around us walked and crawled and moaned, and all of it decayed in the summer heat, melting and dripping and decomposing into the grass where maggots were born and scavenging animals fed.

There were two or three of our teachers wandering the parking lot, pencil skirts and slacks torn. If I'd had anything in my stomach, I'm sure it would've landed on the gravel roof in an acidic pool. I walked to the edge of the roof and looked down. Peter pulled me back into the rooftop stairwell.

"Death is everywhere," he told me. "Even before this happened. Death was still everywhere, it was just harder to see. Millions of animals, people, organisms like germs, all of that dies every second of every day, but we never saw it before. I wish you didn't have to see it." He rubbed my back. The heat was stifling in the stairwell, but it smelled like dirt and sweat instead of dead people's rotting limbs. I laid my head on his shoulder. I remember feeling goosebumps at his touch for a split second between deep breaths.

"Ernest Hemingway shot himself in the face with his favorite shotgun," I said to Peter. I stared at my heinous gym shoes that should've been replaced at the beginning of the year. They almost embarrassed me in that moment. I'd never been embarrassed before; no one had ever noticed me enough to allow me to be embarrassed. My stomach lurched to know that I'd fallen in love for the first time during the Zombie Apocalypse.

"Maybe we'll see him around then," Peter told me. He ate one of the stale graham crackers I had for our breakfast and made me eat the other. I couldn't remember what fresh crackers tasted like anymore and it made me want to cry.

"*Fuck you!*" we heard from the vents below us, not giving me the chance to start sobbing on Peter's shoulder. The stairs to the roof were from the cafeteria kitchen. The voice was female. It sounded sharp and angry but masked by terror and disgust.

"It's a solution to a problem," a male voice answered.

"She's dead," the female voice said. "She was our friend. You can't eat her, you creep."

Peter's grip around my shoulder tightened. My stomach lurched for the millionth time that day.

"It's my birthday," I told Peter quietly. "I'm fourteen years old today, and there are kids down there arguing about eating a dead girl. A girl died on my birthday and they're going to eat her. No one's ever wished me a happy birthday outside of my family, and I've always hated it. But I would take it in a heartbeat over an argument over when we start eating our dead classmates. I would take loneliness everyday for the rest of my life."

Peter Rancowski stood up and pulled me up next to him. He wiped the tears I didn't realize started burning lines into my cheeks.

"Happy birthday, Carly Stevens," he whispered to me, and kissed me so softly on the mouth I was barely aware it had happened.

He held my hand all the way down the stairs.

"Nobody is eating Toni," Peter told the two voices firmly when he finally saw the body on the floor.

Toni Racine was one of those popular girls who was really nice, but who you also wanted to slap because she would only be your friend when the other popular kids weren't around. But it didn't mean that I wanted her to die and it didn't mean that I wanted anyone to eat her on my birthday.

"And who's gonna stop me?" the male voice asked. The voice belonged to James Crain, a six foot tall football player who looked twenty-three instead of fourteen, and who was dating the female voice in the situation, Gwen Michaelson. She was standing defensively in front of her dead best friend. Toni was flat on her stomach with her hands splayed out by her head. Her dirty blonde hair fell over her hands, and a small trickle of blood stained her cheek by her nose. Gwen's hazel eyes were red and puffed out, and her nose was running.

"She had leukemia," Gwen said, and even though we all knew the story, we let her keep talking. "She'd been in remission since we were eight. All of sudden last year it came back, even though we all thought she was fine. Her hair wasn't falling out, I know, but it's because she didn't have the chemo she needed. She was supposed to start Thursday, the day after all this crap started happening. She shouldn't have even been here, she should've been resting at home. But she wanted to be normal. And then this all happened and she's not just abnormal, she's dead. Toni is dead."

"Yea, Toni is dead, and we're seriously low on food, babe, so get out of my fucking way." James pushed Gwen out of the way and reached down for Toni.

"No," Peter demanded. "Nobody is eating Toni or anyone else." He pushed his thick black hair out of his eyes.

Gary Smith walked into the kitchen at that moment and glared at James. Gary wasn't as big as James, not many eighth graders were. But he was built from running and swimming his whole life, so when he walked up to James and punched him in the face, James fell backward onto the metal prep table and nearly collapsed it.

"You're sick," Gary said to James as Gwen yelped from the side. She ran back to Toni's side and clutched her friend's hand. James immediately stood up and charged at Gary, knocking him down to the tiled floor. He straddled him and grabbed him by the ears, pounding his skull into the floor until we heard the violent, sad pop, and the blood started pouring out of the back of Gary's head. It was thick but spread quickly, and it seemed like it would never stop spreading outward, like it would gush and cover the floors until we were up to our ankles in Gary's blood and brain matter.

For the first time, my intense fear of staying in the school overpowered my fear of the walking dead outside this school.

"You're no better than them," I whispered. I looked at Peter and saw the tears streaking his face and I was desperate to erase the scene from his memory, to make him whole again after this massive piece of his childhood had been ripped out of him.

"What did you just say to me?" James barked. He was still straddling Gary's lifeless body, his jeans soaking up his old friend's blood. He didn't even look at me. "Who are you?"

"My name's Carly Stevens and I've been in class with you since the second grade. And you're no better than the zombies out there bashing at our windows. They tear each other's limbs off and they eat each other and they eat us. Animals have more compassion than you, you monster!"

"Bitch," he said, but he didn't move. He just stared at me with his buzzed hair and green eyes that reminded me of springtime. This notion sickened me even more.

"We'll organize a food mission," Peter said. He'd stopped crying. "We'll get the best runners, give them some bats and golf clubs from the gym, and go to the Wal-Mart a mile down the street. They'll get food and clothes and come back. We'll take a teacher's car, one or two were left behind. There's got to be keys somewhere in here. We'll plan tonight and leave in the morning. Spread the word, be at the gym at sundown. And yes, Gwen, we'll give Toni and Gary proper burials. We'll figure it out somehow." He turned to face James. "And if you ever call Carly a bitch again, you fucking jerk, I'll bleed you dry." Peter grabbed my hand and stomped off down the hall, with a look on his face that screamed fire and rage.

Peter and I went to watch a movie together in the AV room. There weren't many choices so we settled on 'Toy Story' in Spanish.

"I got Mr. Farkas' keys out of his desk," Peter told me. We were sitting on the cold floor, our knees barely touching. "We could go. We could get out of here, me and you."

I silently considered the idea—the idea of Peter and I driving away from this junior high, the mess of books and old white tile and red bricks and zombie covered windows. We were too young to drive, but if we just did it, we wouldn't have to worry about dead cheerleaders being eaten by their classmates or fourteen-year-olds beating each other to death. The idea was so incredibly appealing that my palms began to sweat at the notion of driving until we found someone else. Someone that wasn't going too crazy from the idea of being abandoned by the people they'd been trained to trust since they were old enough to talk.

"I'll go," I told him. It was the first time I truly looked at him, really studied the flecks of gray in his blue eyes, the sun freckles on the bridge of his nose that his caramel-colored skin barely let show. It was the first time I'd really let him look at me, too, as he studied the pale fragility of my cheeks and the hollowness behind my brown eyes. I knew down in the pit of my stomach that if things had never changed, if we were sitting in Honors science and that zombie never smashed its greening, purplish face again the window, and he had asked me to run away with him for no reason, that I would've gone, zombies or not, because I was in love with him, in the only desperate and untainted way a fourteen-year-old girl could be.

Peter and I went to the meeting, he commanded the room with his new sense of purpose. We sacrificed ourselves to be the ones to go on the expedition for food, and of course, no one objected.

We gave the cross country and track runners the task of making a mad dash around the school to attract all the walking dead away from the teachers' exit, and two running backs from the football team to distract the zombies for long enough to bury our dead. I felt bad for their heaving bodies when they got back, malnourished and thin, trying to keep running in the excruciating heat.

Peter dug the graves with six other kids to get it done fast enough, and there was no time for Gwen to honor her best friend. James didn't show his face and no one asked why. Word had spread fast about what he'd done, and it had taken a lot to convince the other boys not to find him and hang him out a window for the zombies to get.

Before the bodies were buried, I was elected to drive a scalpel through their spinal cords. After all, I was the only student who could remove a frog's brain intact. Nobody wanted it to be messy, but we also needed reassurance that our friends wouldn't crawl out of their shallow graves during a thunderstorm.

The pops of their spinal cords were more violent than the frog's jaw. I was wearing gloves, but I could smell the spinal fluid on my hands for days after that, salty and slightly bloody.

I can still smell it in my nightmares sometimes. I wanted to vomit, but the things that you do when you have to, even at fourteen, are always surprising. I mustered my brave face and prayed to whatever god let this happen that it would be the last time I had to do something of the sort, even though I knew it wouldn't be.

And then, two days after we buried Toni and Gary together outside of the gym doors, Peter Rancowski was pulling me along as fast as we could manage while we still held on to garden shears, baseball bats, a hammer, and a bow and arrow from archery class. I didn't do well in that class so I silently hoped Peter knew how to shoot.

We reached Mr. Farkas' Toyota and I heard the runners go around the corner of the gym, where some kids would be ready to pull them inside the doors and nail the boards back in place. I hoped they made it back, but never turned to check.

We made it to the store without any problem, and the Wal-Mart parking lot was mostly empty. The heat and smell made me want to lie down on the pavement and give up, to just melt right into it and let the zombies come and pull my bones apart.

After we went for the main doors, walking quietly to avoid drawing attention, we entered, not surprised to find the doors unlocked. We moved slowly through the aisles, and quietly put as many cans of food, boxes of crackers , bottles of water and cans of soda pop into plastic shopping bags. We heard the first footsteps behind us when we were in the chip and snack aisle, and for a split second I smiled, thinking maybe, just maybe, someone with a pulse had found us. But almost immediately I heard the dragging noise, the scraping of bone on tile and unevenness of the steps.

My heart sank.

I reached for the bat in the backpack I was wearing and turned, swinging as hard as I could. Teeth and pieces of rotting cheeks, tongue and nose went flying, splattering my clothes and Peter's back.

"More of them are here," I whispered to Peter, wishing it wasn't true, but feeling it all the way through my bones and down to my slightly weakened knees. My arms were shaking with adrenalin and my knuckles were white from gripping my bat so tight. "Move slow," I said.

Peter took a step backward, whiter than I'd ever seen him. We moved slowly, perfectly matched in each other's steps.

We made it to the clothing section in near silence, Peter stuffing underwear, socks, jeans, and t-shirts in packages of every size into backpacks and bags. We took as much as we possibly could. I circled around him watching out, knowing that we'd have to make one or two more trips to get enough stuff for everyone. My stomach churned at the thought of repeating this process.

I bit my lip hard the entire time, trying to distract myself from the scene around me, from the idea that the last time I'd been to Wal-Mart had been with Jackson. My mother explained that we needed black socks for a benefit dinner she was going to be hosting next month. White socks weren't appropriate for the black pants we'd be wearing. She sent us out with forty dollars for socks and a tie for Jackson, and we'd gone to Wal-Mart instead to spend only ten dollars on socks and a tie. Then we spent the rest on peanut M&M's and Cokes. We'd sat on the benches outside and made up stories for the people walking in.

"That guy in the wife beater," he'd said, pointing to a tiny man stepping out of a big black truck. He was covered in sweat stains. "I can tell from here he smells like whiskey and beer nuts. And he wears that wife beater to cover up the fact that his fat wife beats him with a stick from the couch because she's too damn fat to get up and do it."

"If that's true, I feel bad for him," I said as I took a swig from my two liter of Coke. "I'd like to think he's just white trash."

"There's no white trash here, sister," he laughed. "That guy just couldn't manage to get dressed this morning. Probably too much drinking last night. But there might be prostitutes in Wheaton." He pointed at a woman in leopard print pants and five inch patent-leather heels. I laughed with him. I missed the sound of his laugh so badly in that moment. I shook my head and kept moving.

We ended up going back and forth to the car four more times to unload our supplies. The fourth time we were on our way out when we heard a terrible screech, an inhuman screech of pain that caused Peter to turn so quickly and shoot that I barely saw the arrow fly and hit the zombie in the chest. Or what would've been its chest before its muscles had fallen away to show its ribcage. The impact of the arrow made it stagger back a couple of steps but it didn't look down to investigate the arrow protruding from its chest. The next arrow hit its left arm, and then the next right between the eyes. The zombie dropped backward with an almost comic splat, like a sound effect from the old Batman TV series, like the word SPLAT should have popped out over the scene. Its limbs went lax, and its feet fell outward.

That's when it hit me.

Vintage Superman Chuck Taylor high tops and a tiny drawing of Batman and Robin on the inside heel of one of them. The zombie was Jackson, my seventeen year old brother, with half a chest and an arrow between his eyes.

My heart felt so heavy I thought it might have sank right through to my intestines. The adrenalin leaked out of me until I was completely still, just staring at Jackson's eyes, identical to mine, except totally lifeless and unaware. My stomach revolted at the sight and I turned away from him, away from the confirmation of my devastating loneliness and lack of family.

Peter got me back into the Toyota as quietly as possible and didn't say a word when I promptly reopened the door and retched up the popcorn we'd found inside the store onto the scalding hot blacktop.

"We have to go back," I told him as I wiped my mouth with the back of my hand. I swished some water and spit it out the window.

"I know, Carly," Peter said. He put the car into drive and took my hand. The look of desperation on his face weighed on my empty stomach. We spent the rest of the short ride in silence watching the nameless, wandering dead stumble through the town we used to know.

When we returned to the school, it occurred to us that we had no clue how we'd get back in. We didn't plan on coming back, so we hadn't bothered to think it through.

"Do you trust me?" I asked Peter quietly. He nodded, then leaned over and kissed my cheek, which immediately turned pink as I blushed. "Get ready, and don't lock the door when you leave. Grab everything you can. Count of three. One. Two. Three."

On three, I honked the horn, long, long, long, short, long, long, long, and watched the zombies stumble toward the sound. The exposed bones and sagging flesh was still a shock to me, especially in these numbers, and especially when they were that close to us.

"Go!" I screamed at Peter, and I shoved him out the driver's door. He ran for his life with the five bags he managed to carry, his thin legs scrambling toward the door, tears streaking through the dirt on his cheeks. I drove the car, smashing through zombies that used to be our grandparents, mailmen, little sisters and dog groomers.

Limbs flew and bounced off the Toyota's, hood, fenders and windows, leaving black streaks and congealed blood in long trails. I stopped the car in front of the gym doors, where twelve kids, including Peter, were waiting with bats and golf clubs, plus Peter's bow and arrow.

"Out!" he yelled at me. His voice was so stern I wasn't sure how to react, like when a big rig truck honks at you and you just speed up, unsure of what else to do. So I grabbed a couple of bags and ran as Peter picked a zombie off whose hand reached so close to my arm I could feel the wind move near it.

Then I was in the school. The doors slammed behind me and Peter grabbed me and held my head close to his chest.

"Next time you ask if I trust you, don't ask me to risk your life," he said to me. Then he tilted my head back, and for the first time in my life, I was kissed hard, like he couldn't breathe without kissing me, like a girl should be kissed, at least at fourteen.

We let the other kids run back and forth from the car for the supplies as they dodged the zombies. Peter and I took showers, and fell asleep in the library together, on the couch, clutching each other's shirts as if they were the anchor to the world.

For three weeks we rationed the food taken from Wal-Mart so well I thought we'd be able to live off it for months. But one Friday morning in early August we woke up to Vince Relena standing over Gina Martin's body, and I knew something had gone wrong.

"She ate all the chips," Vince told us while still looking at Gina. She was flat on her back, and a screwdriver was sticking out of her right ear, blood pooling around it. It didn't spread as fast as Gary Smith's had; the screwdriver was stopping the flow somehow. "I told her to stop and she told me to fuck off. She can't just eat whatever she wants."

"It's fine, Vince," Peter said. Vince leaned down and yanked the screwdriver out of Gina's ear with a wet pop. He stood back up slowly, watching the blood pump out in gushing waves.

"Is it fine, Pete?" Vince asked. "Is it fine that she ate all the chips, or is it fine that I killed her over it? Tell me which one is fine, because I think both are totally out of line. Both deserve consequences, I'm sure."

He took a step toward Peter, then he took another one. His head was cocked to the left, his green eyes as emotionless as his voice. I moved backward, holding my breath at the reenactment of this awful scene, the image of Toni Racine bleeding out flashing before my eyes, watching an arrow hit Jackson between the eyes, the pictures of Gary Smith's head popping open on the cafeteria kitchen floor, all of it racing through my head. I grabbed a long knife from a table and tried to stab Vince with it. He immediately grabbed me around the neck and pressed the screwdriver to it.

"I don't see why I couldn't do it again," Vince explained to Peter. "It's gross the first time, but I think I'd get used to it. I don't think it would be that hard. All those dead fuckers can do it, why can't I?"

Peter nodded at Vince slowly. He took a step toward me and I realized I was still holding my breath. I exhaled slowly and Peter looked me right in the eye, grabbed the knife from my hand, and drove it into Vince's stomach. He pulled it back out and Vince's grip on me failed. Vince collapsed forward. Peter's eyes were closed and he looked tired. I didn't know what to do, or how to comfort him. I just stared at the bodies on the floor, at the blood pouring out of Vince's mouth and stomach, his hand clutching at the once white t-shirt that covered his wound as he sputtered dots of blood on the tile as he died.

"We're leaving tomorrow," I told Peter.

The bloody knife fell out of his hand and clattered to the floor, and I led Peter out of the kitchen, telling a couple of kids that they needed to bury the two bodies in the kitchen, and that I'd explain later. We went to the gym showers and I washed the blood off his caramel skin, his blue eyes staring at his hands the entire time, as if they'd betrayed him. I kissed his cheeks, forehead, eyes, and his chest. I felt his heartbeat under his ribs, my tank top and underwear soaking through. That night I slept with my head on his chest, needing the constant reassurance he was still alive, that he hadn't broken his own heart in too many places for it to keep beating.

The next night Peter and I left in much the same fashion as the teachers did. We slipped out quietly, nailing the front door shut from the outside to keep the kids safe, only bringing a day or two's worth of food for ourselves. I figured we could find food again somewhere else, and wanted to leave the others with as much as possible.

I felt like a coward leaving, abandoning them like the teachers had. I hated them for abandoning us. Instead of staying to fix what was wrong, I decided to run, to seek refuge in my solitude like I did before the world turned to some chaotic disaster from which it would probably never recover. No one was ready, least of all us, the children.

We weren't ready to wield guns and ration our food so that we wouldn't have to leave the school we should've left months ago.

I'd like to say that now, at eighteen, I would know how to pick up the pieces of the kids I once knew, but I still don't think I would even know where to start.

I sometimes wonder about going back to that school. About going to see the kids we left behind, see if they've finally given up, eaten each other, beaten each other to death, or maybe had the guts to escape.

We've driven from west coast to east coast maybe four thousand times in four thousand different routes, and we've run into people. People that have built safe houses and fortresses to guard themselves from the evil that stumbles near them every day.

We never stay, because after a night or two, the people's faces start turning into Gary and Toni and Vince's faces—faces that we'd once seen alive and that had betrayed us. The faces that once laughed and had first kisses and believed that in a few years they'd be at the prom and promising their first loves that they'd still love them even when they left for college. But they were lifeless and sad now, underground with severed spinal cords just to be safe.

So Peter and I would eat dinner with the people we met, maybe trade for a shower and some new clothes, and then we'd move on, like we're still moving on now.

We never speak about what could happen. We never speak about the fact that one day we might not be able to find gas and we'll have no way to keep driving. We never speak about how we'll never bring children into this world or how we'll never be able to get married. I just hold Peter's hand, as we drive west, then east again, and dream about that first violent pop a frog's jaw makes when you want to remove its brain whole.

THE ANGRY PRINCESS

JESUS "DARK RIDDLE" MORALES

*R*evelation #0: A very bad buzzing

The sound of the particle accelerator was so drowning, that they could hardly hear any other noise. Even so, Ryan Goldstein managed to get his two-man crew to the portside of the main stabilizer. Once there, they shouted to one another, frightened at the computer-controlled analogue of the mainframe.

"You got to stop it manually!" Greg Ferns yelled. "This thing is finally out of control. I told you not to let the EPA regulate the gene-coders."

Ryan knew what his partner was talking about. Just days ago, NATO had grown worried enough about the CERN covert physics experiments to send an international science envoy to gauge their intentions. Physicists led by the EPA gave the green-flag for the operation of the particle accelerator, but they had tinkered with the huge collider's gene-coder. In particular, they were worried about what some called the Rodrigo Principle.

It was basically a theory that mathematician Fernando Rodrigo hypothesized on, a theory that the accelerator could lock on to human DNA—except for DNA that was damaged. Ironically, Rodrigo himself had damaged DNA from a rare genetic disorder, thus he knew more about it than anyone else.

"I think the mainframe is going haywire here. I can't control the initial programming; it's as if the collider is on autopilot."

Ryan and his team had recently programmed the accelerator to lock on to human DNA purposely. It was an experiment that was meant to decode parts of DNA strands. The funding for this type of experimenting was incredible and Ryan also liked the idea that the accelerator might be able to be used as a DNA scrambler—one that could fix a target on cancer cells and literally delete them. In this way, Ryan and his team had thought they were close to finding a cure for cancer, and any other ailment that was related to DNA disruption.

"Greg, tell Bill to pull the heat-blocks on the port. We don't want this thing to overheat!"

Bill Drake followed the foreman's orders and a halt to the screeching noise occurred. Suddenly the air about them was filled with silence.

"Well, it looks like we pulled it off," Ryan said as he wiped the sweat from his brow. Bill and Greg were similarly relieved, but quickly took notice of Ryan's new dismay. Ryan stood before them, spewing a freakish blue blood from his pores. Seconds later, the same blue blood began dripping from the other two men.

"What, I'm bleeding—we're all bleeding, but why? How?" Ryan asked in puzzlement.

Bill turned to read the log statistics from the particle accelerator's codex screen. He stood silent for a long moment, trying to grasp the sheer vastness of an impeding doom.

"Sweet God, the accelerator—it's locked on to our DNA!"

"But how?" Greg asked. "The computer's gene-coder is locked down, there's no way it could act on its own."

Still bleeding and trying to hold off the shock now enveloping his body, Ryan answered their questions. "Damn those EPA inspectors, they didn't compensate the heat factor. When they regulated the accelerator, they misgauged the heat output. The damn thing overheated and the coder went online by itself!"

Bill stood in total fright. "But our blood? Why are we bleeding like this? Why is it blue? Blood usually turns red when it hits the air, this doesn't make sense."

"It'd the particle accelerator, it's bending our DNA even as we speak. Our blood won't turn red because our bodies aren't dealing with the Earth's physics properly. It's breaking fractals. Remember the Fernando Rodrigo Principle? If the collider locks on to a certain fractal pattern, it'll soak in that entire design. That design in this case is our DNA...us. Our bodies are in flux. Hurry up, Ferns, we need to reverse the code-lock!"

"We can't. It's still working, it's still online!" Ferns replied.

"How many people has it locked on to?" Ryan asked drearily.

"It says over..." There was a long pause. "It says over six-billion."

Ryan's eyes grew wide in stark acknowledgement. "Jesus, that's...that's..." He couldn't finish his sentence, so overwhelming was the knowledge.

Bill said it for him. He said it right before they vanished. "That's...everyone."

Revelation #1: Echoes
1 day after people
Chicago, Illinois, the United States

"Hello?"

"Hello? Is anyone out there? Anyone?"

Laughter followed that call, a hollow and maddening laugh.

"Don't wanna answer me, huh? Well, then y'all can just piss off! All of you bleedin' heart nobodies. Just piss off!"

The sky.

It was so very beautiful in this August month. The streets were still cramped with dozens of cars, many piled up with motors still revving. Some were still billowing dark plumes of smoke as they melted into metal cinders; mere wheeled headstones to people that no longer existed. Where did they all go? Where were their bodies? Where were we?

A man walked past his reflection and screamed. So there it was deemed, that no stick, stone, rattle or hum would ever come. What have we become? When we lost the power to feel, did monsters become real?

Cowboy had traveled far and wide. He didn't know how far or where he traveled from, since his memories were as scattered and schizophrenic as the lonely landscape. But he did know that he crossed into the city a day ago. He didn't know his name. He didn't know his age—though he wasn't older than sixteen due to the peach fuzz where a beard would one day be—and he didn't know why he was here.

He stared at his reflection in a shiny glass building. It was one of the tall and wondrous skyscrapers that lined the beauty of the wide lakefront. He wore a cowboy hat, a thin flannel shirt, dark blue jeans and a pair of rattlesnake boots.

His face was dotted with the shade of a thin, incoming beard. Rugged-looking and well muscled, he dubbed himself by a generic name—Cowboy—until his memories would return, if ever.

One of the things he noticed outright was a discoloration in his left eye. It appeared he had one brown eye and one blue eye. This intrigued him, although it didn't scare him, as he figured it was something of a birth defect. He seemed to recall how that oddity took some getting used to in his childhood, despite the fact he couldn't remember any real details about his mysterious past.

By now Cowboy was near the large and monumental Chicago Conservatory. The preened gardens around it swayed like lovely welcoming hands. He moved closer, though tired. For every mile or so, the giant parkway was lined with an assortment of fine water fountains. The place was called Garfield Park Conservatory and it was ominously gorgeous, yet Cowboy rarely smiled. He peered through the thick glass of the conservatory, where he could see a fantastic menagerie of trees and other plants of exotic wonder. About to enter the already opened door of the facility, he stopped dead in his tracks.

A woman cold and alone, spoke few words. Madness twisted her lines, the vines of her voice giving her little choice. Through the land, all was hollow, yet still her voice was followed. Move as fast as you can, I thought I heard a man. But morality measured, reality treasured, for this voice was merely tethered to the loyal and the feathered.

A faint voice was heard. Cowboy cocked his head curiously. Was it the reverberating sound of his own voice haunting him? For over six hours, echoes had fooled him, echoes of his own voice being driven back to him from distant miles away. Distorted and mired in the wind, they fooled him during his lonely venture to the city, but this new voice appeared to be one of other origins.

"I...I heard you. You know I done heard you!" Cowboy yelled.

He ran outside the conservatory, towards a row of peach trees growing in the park's paths. His heart pumped, excited now, when he saw a thin silk blouse of a woman caught between the branches of a peach tree. Once again, the high-pitched voice spoke. This time the words were more audible and Cowboy could hear what they were saying.

"Sleepy time. Go dark now. Sleepy time."

Cowboy wrestled to keep his excitement at bay. He heard the voice. It was not only a clear voice, but it was real. It was not like the ones he imagined hours ago, but one of female origin, too, or so it seemed.

Glancing upward to where the voice was coming, he expected to see a small woman, perhaps afraid and clinging to the branches, but he saw nothing but leaves and birds. This made no sense. Slumping to the grassy floor, his spirit beat and severely disappointed, the voice came rushing back to him.

"Sleepy time. Sleepy time. Go dark now."

"Damn it, I said I heard ya, girly! Now come outta hidin' already. I swear, by sweet Jesus, woman, I ain't fixin' on hurtin' you none!" he yelled angrily.

Shaking his heavy fist at the trees, leaves began to fall from above, brushing past the redness of his hot face. Cowboy calmed himself once more. This time, he closed his eyes, focusing on the spot where he heard the girl's strange voice, and like a sonic-enhanced bloodhound, he found it.

"Go dark now. Sleepy time. Sleepy time for you. For you."

"What in the hell? What?" Cowboy giggled uncontrollably.

The edge of madness was gripping him. *Where is the edge? Without the edge we're in trouble.* The madness of loneliness was crushing him as if he were in an ocean of wild insanity, and this, after only one very long day.

Atop him, from branches adorned by the lime green leaves of the peach trees, they spoke. Four big parrots, talented birds, probably refugees from the nearby conservatory, they spoke some of the last vestiges of human words.

"Sleepy time. Sleepy time. Go dark now."

In another land, skipping through the sand, the virgin, young and tender, flipped the keys among our gender. Her hair was short, her face pout, and the likes of children's court, lean or stout. Brazen and sassy, tart and classy, the one awaits her fate. For this reason, the man lives to meet the date, so very far from late.

Madrid, Spain: The Shopping District

The child simply called Girl stood just over four feet tall. Her hair was black and neatly cut into an Asian-styled hem. Light-skinned and slightly freckle-faced, she gingerly jumped from car to car, wondering how some on the desolate streets kept moving with no people in them. At ten years old, the sassy tart didn't seem bothered by the disappearance of her mother, her father, or her lost family. And why should she? She couldn't remember them, nor if she even had a family. Her name, too, was a mystery. It, along with the population of Spain, and perhaps the entire world, was lost to circumstance. Yet no matter how she tried, she couldn't figure just what circumstance could do. It felt like she was in a dream, so in accordance, she acted like it was, at least for the time being.

Skipping merrily down the lonely streets, her hopscotch adventure was nearing the later evening, but the sun still shined bright over her. Faithfully, a memory came to her. It was of her mother. She remembered what she told her the last time they spoke: boys are bad and men are the same. She recalled her mother arguing with a tall man. Was this her father? She didn't know.

"Yo magusta eres. Si. Eres muy bueno," Girl replied.

Soon her Spanish gave way to plain thought and her words met the obvious fondness of the Shopping District's goodies.

"I like these a lot," Girl said while spinning around in joyous circles.

A torn black t-shirt and a bright, pink pair of short panties is all the barefoot girl wore, while she romped around the abandoned market place. But soon, she discovered a great deal of exciting things to play with and possess. In her hand was a fine sundress that was decorated in attractive floral designs. Whatever her past was, it seemed she had never had the perks of high-end clothing. Before her eyes, blowing wispily in the bright yellow sunlight, lines of female clothing of all makes and design could be seen. Now untended by vendors, clothing and an assortment of market-side sweet shops held an alluring sign of temptation for the partially clothed Spanish girl.

A child was born by a river. There, long dead parents did quiver. Love was lost, shifting the cost. Now payment was in need, but acceptance never faced the deed. Cursed, or worse, hearts fled, words gone, quiet and unsaid, for those that bled, they inherited only trinkets left by the dead.

"I make claim to this spot. This is...uh..."

Her name again—wait, what was it? Girl couldn't remember. In her mind, it seemed to flee from her every time she tried to grasp it.

"Huh? Okay then, this spot I claim as Girl's spot!" she shouted in some quasi-victorious gesture.

She jumped on top of a table and looked around as if expecting someone to object to her new tyrannical domination. As usual, no one could be seen.

"Ha, fine then. This is my city now. 'Hide and seek' is a stupid game anyway!"

Girl curled her lips in a smirked pout and folded her arms in sheer bratty rebellion.

"We'll see who can last longer. I can play this game better than anyone. You hear me out there? Anyone!"

Jumping from the patio table, she resumed going through the vast presence of clothing at the apparel hall. In one hand—the one not holding four very expensive skirts—a large, strawberry ice-cream-cone was steadily melting. That proved time was moving normally, but normalcy would have no bearing on her time.

Revelation #2: The Angry Princess

24 days after people
Geneva, Switzerland
CERN—it's the now vanished corporation that funded the production and arcane experiments to the world's largest particle accelerator. With no one left to operate it, the last rotations of the super-conducting magnets finally halted. In tune with its stifling blockage, a computer message put out huge red letters on a warning screen that no one was present to see.

Population Enhancement Compromised! Population Enhancement Compromised! Europe: 1,17,389 deleted. Asia: 2,313,787 deleted. North America: 12,89,998 deleted. South America: 34,74,125 deleted. Indonesian Islands: 45,170 deleted. Archipelago Islands: 450,002 deleted. Antilles Islands: 7,415 deleted...

The list went on, and on, and on. Yet none would ever know.

By sunset's weary arch they seek, near crows and ravens harkened beaks, the lot was laid, primed and seeded, but warnings ever gone unheeded. Bristles and pines, and hordes of swine were all left to precede it. And where and who, and how and when, begot the lust for the lion's den? In past or dream or future deem, the growing silence still, for now the man apart from them could have this land to till.

Madrid, Spain

Girl cursed wildly in anger. For a petite child, her anger and wild bouts of spoiled frustration often brought on tantrums of uncontrolled fury. This time, she was backing up in an elevator, before getting up enough courage to chase wild boars through the lush halls of Madrid's most famous casino.

"Get out of here, you stinky pigs! Get off of my property!" she roared.

The wild pigs were native to a few of the surrounding forests miles away, but without the noisy entourage of people and their automobiles, they teamed up with more domestic varieties and made a savage campaign to raid the casino's concession stands.

Unwilling to share the little fresh food available, Girl spent a lot of her time chasing the pigs from the casino grounds. In what would look outrageously funny to anyone in real time, she often used a large broom to slap the boars on their backs in an effort to send them out of her prized territory. Now dirty-faced and wearing a thin black dress, Girl looked like a tiny witch, fending off some mystical beasts, but unknown to her, the real competition for food sources was just beginning.

"I'm the princess here. I'm princess and ruler of all of this land! You little monsters better get away from my food!" Girl shouted.

Yet this was an ironic statement for her to make, as she had threw a big can of fruit cocktail at the fleeing pigs. Noticing she might lose one of her favorite treats, she ran back for the can.

Gro-o-wl, hr-r-rmph!

She peered upward to see a huge wild boar, with tusk-like teeth, staring back at her. Unwilling to give up ground, the big pig rushed her, tearing a long well into her arm, before rearing up to attack again.

"Owie!" Girl shouted. "That hurt, you stupid ham-hock!"

She raised her broomstick and began whacking the pig with the wide end of it to no avail. Knowing the boar could inflict more harm than she could, Girl made a mad dash back into the casino with the alpha-status boar in hot pursuit.

"Ugly boogers, I hate you fat booger-pigs!" she yelled as she ran into an open elevator.

As the elevator doors closed, the big boar could be heard scraping the outside with its sharp tusks. But soon, the noise faded as she was lifted upward toward the higher floors. However, she suddenly felt a nauseating wave in her stomach as the elevator stopped cold. Then the inside lights turned off, while the instrumental music version of *Shakira's Whenever, Wherever ended.*

"Uh-oh, this isn't good," she remarked dreadfully.

As she had feared, the electricity in Madrid had finally gone out...and at a really inconvenient time as well.

"Oh no. I...I'm stuck in here!" she called out in a panic.

After crying in the dark of the cubicle prison she was in, Girl finally calmed down enough to think straight. She let her panic flow out of her, and then began her plan. Being too short to reach the top flap of the elevator's ceiling, she started using her broom as a leverage tool. Pushing as hard as she could in between the elevator doors, she was able to pry the doors open, if only a few inches.

"Good, I'm getting there. I'm a princess; I can do anything...anything!" she said, repeating this over and over to herself.

Building up her confidence by the second, she also built up her strength, and within three minutes, had the broom prying open a large enough space to climb through. But as she pushed her little body out, she nearly fell seven stories down.

"Oh, God!" she screamed, now hanging from the edge of the elevator's metal floor mat.

She looked down and felt a wave of vertigo grip her. For a second, she nearly lost hold and fell, but her survival instincts were strong and she put all her strength into her petite hands. Below her, she could see the sunlight illuminating several open doorways that the elevator would normally merge with. The nearest was some ten feet below her and at least three feet to her side. And her strength was quickly waning and she knew she had to do something or perish in a most gruesome fall.

"I can't die like this! I won't die like this!" she shouted, using her anger to strengthen her frail body.

Turning to her right, she began swinging her body as hard as she could, and gambling on a most daring maneuver. Girl swiftly swung her body with such force that she sent herself flying over to the nearest sunlit floor. Turning her body in midair like some flung cat, she quickly gripped the open space of the empty doorway, only to find herself hanging in a pitiful dangle.

No! I'm—I'm falling! she thought.

But once again, the angry princess exerted her strength and finally rolled herself on solid ground, namely, the sixth floor of the casino's hotel region. Girl let out a big sigh and began to laugh uncontrollably, though she didn't know why. Tears ran down her face, while she spotted the nearby stairwell. It would be a long climb down in her weakened state, but at least this time she could take the stairs.

Standing up on wobbly legs, she cursed openly and sought something to blame for her misfortune. Now that the electricity was gone and she was in heavy competition with wild boars for the casino's quickly fading resources, she thought it best to leave for more plentiful prospects.

"I hate those stupid pigs! Dumb booger-noses! Now I have to leave here. I hate ham anyway."

Revelation #3: Canine Rodeo
Chicago, Illinois

The smell of fresh pancakes was in the air as Cowboy dreamed. The sound of bacon and eggs on the griddle and the morning sunshine through the wide farmhouse window had Cowboy stretch for the dawn's good omens. As an assistant crop duster to his father, he'd have to get up pretty early to help him cover both the McFarland and June's acres before his dad headed to Barney's Barnyard to refuel. But this was a good life, his life, once.

Burk! Bu-a-urk, a-a-a-rk, ba-ark, ba-a-ark!

"God-dang-it! What in the hell is this crap?" Cowboy shouted, being awakened by a brown dog.

Cowboy spun around slowly. He took a good look at the skinny dog. It was a bloodhound. Oddly enough, he remembered this particular kind of dog. He even wondered if he owned it at one time or another, being as how his memory had slipped him so badly.

"What—what do you want, boy? There's plenty of food in this place for the findin' so you just get. You hear me now? Get!"

But the big bloodhound merely paced around him in playful fashion. Apparently, it hadn't seen anyone living for some time, and after spending a lot of time barking at window mannequins, the dog was a little surprised to see this sleeping one get up and move.

"Dog gone it, you don't take to threats too serious like, do you? Well, I guess I got myself a partner now, ain't I? But your timing's really bad, let me tell you that, lil' doggy. You plumb ruined a great dream I was having; one that could have told me who I was, too!"

As if it understood, the bloodhound whined and slid on the marble floor of the huge library's stairs, to which Cowboy had been sleeping. The dog put its paws over its face, while Cowboy reprimanded its previously loud barking.

"Ah hell, it wasn't that bad, doggy. I could have been dreaming about stuff that wasn't real anyway."

Looking past the two large, stone lions that adorned the Chicago Art Institute, Cowboy pulled out a big packet of Slim-Jims that he'd taken from a White Hen convenience store and began his breakfast for the day. Empathetic to the dog following him, he gave two to the bloodhound and started for the huge museum ahead.

Before he slept, he noticed that power to some of the buildings was still on. During earlier days, most lights were still glaring in the night, but by thirty days in, nearly all the lights had gone out...all except places like the art museum, to which he, and his newfound canine friend, was now heading.

On the way there, he saw three very fancy apartment buildings standing tall and proud among the dawn sun. Like many others that were near the Lakeshore Drive area, they were fantastically impressive.

"Huh? Well would ya' take a gander at those things. I guess no rich folks will be spilling outta there anytime soon, huh?" Cowboy remarked to the wary bloodhound.

Nonchalantly passing by the buildings, Cowboy's dog began to bark frantically.

"Oh, come on now, doggy. You gonna' get all riled up again over nothing but birds and wind?"

However, he slowly began to notice what his dog was barking about. Trapped in the lobbies of the buildings were several dogs, ranging from near tiny to huge.

"So that's what you were yapping on for?"

Figuring the dogs would starve if not released, he began to head for the first building with intentions to do the same for the next two neighboring it. Upon arriving at the first, he noticed the door was firmly locked and the windows that encompassed the doors were thick. Peering inside, he saw seven dogs; four were already dead, leaving behind three living: a medium-sized Bulldog, a small Pug, and a white Chihuahua. The dogs immediately began scratching and barking at the window, now seeing that Cowboy was just outside the glass. Yet he had to find something strong enough to crack the thick glass without hurting himself.

"Alright, alright, you sassy ass varmints. I'll get to rescuing ya soon as I figure this door out."

Seeing a huge metal chain once used to herd cars into the museum's private parking lot, He unhooked the ringed chain and started back toward the building. Once there, he heaved heavily in a long, swinging arch. The weight of the steel chain came crashing against the door and the glass shattered into thousands of small shards.

"Jupiter's balls, that was a bit smart on my hands! Hell, I should've worn gloves for that kind of thing..."

Before he could say another word, the dogs came rushing out, running off into the hot weather of the Chicago summer. He watched the canines all head for a certain street where water from an open fire hydrant could be seen far in the distance. Turning to his bloodhound, the only dog that hadn't left him behind, he smirked and made a condescending remark on the seemingly ungrateful dogs.

"Damn mangy pooches! You'd have thought maybe one of 'em would have given me a bit of respect."

Inside the empty lobby, Cowboy noticed a series of chairs and a small table with several magazines on it. Picking up a stack of them, he sifted through the magazines for any of interest. One by one, he flicked them to the floor. About to sift through more literature, he heard barking again. It was coming from the last of the luxurious buildings.

"Well, here we go again, partner."

Eight minutes later, Cowboy was in front of the skyscraper's glass doorway. He used the same chain-crashing tactic he did on the last door, and several more dogs were free; and like the others, none stopped to lick his face or rub his leg. But by this time, Cowboy figured the dogs weren't rude, but simply aching badly for something to drink or eat. With one last door to crash through, he took a handkerchief from his back pocket and wrapped it around his hands. The last door he bashed open had caused a series of small cuts to form on the outside of his hands, and now a tiny stream of blood was trickling from them. This time he noticed only two dogs. Even so, they were huge. One was a skinny Doberman Pincher and the other, a stocky Rottweiler. The two dogs dwarfed Cowboy's loyal bloodhound, but they appeared friendly enough.

With a crash the last glass door was shattered and as in the other cases, the dogs leapt out with excitement. However, the Doberman suddenly stopped and cocked its head in a curious gesture. A frightening second later, it jumped on top of Cowboy, ripping at his arms and fingers in some rabid attempt to tear off his face. To make matters worse, the big Rottweiler joined the canine's wild fray, and soon, the dogs' combined weight and sharp teeth were overcoming him.

"Get the hell off me, you mangy mutts!"

The starving dogs had been spurred to attack due to Cowboy's already bleeding hands. This made them fall into a primal feeding frenzy. Cowboy, now infirmed with several deep lacerations on his arms, was in deep trouble. But through all the growling, he heard his bloodhound tearing at the tail end of the big Rottweiler. With one of the dogs distracted enough to leave the primary target to attack his bloodhound, Cowboy took the opportunity to pick up one of the chairs from the lobby and bash it over the Doberman's head. That blow nearly crushed the dog's weak skull and it turned tale and headed for the street. Cowboy turned behind to see the Rottweiler tearing into the midsection of his bloodhound. Eager to return the favor, he swung the chair at the huge black dog. But unlike the skinnier Doberman, this dog was in it for the fight…and the food.

"Get off of my pal, you raggedy sack of crap!"

Being too complacent for a single moment, the big black dog chomped on Cowboy's left hand, sending blood spurting in all directions. Yet his bloodhound took a deep bite into the other dog's neck. This assault forced the Rottweiler to release its grip, and finally, the hunger-crazed beast ran for the desolate street, leaving both Cowboy and his dog in bad condition.

"You did good, boy. I'd have been ripped apart if it weren't for you!" Cowboy spat, addressing the injured bloodhound in genuine appreciation.

Needing to compress his wounds, Cowboy ripped off his shirt and began to wrap it around his left hand, where the deepest bite marks were. He needed stitches, there was no doubt, but he'd have to compromise decent medical treatment for something more immediate. The bloodhound rubbed up against Cowboy as its master slumped to the floor of the lobby in a bloody mess.

"Well, that was a stupid idea. We won't be doing that again, will we, boy?"

Cowboy rubbed the dog's head in a boyish nod, but the bloodhound didn't respond. He looked over to see a major gash in the dog's side and neck. The bloodhound's eyes were watery and in the moment it took him to gently brush the dog's pelt in a last gesture of empathy, the dog passed on.

"Oh, you—you dirty—damn it, this isn't fair!" Cowboy roared, now crazed with anger. "Ha, I'm the last man on Earth…and…and you give me a friend, only to take him away from me like this? What kind of horse crap is that?"

He stumbled outside as the sun began to set over the city's wide skyline. He shook his fist upward, cursing God in a mad fit of frustration.

"What did I do to deserve this? Answer me, damn it! I know you're up there... somewhere. What did I do, huh? What the hell did I do?"

Madrid Spain
Revelation #4: Birth of the Scramblers
Girl found a new spot to inhabit; it was the city's biggest park. Here, everything was growing out of control, for there were no people to tend to the ever-growing gardens of flowers or weeds that sprouted from the cracks in the streets.

The pavement was almost unrecognizable, being overtaken by mats of lichen and moss. In truth, Girl could hardly tell where the street, the park, and the pavement began or ended, such was the overgrowth of vegetation. The houses seemed to be taking a beating as well. It had rained fairly hard this month and she could see the thin cracks of erosion starting to split the homes' pristine paint jobs.

Girl remembered coming to the park when she was younger. Her memories were starting to return in small flashbacks, despite the fact she still couldn't quite place her own name. After twenty days not knowing what her name was, she was growing frustrated and was looking around the abandoned city, trying to pick out a good name to adopt for herself. In both her hands, she held two household products. One was an empty box of crackers and the other was a sealed jar of petroleum jelly. Both were random items she'd picked up during her travel to the big park.

"Hmm...what should it be, Saltine or Vaseline? Those are both pretty names. Which one should I use, which one is the prettiest?" she muttered under her breath.

"Let's see, what goes best with the title of princess—Princess Saltine? Ah, no, that doesn't sound right. How about Princess Vaseline? Yes, I'm Princess Vaseline, ruler of Madrid." She practiced her royal greeting to an empty world.

"Yes, I like that very much. From this point forward, I'll be Princess Vaseline of Madrid. Do you hear me, noisy birds? Do you hear me, you smelly pigs? Do you hear me, bad dogs? I'm Princess Vaseline, and I rule this country!" she shouted loudly.

Girl—that is Vaseline—jumped atop of a weed-covered assemblage of rusty monkey-bars. Balancing herself at the playground's highest point, she playfully beat on her flat chest like Tarzan.

"I will command the birds of the air, uhm—and all those cats that make noise all the time at night. And then I…"

Suddenly, Vaseline was shaken off the monkey-bars, landing on the soft peat below. She got up quickly to see the buildings around her shaking violently. In fact, the very ground beneath her was shaking, too.

"Oh no, is this an earthquake?" she shouted as she ran to duck under a moss-covered swing-set.

The earth shook for over thirty seconds and she had lost her balance and skidded against the ground, tearing a long scrape on her left forearm. She shrieked in fear, but as quickly as it started, the violent shaking ended. Princess Vaseline looked around the buildings that lined the huge park. By now many were dilapidated, having been reduced to half-collapsed fixtures of the once brawny urban stronghold.

"All my pretty buildings; they're all smashed and stuff!" Vaseline cried.

But she got distracted by the blood dripping from her cut. Looking at the shallow wound, she jerked back her head, not understanding what had occurred.

"My blood is blue! What's wrong with my blood?"

Unknown to her, Vaseline had just survived another wave of metaphysics. The far off accelerator had attempted to recalibrate its mistake with one last ditch effort to bring back the people that it had accidentally deleted. In the process, the world's physics was slightly altered and for a period of time, Princess Vaseline's blood dripped bright blue. But now it began to change from a deep purple, and finally back to red, a sure sign that the flux in the worldwide DNA swap was over.

She was amazed at her multicolor wound, but was soon noting a great many sounds. It was the sound of people, moaning and gurgling. The sounds grew louder until she could see many forms stumbling around the darkening park. It seemed that the people were back…lots of them.

"Hey, I'm over here!" she cried. "Hey, you guys, I'm over here—where have you all been? Have any of you seen my mother?"

But her questions remained unanswered. As she drew closer, the clumsy, stumbling folk began to grow sharper in focus. Vaseline saw at least a dozen or more coming quickly towards her. Her greeting smile rapidly turned into a frown when she noticed that many were monstrous looking, as if they'd been turned inside out. Some even had extra arms and legs and many, that is to say the great majority of them, looked as if they had been dead for a long time. And the smell—Vaseline nearly vomited as even more approached her.

"Ha, you're not real people. You're are all scrambled up!" Vaseline shouted as she dodged the grasps of the slow-moving freaks of nature. "Yuck, you're all scramblers!"

Knowing she had to get past a great multitude of them, Vaseline nimbly ran towards the boathouse at the park's end. Jumping into a small rowboat, she barely got to the deeper part of the placid lake before a pair of so-called 'Scramblers' got the chance to nab her.

"Golly, that was close. Those...Scramblers almost got me!" she exclaimed, still trembling in fear.

Even so, she seemed to sense that the deformed ghouls, the ones that replaced the real people, couldn't swim. *How could they?* she thought. *They're all dead-like, slow and severely mangled.*

That noted, she let out one of her bratty tantrum-spawned rants.

"You ugly poo-poo smelling people want to steal my country? I'll kill you all. I'll figure out a way to get you nasty booger Scramblers out of my kingdom—you just watch and see!"

Vaseline finally sat peacefully on the boat as the sun began to set. It would be a long night out in the middle of the lake, but she was already scheming.

However, if she'd known that the morbid figures she suddenly encountered were far more deadly than she thought, and in vastly more numbers than those in the park, she might not have been so confident.

Revelation #5: We're not in Kansas anymore

Cowboy got up. He dusted off his hat, still trying to make out what all the shaking was about. Was it an earthquake? Just moments earlier, he was holding onto an old parking meter, trying not to lose his balance, while the ground shook violently under him. This time the urban cowboy found himself in a strange land. The city was still a city, but there was a different look to it. Many of the larger buildings were strewn with broken windows and piles of rubble now littered the already overly vegetated streets. More so, he noticed that the street signs and grimy advertising billboards that lined the main roads were all in a different language. On closer examination he could see they were all in Spanish.

What the hell just happened? he wondered. I'm sure as hell ain't in Chicago anymore. I must have been moved some how— got a strange tingling in my body, as if all the parts of me have been reintroduced. Hell, that's a strange thing to say, a strange thing to even think, he pondered.

He began walking past some of the bigger streets. It had been some time since anybody catered to this place as well, and it too, was in rugged condition—the same as Chicago. Cowboy still couldn't recall his past, but in his dreams certain flickering thoughts and images gave him the impression that he wasn't really from Chicago but rather from the south western states. He recalled images of flying in a small plane, as well as planting crops and rearing cattle with his father. It was no doubt that when he woke up in Chicago, he had somehow been planted there. It was this knowledge that helped him maintain his grip on logic. He now suspected that whatever force moved him to Chicago months ago, had done so again, yet he still didn't know where he'd ended up.

"Yep. I done got swapped to another place again," he muttered to himself. "Well, if this ain't a dream, than I figure God wants me here for a reason. I ain't never been a big fan of church and all, but I pray that God's playing nice with me."

The dark plain, the rhythmic rain, the odds that men are always sane, these are thoughts of the bold and the vain, When the earth shakes, and the body quakes, the real falls to fake, as one waits at the golden lake. The envy of rot and flesh are here, they wish to hold you, but not for dear, for at their sight your soul will fear.

Cowboy saw people, lots and lots of people. This was so sudden that his tongue seemed tied by the shock of them. He hadn't seen a living person in months, and in some way he still hadn't. Even so, he quickly rushed up to the nearest couple. Two people stood before him. One was a short woman with black hair matted down in dark, nearly black blood. The other was taller, bald and very sickly looking. It was clear they were a pair, since they held hands rather tightly.

"Hey, y'all, I sure as hell am glad to see the likes of you. I ain't seen any folks for…well damn it, I don't even know how long. I got lots of questions and I…"

Cowboy leapt to his side as the woman leaned forward and tried to take a bite out of him. He moved just in time, and instead of the zombie woman nabbing his arm, she bit down hard on a leather sack he was carrying. Cowboy jerked the sack away from her, hard, sending the lady ghoul faltering backwards. The other one rushed him, too, but he noticed that even moving fairly fast, they were still clumsy, and were slow walkers indeed. The bald man's eyes were washed over with an opaque milky film of white and a tinge of greenish yellow. He noticed this condition in the woman as well.

"Hey, what in tarnation is wrong with you crazy folks? Is y'all sick? You sure got a look of the jaundice in your eyes!" Cowboy snapped. "Maybe I should try to find a hospital that ain't abandoned. You folks look plum-ass horrible."

But Cowboy still received no response. Instead, the ghouls moved toward him with more excitement with their black-line mouths agape in hunger. Cowboy swung his heavy backpack as hard as he could, and it easily sent the bigger ghoul to the ground, while the undead woman kept staggering toward Cowboy with malicious intent. Then he realized he'd drawn a lot of attention from more zombies. They too, seemed to be afflicted by the odd disease, but some of them were even nastier looking than his first encounter. Many were bent up in odd shapes and some could hardly walk, having their arms twisted at opposite ends and the like. One particular ghoul made Cowboy shudder in his boots. It seemed to have no legs or lower portion of a body. But it still crawled quickly on the ground with its hands dragging its intestines along behind it, while taking a rabid chase to him.

"What the hell? You ain't real folks, you're all monsters!" he yelled as he ran and dodged the many more Scramblers heading his way.

Cowboy got to a lower part of the wide street and stumbled down a long hill. The street, being covered in clover patches, was slippery and he fell hard. He found himself under a huge viaduct and all around him, massive swarms of zomboid Scramblers were coming in from all sides. He knew if he didn't move fast, the slow Scramblers would trap him in the trench-like roadway. Yet he saw a glimmer of hope, literally, for not more than a hundred yards from him was the soggy coastline of a large lake. The setting sun was shining a beautiful gold hue over it that Cowboy found strangely ironic in his grisly circumstance.

"Heh, damn you all to hell!" Cowboy shouted while making a mad dash for the lakeside.

An obese dead woman with her head fixated backward, used her stubby arms to try to wrestle Cowboy to the ground. He was surprised at how strong she was, being as how she was very misshapen and plagued with some horrific ailment that rotted nearly all of the flesh off the left side of her face.

"Get yourself another boyfriend, you freak. I ain't courtin' no ghoulie!" he shouted as he sent a hard kick into her midsection.

The fat woman rolled on the ground and he could see that the spurs on his boots cleaved off even more loose flesh from the flabby monster he'd just assaulted. Turning to the right, he noticed with very stark horror, that the mob of ghouls were dangerously close. His short wrestling match with the fat fiend had cost him precious time. Once more, he leapt away from a lunging Scrambler. This one was a punk-rock-looking teen, but seemed to be decomposed in a manner that was unimaginable to Cowboy until he laid eyes on the monstrosity.

"Good Lord, that was too damn close!"

He rushed into the water, hoping on his life that the vast mob of nasty creatures would not have the stamina to follow him. After getting chest-deep in the lake, he discovered that the ghouls stopped short from fully entering the warm lake only a few feet in. He wasn't sure if they actually feared the water, or whether they simply couldn't swim. Whatever the case, Cowboy was a very adept swimmer and began making his way past the tall tree line that would block his view from the demonic mobs. He heaved for air and suddenly saw a quick moving boat in the distance. He had seen a small girl rapidly paddling the rowboat away from him.

"Hey, come back here. I'm stuck with these things, too!" he yelled loudly.

In the boat, Vaseline saw Cowboy only as another threat and was paddling as quickly as she could the other way.

"Gosh-darn-it, that little sprite wasn't a monster. Why the hell did she bolt on me?" Cowboy cursed. Still complaining, he swam to the other side of the lake. It was a clear and oddly serene place where he saw no ghoul's roaming about. Huffing and puffing in exhaustion from his long swim, he plopped down on the coastline, still trying to catch his breath. But just as he did so, he peeked another figure slowing easing toward him. Quickly grabbing a water-logged tree branch, he swatted the slow moving figure so hard that the thing rolled down the sandbank. About to bash the ghoul's head in, Cowboy realized it wasn't a ghoul at all but a skinny and frail old man.

"Ouch! Don't do that again— eres no bueno!" the old Spaniard croaked.

Cowboy didn't speak; it was the first time he actually heard another person talk in quite a while and he was so full of questions, he didn't know where to start.

"Dear Lordy; you're a real man—a plum genuine real person!"

"Of course, I'm real, you pandejo. But you almost killed me!" The aged man cursed in a thick Spanish accent. "I haven't seen another man, woman, or child in many weeks. I'm not even sure what month it is. But I'm glad to see you here, my friend."

For a moment, the two of them simply gawked at each other, taking quick notice that they both had different color eyes—one blue and one brown. Was this a coincidence, or did it have a deeper meaning? Whatever the case, neither one brought up the issue, feeling that the monsters abroad were of more concern.

"Hell, I thought I was the last person on the damn planet, amigo—do you have the slightest idea what the hell is going on around here?" Cowboy asked.

"I don't know much but I know we're in Spain, my hometown of Madrid. I was on vacation in Italy and then suddenly I woke up and found myself back here. I couldn't remember a lot of things at first, not even my name, but after a few weeks, I started to get some of my memories back. My name is Fernando, I still don't know what my last name is, but I hope I'll remember as time goes by."

"That sounds damn similar to what happened with me, but I'm American. I think I'm from Texas, though I can't be sure. I wasn't lucky enough to remember my name, not yet anyway, so I just call myself Cowboy—hell, I do know I was a real cattleman with my father some time in the past, so it figures well enough."

"Heh, you talk funny, Yankee, I'm sure you're a Cowboy, but madre-de-dios, what the hell are those monsters that are taking over the city? I haven't seen a soul for weeks on end, and then suddenly there are thousands of these...how do you say...los Cucuy."

"Hell, I thought you would know," Cowboy spat back. "From what I can tell, they're all sick and twisted up. It's got to be some kind of wicked disease, a real bad one, too. Maybe it's affecting our minds, making us forget who we are and where we come from. Whatever the case, I sure as hell hope we don't end up like those poor bastards."

Fernando stood up. Still rubbing the aching bruise that Cowboy made when he smacked the old man with a tree branch, Cowboy suddenly realized he hadn't apologized.

"Hey there, Fernando, I sure am sorry about swatting you and all. It's just that..."

"Forget about it. I was thinking about what you said about those monsters...those people. I don't think they are sick. I seen a lot of them and they're all rotten up pretty badly. Many of them don't even have legs. And some of their arms are missing. No sick people could survive that," Fernando reasoned.

"Aw shoot, mister, if they ain't sick, then what in blazes is wrong with the lot of 'em?"

"I think they're dead— dead people that have come back to life," the old man said.

Cowboy stepped back, shocked at the old man's proposal. Even so, he had to admit that he thought the same thing when he first saw how decomposed and rigid they were. Nevertheless this seemed impossible. But in a world where he seemed to be teleported from one place to another, and one devoid of any real people, this concept held as much credit as any other.

"Well, dead or not, we need to stick together, pal. Ain't no telling what kind of boogie-men are going to show up next, right?" Cowboy suggested.

"That is a very good idea, señor. We'll never survive alone, not with all of those...*things* out there."

Cowboy was soaked from his swim and took off his shirt, twisting it to drain the water from it. The sun was setting fast and he didn't want to get caught completely wet in a cold night. Turning away from Fernando, the old man saw a familiar mark. It was a pattern of diamond-shaped blemishes on Cowboy's back. It was another similarity they shared, just like the odd, mismatched coloration of their eyes.

The old spinster couldn't help to inquire about the weird markings. "Señor, your back—you have many marks on it. How did you get that way?"

Cowboy seemed offended at first, wondering why the aged Spaniard would ask such a trivial question at such a dire time. "We should be worried about making a shelter to keep those nasty things away from us, not talking about our skin care," Cowboy barked rudely. "Hell, what's so important about my skin anyhow?"

Fernando answered by lifting his own shirt. He revealed a series of patches that had the very same blemishes on it. "I was born this way. It's nothing bad, mind you, but my doctor said it was a genetic condition, something...wrong with my DNA."

Cowboy quickly realized there was a connection between him and the old Spaniard.

"Hmm, I don't know squat about any DNA thingies, but I done had these here marks since I was a wee youngin', too. I seem to remember that quite well. This can't be a coincidence. Hell, I'm getting' to wonderin' if that lil' gal I saw in the boat got the same blots on her. It wouldn't surprise me at all, given what I've seen so far."

Fernando keenly squinted his eyes. "What girl?"

"Didn't you see her? She's a pretty lil' thing. She got short black hair and can't be no older than ten or eleven. I thought maybe she was your daughter."

"No, I haven't seen anyone, and certainly no girl," Fernando answered ruefully. "However, I did see a huge tree house just off of the main street. I was thinking that maybe you came from there."

"You say a tree house?" Cowboy inquired. "What do you mean?"

"I had seen lights flickering in it during the night, but the tree house is set in the middle of the largest tree in the park. It's very close to the abandoned hospital. Someone must have been able to get inside the building and was able to build a tree house from there. You see, the tree and the old building are very close. I saw boards leading from the collapsed hospital to that giant tree. It's very high, I thought another man made it, but since you seen a child, it might be possible that this girl you saw did this."

Cowboy cocked his head in thought for a long moment. "Well, I don't know about that. I can't see a lil' girl doing all that. Seems to me it would be hard as hell to make a tree house so darn high, and even so, I doubt she'd have the muscle to pull it off."

Fernando considered his words, and then said, "That may be true, señor, but the girl might have been able to do it, little-by-little. After all, it's been weeks since this insane holocaust happened, and it's been a long time since anyone was able to stop her. These monsters just came into being only hours ago if I'm right. And besides, who else would make a tree house? Only a child would do that."

And that did it for Cowboy. The old man made sense. An adult would have taken the time to build a bunker or reinforced room, or even take refuge in the top floor of an apartment building. But building a tree house—that was truly a concept that would only have come from a child.

"I think you're right, Fernando, and I think it's time for you to show me this tree house. Maybe, just maybe, we'll get to the bottom of all this!"

Revelation # 7: No boys allowed

Cowboy and Fernando crouched gingerly near one of the larger trees in the park. The fact there was no one around to trim the grass made it much easier for them to hide. They peeked up at the tree house above. Indeed, as Fernando described earlier, it was very high. Cowboy could also tell that it was constructed by using a set of boards to traverse a high crevice between the abandoned hospital and the tree house. They noticed that the flanking boards to the hospital's dilapidated roof were pulled inward. This indicated it was the way the owner came to-and-from it.

"Look, the lights are flickering—there's someone up there," Fernando said.

"Maybe we should just call out. Whoever's in there will probably be as happy to see us as we were to find each other earlier."

"No way, señor, those monsters out there would hear us and come at us. If you haven't noticed, there are many more around here than before. Perhaps they can smell us."

"I sure hope not," Cowboy added, as he peeked over the high grass, taking stern notice of the vast mobs of clumsy ghouls lining the nearby street.

"Damn, there seems to be a whole herd of the things in front of the hospital. To get to the tree house, we'd have to find the same path its owner took, and I think it's somewhere in that big, building," Cowboy said.

"Statistically speaking that would seem unsound. We need to find another way in the building and into the collapsed apartment next to the tree house. I'm sure that's how the owner got in."

"You sound very sure of yourself, mister. Do you mind if I asked you what you do—uhm, I mean, what you once did for a living? It seems to me you might have been a professor of somethin'," Cowboy prodded.

"Your senses are keen, my boy, I was an academic man—not a professor—but a mathematician, an expert at fractals."

"Huh, an expert at what? Fractions you say?"

"Not fractions, señor, fractals, they're the basic structures to all things in nature. I fear that something concerning the tie to our biological fractals may be the cause of all this."

"What are you sayin'? That we got knocked out of the order of things? I thought God was testing us; sure, that's what must really be going on," Cowboy responded.

"We can't be sure until we see that girl. I still think she's the one in the tree house. If I suspect correctly, she'll bare a connection to us, and then, señor, I will prove what must have occurred to our kind."

"Ah, whatever, you eggheads always claim to have the answers. Let's just get in to the hospital and see if we can get into that tree house. If it's been safe for the owner—the girl—then it should do right and fine by us, too."

Agreeing on that premise, Cowboy pointed to the north side of the park's jogging path. It was cluttered pretty high with weeds and cattails.

"That narrow pathway seems to be our best bet. The grass is higher than a big bull. It'll be hard for those darn creatures to get a bead on us if we trek through there quietly enough."

Fernando considered Cowboy's proposal. It appeared to be the best option, since the old winding pathway did lead directly into the hospital's parking lot. "Right then, let's get to it before it gets even darker. I don't know if those things could see better at night, so we'd better move quickly."

Meanwhile, from up in the tree house, Princess Vaseline saw two figures rummaging quickly through the tall stalks of weeds below. She could tell they were different from the normal Scramblers she'd encountered earlier, as they moved quite quickly but didn't stumble.

What the two men didn't know was that they were heading straight into a nest of sleeping Scramblers that rested in the midst of the tall grass. Suddenly, Vaseline was forced to act.

"I have to do something," she whispered. "That looks like the cowboy I saw when I was on the boat. I didn't want him to see me back then; my mom always said boys, especially men, were bad. But if I don't do something, they might get killed. I don't want that on my mind, they might be the only other people that aren't booger-men."

From above, Vaseline waved a small torch to get the men's attention, and it worked.

"Hey, turn around and go through the emergency room. I locked the fence there," she called. "You'll have to jump the fence though. Hurry, hurry, there are Scramblers real close to you!"

Cowboy and Fernando looked up and saw the littler girl yelling down at them. At first it was all noise to Cowboy, who only heard the girl's hectic warnings in Spanish, but soon she spoke in English, too, which made things understandable even for him and the old Spaniard. Even so, the yelling quickly excited the mob of ghouls around them, yet they still couldn't see the daring men among the tall grass.

"I hear ya girly, but keep your mouth shut. Those things will come closer if they keep hearing you shout," Cowboy explained.

Vaseline could now see that the nest of resting ghouls, which were just mere meters ahead of the men in the tall grass, were rapidly waking. Clearly, the two men couldn't see the danger ahead of them, for the very grass they took refuge in was also acting as an ambush spot for the undead Scramblers.

"Hurry, those booger-people know you're there. You have to run for the fence!" Vaseline warned.

But it was too late, the nest of six zombies burst from the grass stalks like nightmare predators. In an instance, three of them grabbed Fernando, but the old mathematician kept spinning and turning, successfully avoiding the rabid jaws on the ghoulish fiends. At once, Cowboy came to his aid, kicking and punching the slow moving flesh-eaters. In mere seconds, he managed to free Fernando, but realized they were being surrounded by dozens more of the rancid creatures.

"Jesus, Mary and Joseph, these boys are all messed up!" Cowboy spat.

He could see that many of the monstrosities were mangled and had limbs sprouting in the wrong places. He immediately knew why the little girl referred to them as Scramblers, as their decomposed bodies did seem to be scrambled about.

"Mira, Mira—look, there's the fence, let's run for it, señor!"

Cowboy took off running as fast as he could. Surprisingly, the old man was keeping pace quite well and they were able to dodge a dozen of the nasty ghouls without incident.

"Rapido, rapido, hombre—we need to move fast!" Fernando yelled as he climbed over the tall fence.

Cowboy watched Fernando drag his body over the fence to land on the other side, bleeding from a long patch of welts.

"You're crazy, old man, you done flung yourself over a heap of barbwire. That's the actions of a man with cow-pie for brains, mister," Cowboy said as he landed hard on the other side of the fence.

Unlike Fernando, Cowboy was unscathed, for his time on the ranch was full of dealing with barbwire fences, and even if his mind couldn't recall how to avoid them all, his body sure seemed to remember.

"Alrighty then, let's get to the roof of this here place," Cowboy said.

Fernando didn't move, he stood there, glancing at the sign of the hospital. "I—I think I remember this place," he said while reading the name of the building aloud. "Saint Augustine."

"Who cares what the name of the place is, apparently no saints stuck around here to protect our sorry hides, so we best get!"

The two rushed to the entrance and saw a pair of toy dolls lying near the door. They could now clearly see the spot that Vaseline used to enter, but Cowboy could also see that it had been compromised.

"Wait, don't rush in just yet," Cowboy whispered. "You see that glass panel on the side? It's been busted—busted from the outside."

"Huh, how do you know that?"

"Hell, I thought you said you was smart, mister. Look, the glass on the floor is in the inside of the building, which means something broke it from the outside."

Fernando just sighed in embarrassment and disappointment. "You're right, son. So now what? We can't go back, there are hundreds of those monsters behind us."

"I know that—don't you think I know that, you crazy old coot!"

Cowboy paced around the area for a few precious seconds before coming to a conclusion.

"Aw, shoot, we're just gonna' have to run the gauntlet. I mean run straight past them. You saw how slowly them Scramblers are."

"What? How do you think we'll survive? The corridors in that place are sure to be narrow, it could be crowded with those things. It's too damn risky," Fernando said.

"What other choice do we have? If we wait here any longer, that mob of...*booger-people*, will get large enough to knock down the flimsy fence we just jumped. Than what will we do? It's bad enough they can smell you're bleeding cuts from a mile away," Cowboy chided.

"We don't know if that's true, son."

"We don't? Take a peek behind you, mister."

Fernando did as Cowboy asked and saw a great multitude of deformed ghouls now shaking the thin fence that they had leapt over.

"Dammit, it won't take long for those things to push the fence down—we gotta move and do it now!" Cowboy yelled.

With Cowboy taking the lead, the two men rushed in the entrance way. Cowboy picked up a long crutch he found on the floor and tightly held it as if it were a real weapon. In similar method, Fernando held a broken-off tire from an old wheelchair. It was wide enough and sported a series of sharp spokes that were broken and bent. The two made it to the second floor hallway without any sign of the ghouls, but by the time they reached the third floor, they were shocked at what they found.

"Gees, why the hell is this particular hall so filled with these bastards?" Cowboy asked.

Fernando was equally puzzled, for the first two halls they ran through were virtually ghoul-free. But now, nearly at the rooftop, the long hall ahead of them was full of stumbling Scramblers. They were situated at the end of the hallway, where two radiologist rooms were set facing each other. Then, as Fernando peered deeper into the dark hallway, he could see why this hall was so filled with the ghoul scourge.

"Look, past the waiting room, son, there's another hallway connecting this building to the hospital's older one. They must have been able to get from the older building to this one using the bridge-way."

Cowboy could now see what the mathematician meant. The older hall ahead of them was actually composed of a bridge-way that connected the new building to the old one. It was a common architectural feature in most American hospitals as well.

"Damn, we'll never make it past that mob, and we were so close, too," Cowboy cursed.

Fernando appeared un-wavered. "We can still win this, my boy."

"What—how? We're done for, mister. We can't move forward, and we can't move backward. By now that fence must be down and hundreds of them are crawling up here to take a bite out of our asses."

"We may not be able to make it to the tree house together, but you can do it alone."

"I don't follow your thinking, mister."

"Listen to me, señor. I'm bleeding already, so the monsters will be sure to follow my scent. There are two rooms here at this hall's beginning. Since we're both in one and the other is empty, we should separate."

"I still don't get your meaning."

"I'll distract them—they'll all be paying attention to this room, the one I'll be in. You'll take cover in the other room. When they're busy trying get into my room, you open yours and run for the roof. It's the only way."

Cowboy thought about it for a long second. It seemed to be a great plan, but it would mean that Fernando would have to sacrifice himself.

"Oh hell, no sir, I ain't gonna have your sacrifice on my conscious. We have to find another way," Cowboy retorted.

"Look, they already smell my blood, there's no other way, and if we don't do this quickly, we'll both die."

Cowboy cautiously peeked toward the hall and could see the mob of Scramblers starting to stumble towards them. It certainly seemed to be exactly as the old Spaniard predicted.

"Damn it, maybe we should just try to push through."

"No, son, now come on, we don't have much time. Listen to me. I didn't tell you this before, because I wasn't certain, but now I am. It' very important, so please listen closely."

Cowboy just narrowed his brow, wondering what other non-sense the old man was about to conjure up.

"There is a similarity between you and I. It's the markings on our skin and the way our eyes are mismatched by color. You and I have a genetic disorder, an anomaly in our DNA. I suspect the girl has this also. Make sure to look for these traits on her, too."

"What the hell are you yapping about, old timer? This is no time to jab about this crap. Those ghouls are starting to close in on us!"

"Just shut up and listen to me. After you get the girl, you'll have to find a machine—a gigantic machine. I don't know where it is, because my memory hasn't fully returned, but I do know it's up north. I also remember that it's called CERN. For some reason I always remembered that name. There is a way to reverse this mess—this whole mess. You have to find it, son. I wish I could help you more, but I just can't remember any more than that."

"Okay, I done heard your crazy ranting, now what?"

Fernando suddenly interrupted Cowboy and pushed him out of the small room. He locked the door from the inside, knowing that Cowboy would have to run to the other room for shelter. As the Spaniard predicted, Cowboy rushed into the other room and locked the door.

Cowboy could now hear the Scramblers scratching at the other room's door, no doubt after the scent of Fernando's fresh blood.

"Shoot, that old coot is doing it, and the foolish son-of-a-bitch done put his plan in action without my consent, too." Cowboy was at an impasse, he had to go along with the plan now or Fernando's valiant sacrifice would be in vain. But what was all that ranting about? He spoke of giant machines and the weird marks the two men had in common. Cowboy didn't even know what DNA meant let alone understood the old man's incomplete theory. But some-how, he felt it was important...and more importantly, that the old Spaniard was right about it being the root to the world's rotted demise.

"Damn, they're piled up against Fernando's room," Cowboy muttered as he peeked through a crack in the door.

Then suddenly the room to Fernando's door opened. At first, he thought the ghouls finally broke through, but he suspected the old man had simply let them in. Now was the time, with the majority of Scramblers rushing in to eat the poor old man, Cowboy finally had a chance to make a break for it.

"Here goes nothing," Cowboy remarked under his breath as he dashed out of the room with the crutch held out like a baseball bat.

In moments he was at the door that lead to the rooftop, but three Scramblers stood in his way, they must have been slow learners, as most of them were already tearing into Fernando's body. Cowboy tried to keep his focus on the incoming Scramblers, rather then the gurgling screams he heard as the ghouls behind him ripped into his friend. Cowboy was scared, but he had to take charge of fear. He mustered up his strength and went after the three zombies with the crutch waving in the air.

"You dumb sons-of bitches, I got more spunk than the Duke himself!" he yelled while swatting away the slow ghouls.

It took just over six seconds to swat all three zombies to the floor with bloody hammering of the steel crutch, and then he rushed through the door and up a small stairwell to the rooftop. Finally he was at the point he'd seen from the ground. The roof was dilapidated and dirty, but he could see the big tree house situated just ten feet or so from the roof's ledge. But as he got to the edge, he noticed that the planks of wood that acted as a passageway to the tree house were pulled in. He also noticed the distinct thumping of the Scramblers hitting the locked roof door behind him. It appeared they were through with Fernando and were now focusing their attention on getting at him on the roof. If he didn't get to the tree house soon, he'd be doomed to suffer the same fate as his friend.

"Hey, girly, put out those wood planks and let me come over!" Cowboy yelled.

From a porthole in the tree house, Vaseline poked her head out and pointed to a big sign atop the arboreal makeshift shelter. The sign read: ***No Boys Allowed!***

"Can't you read, stupid-head. I wrote it in English, too!" Vaseline shot back.

Cowboy was shocked at the sheer silliness of her response.

"Girly, you best let me in there, 'cause those damn Scrambler things are aiming on eatin' me!"

"I can't," Vaseline answered. "My mom always said boys are bad, especially the older ones. That's one thing I remember her saying before she vanished. You're an older boy, aren't you?"

"Hey, girly, there's no time for this tom-foolery. I need to get in there with you or else I'm gonna be ghoul-munch. Can't you understand that?" Cowboy pleaded.

"That's not my problem, booger-boy."

"Why you stuck-up little snot! You set out them planks and let me in or else I..."

A loud crash came from behind him.

Cowboy looked back and saw that the door had been forced open from the pure weight of dozens of rotten ghouls. They moved more quickly now, excited at tearing into the flesh of Cowboy. There seemed to be nowhere to go but down, or into the rabid mob. However, a quick thought passed through Cowboy's mind. The tree house was very high and a fall would be certain death, but it was only ten feet or less from the ledge. Was it possible for him to jump that distance? Whatever the case, he was going to find out. Taking a few steps back, he took a long running sprint and jumped for the tree house. Being too far to make contact with his feet, he grabbed out and nabbed the ledge of the tree house with his outstretched hands.

"Sweet mother-of-pearl, I almost did myself in!" Cowboy grunted as he tried to pull himself up on the narrow ledge of Vaseline's rickety home.

Behind him dozens of warped ghouls were determined to follow, but their slow gait and lack of musculature made it certain they couldn't make the jump. Over twenty of them fell below to splat on the hard ground. Then the rest of them figured out it was too far across to reach.

Cowboy was losing his grip and his strength. But then the little girl poked her head out of her house and peered out the window to see Cowboy struggling to pull himself up.

"I thought I said no boys allowed!" Vaseline shrieked in anger. "You're going to bring all the booger-heads over here."

"Hell, little lady, I'm just trying to survive out here; you... got...to help me up!"

Cowboy expected her to open the small door leading into the tree house, but instead she came out with a broom. Standing there with the broom in her hand and her face scrunched up in anger, she looked like a bratty witch. Cowboy had no doubt the girl was going to push him off the edge and to his death.

"Hey, hey there, girly, I ain't aiming on hurtin' you none. I…"

"Shut up and grab the broom, I tied it to the tree. I'm too small to pick your big dumb body up!"

Cowboy quickly grabbed the broom and finally hoisted himself to safety. He plopped down in the tree house, exhausted and still shivering from the fear of the ghouls and the crazed jump. Looking around, he saw that the girl had made the tree house quite comfortable, but his attention was quickly demanded elsewhere.

Sticking her finger in Cowboy's face, Vaseline began to rant on. "Listen up! I'm Princess Vaseline and I own this tree house, and I own all the land around here. If you want to stay with me, you have to swear an oath to me!" She shouted in truly bratty-fashion.

Cowboy had a quick thought of grabbing the little tart and throwing her out of the nearest window, but that thought faded quickly. He was a good person at heart and he sure didn't want to spend the rest of his life alone.

"Uh, alright, little lady, whatever you say."

At that point, the pretty little girl's face was close enough for Cowboy to see her eyes. As expected, one was bright green and the other an equally bright blue. This made him think of Fernando's earlier claim and he didn't answer her out of a sense of astonished revelation.

"Well, mister snake-boots? You'll swear an oath to me. Now say it!"

"Uh, sure, sure…I, uhm…Cowboy, swear to obey the will of Princess…what did you say your name was again?

"It's Vaseline, you booger-head!"

"Vaseline? Who in blazes gave you that nutty name?"

"I did, it's a real pretty name. Now say it!"

"Shoot, alright, girly. I swear to obey the will of Princess…Vaseline."

Finally, she seemed satisfied. She set up a small table and poured some tea. In the other two chairs, a dirty Teddy Bear and a broken toy robot accompanied her.

"Now you can join our tea party. You must be hungry. I have tea and crackers here."

As Vaseline stretched out her hand to offer him some crackers, he noticed a series of blemishes and scars that ran up the side of her left arm...they were the same exact patterns as the ones on his back and they were also the same as the late mathematician's. This proved that Fernando's theory was right all along. Still, Cowboy didn't mention it. If he could hardly understand it himself, how could a ten-year-old girl?

Cowboy sat down lazily on a small chair with his legs stretched out. He took the crackers and began eating them sloppily, while pouring down the tea to quench his thirst. He had a lot of questions and began asking them, even as he ate.

Instead of getting any answers, Vaseline swatted him hard on his hand.

"What the heck did you do that for?" he yelled.

"You have food in your mouth, you're never supposed to talk with your mouth full...it's rude."

Cowboy just smirked and craned his head in frustration. "Well, I didn't know that, girly."

"I know you didn't know."

"Really...and how's that?" he asked smarmily.

"Because boys are stupid."

Six months later
Vaseline had grown a little since the time she and Cowboy met. He tried to get her to change her name for the first month, but gave up, figuring it didn't really matter. They had traversed a great deal of land and Cowboy was teaching the girl how to drive. They were no longer in Spain, but far north. In the course of ransacking long-abandoned stores of many kinds, the two had gained quite a stockpile, far more than they actually needed to survive.

Cowboy now sported a big scar on his left shoulder. It wasn't from a Scrambler, but from a wayward shot of his own rifle, when

Vaseline had accidentally shot him. He was becoming painfully aware of the fact that letting a child wield adult things, such as weapons and the like, was as dangerous as the dreaded Scramblers themselves. Even so, he knew she had to grow up quickly, especially in a world that was put together so very wrongly. Despite this and all things considered, Princess Vaseline, as she called herself, miraculously seemed to hold on to the joys of childhood quite well. Currently, he was hoping that her skill in driving would be better than her shooting.

"Slow down, girly, you're gonna send us to an early grave!" Cowboy shouted.

Vaseline only stepped on the gas pedal, sending them and their spacious jeep faster than Cowboy had ever experienced. Passing by untended houses, they spotted a ghoul or two poking their curious heads out of the gangways and windows of their newfound, post-apocalyptic world.

But strangely they weren't afraid. In fact, besides Cowboy's gestures of rollercoaster-fear from Vaseline's hectic driving, they were quite happy. So happy that he could see the sunrays bounce off of Vaseline's bright white teeth as she smiled. She loved to drive, maybe too much. When they reached a place where the old city and the mountain range met, they got out of the jeep and breathed in the fresh air.

"I drive really well...right, Cowboy?"

In actuality, Cowboy felt she drove like a road-rage maniac, but he didn't say that.

"Sure, you sure as hell do, girly."

Vaseline jumped over and gave Cowboy a big hug, pressing against his waist in a tight squeeze.

"You're the best boy I ever met!" she declared happily.

"You mean the only one," Cowboy said with a crack of soft laughter.

"So, my Prince Cowboy, what are we looking for again?"

Cowboy turned to view the vast panoramic view of the scenery around them. By now nature had taken over a great deal of civilization and the buildings looked more like weird mountains sprouting small trees. Bizarre as this was, it was still oddly beautiful. He finally snapped out of his thoughts and faced the small girl.

"We're looking for a machine—a very special machine," he said.

"But we passed by a lot of machines on the way here. How will we know if we find the right one?" she asked.

"Well, because it's a big machine...a really, really, big machine."

The wind and the chime are never still, when mankind swallows the fatal pill. Yet from the roots of fallen earth, comes the child, the man, the birth. A new dawn will arise and once again behold a very precious prize.

LORD OF THE FLIES

DANE T. HATCHELL

"**S**ay it! *King Zeke.* Come on, say it! Call me *King Zeke*!"

Jeremiah's face was turning a deep purple. His brother, Zeke, had him from behind in a choke hold. He couldn't speak, he almost couldn't breathe, the tips of his toes barely touching the floor. He struggled to pull out of the deadly grip, digging his fingers deeply into the hairy forearms of his older brother.

"Stop it, Zeke, you're going to kill him!" Sarah pleaded.

Zeke gave her a wicked grin, exposing his left canine. "I ain't going to kill him. He just needs to learn a lesson."

"He's trying to say something but you're squeezing him too hard." Solomon was only eleven, but puberty was kicking in early with him. The extra testosterone helped him find his voice against his older brother.

Spit was foaming at the corner of Jeremiah's lips. His eyes started to rattle in his sockets as if they were going to roll into the back of his head.

"Zeke!" Sarah shouted. Little Esther started crying, building the tension in the room to a final crescendo.

Zeke relaxed his grip and let Jeremiah slide to the floor. He stood over his younger brother with his hands on his hips, and with an expression on his face that said, *I'm waiting.*

With eyes still bulging, Jeremiah laid on his back, gasping to fill his lungs with life-giving air. He had known better than to cross Zeke, who was seventeen years old, thus four years his elder. But he had an ornery streak that his Paw said he got from his Maw's side of the family, and always had a problem with authority. His Paw kept him in line over the years by beating the fire out of him with an old leather strap that kept the edge on a straight razor.

Since Paw got sick and woke up dead, Zeke had been in charge of the family and farm. Zeke spent time every night talking to his Paw through the cellar door. His Paw was confined to the cellar, now that he had developed a taste for living human flesh.

For the first couple of months, the daily routines went much like before Paw died. But lately, it seemed Zeke was acting on his own authority, saying that *Paw said this*, and *Paw said that.*

Jeremiah didn't believe him, and didn't like the way Zeke was treating him and his six other brothers and sisters. He knew his Paw would never tell them to call his older brother, 'King Zeke.'

"I'm waiting," Zeke placed his boot on Jeremiah's stomach, threatening to step on him.

"King...King Zeke," Jeremiah said.

Zeke gave a smirk of satisfaction, "Well now, I'm glad you see things my way." He looked at his three other siblings in the room, "Let that be a lesson to you all. We all do as Paw says. I tell you what Paw says and you do it. Or else."

Esther was the only one giving him a nod of understanding, her alabaster cheeks wet with tears, her bottom lip pouching out.

Sarah gave him angry eyes but said nothing. Solomon ignored his gloating and helped Jeremiah to his feet.

The door to the kitchen, where the entire ruckus occurred, popped open. Ezra led with his long face, perpetually dropped chin and opened mouth, "They's coming." Ezra was second oldest in the family at sixteen years. Mentally though, he was somewhere around Sarah's age of eight.

"Who's coming?" Zeke asked.

"Rebecca, Beth, and a stranger," Ezra said, his eyebrows lifted.

"Okay now, every one in your place. We's going to do this just like the other times." Zeke clapped his hands together as the children readied for their new guest.

The sounds of footsteps echoed off the wooden porch. Rebecca entered the kitchen and gave Zeke a nod. Behind her was a man somewhere in his late twenties in age. Beth followed.

It was easy to tell by the way he dressed that he wasn't a local. Whatever designer clothing he was wearing had lost its luster a long time ago. This wasn't the first time a city dweller had stumbled upon their farm. The locals stayed on their own land, taking care of their farms. Crops and animals provided food and still had to be cared far. There was no time for locals to wander around. Their time was dedicated to the struggle of survival, and battling the living dead that crawled out of graves looking for fresh meat.

The young man had an olive complexion further darkened by the weeks of grime ground into his oily skin. Standing at five feet seven inches, his oversized clothing hung loosely on his large frame. The deposits of fat from a sedentary lavish lifestyle had withered to half their size as his body cannibalized itself from his stomach going empty for too long. His head was none the smaller and looked unusually large now. Thick gold chains around his neck were a sad reminder of what was once important in his life.

"You guys for real?" he asked, looking about with dull eyes at Zeke and the others.

Zeke's left eye twitched and he forced a smile. "Howdy, partner, my name's Zeke and these are my brothers and sisters." Sarah was at the stove stirring a pot. Solomon and Jeremiah stood at attention, looking at the floor. Ezra, Rebecca, and Beth moved slowly behind Zeke. Esther ran to Beth's side. Beth was only ten, but since their Maw's death, she nurtured Esther like she was her own.

"Name's Pauly, pleased to meet you." His courtesy came automatic, instilled in him from his mother long ago. His eyes darted around the room, and came to rest looking over Zeke's shoulder, at Rebecca and Beth. "The girls, they said that you could give me some water...and something to eat," Pauly said hesitantly.

"Yes, sir, that we can. Solomon, get our guest some water. Put some ice in it, too," Zeke said.

"You have ice?" Pauly looked around and realized that a pot was simmering on the stove and that lights were on in the kitchen.

Zeke indicated to Pauly to sit at the table with a hand gesture. "Yes we have ice. Have a seat and we'll get you a tall glass of water and some stew when it's finished. This here farm has a natural gas well. It fuels the generator for us to make electricity. We got our own water well, too, so there's enough fresh water for us and the live stock."

"What about the zombies? Have many been through here yet?" Pauly asked as Jeremiah served him a large plastic cup with ice water. Pauly quickly picked it up, and turned the bottom towards the ceiling. A small amount of water trickled down his chin. The clink of ice shifting sounded as he placed the cup, now empty, down on the table. He had forgotten he'd even asked a question.

"Zombies? Tell you the truth, I don't much care for that word," Zeke said. He shot a look at Solomon, who filled Pauly's cup again with water. "*Zombie* sounds too much like hoodoo voodoo, black magic, and witches. That ain't what's going on round here."

Pauly drank slowly from his cup this time, crunching a small piece of ice between his teeth.

"Now, when you're asleep and you get up and walk, they call you a sleepwalker, right? So, when you're dead and you get up and walk, that makes you a *deadwalker*. Pretty slick huh? Deadwalker, I made that up myself," Zeke said proudly.

Pauly's stomach gurgled loud enough for everyone to hear. The hearty smell of the stew cooking on the stove wafted through the air. Pauly's eyes were wide in anticipation.

"Sure, we get our share of deadwalkers around here. Fact is, our triple-barbed wire fence keeps our cows in, and keeps *them* out.

Good thing they don't know how to climb. They just walk around and around looking for a way in. We have to walk the fence line on the whole property a few times a day. One reason is to check the fence, the other is to get rid of any deadwalkers that're hanging around. A quick swing of the axe to the head puts them down for good." Zeke kept talking but he wasn't sure if Pauly was listening. It didn't matter as the stew was ready to be served.

Sarah looked at Zeke and lifted the ladle. Zeke nodded. She scooped out two ladles of beef, potatoes, peas, and carrots onto a white plastic plate, then brought the plate to Zeke.

Zeke stood across the table from Pauly. The hot plate of food made Pauly's mouth water. Zeke placed the plate in front of him. "We're just trying to do our Paw proud. Do enjoy his hospitality."

Pauly picked up a fork and looked around the room. "Oh thank you, thank all of you, and your father, too."

Before his fork hit the plate, Jeremiah brought a black iron skillet crashing down on the back of Pauly's head with a low thud, followed by a slight ringing sound from the vibrating metal.

Pauly's head slumped forward and crimson spilled from his broken skull through his thick black hair, down his forehead, and the sides of his face.

Zeke snatched the plate of stew out of the way before anything of Pauly's came in contact with it. "Dangit, Jeremiah, did you have to hit him so hard? Paw likes his food fresh."

"I was scared and I wanted to make sure I knocked him out," Jeremiah said.

Zeke raked the stew off the plate and back into the pot on the stove. "The blood is still pumping out the back of his head, so he's still alive. Good, Paw is awful hungry today."

Ezra came to Zeke's aid and the two dragged Pauly into the pantry and down the stairs that led to the cellar door.

The others stayed behind. They were afraid to go near the cellar. The smell, the flies, the cold eerie presence of evil that emanated from the cellar kept them all away. Only Ezra was brave—or stupid enough—to follow Zeke. As for Zeke, he was no longer the good and reasonable son and big brother they all grew up to admire.

Zeke would stay down by the cellar door and talk—sometimes for hours—to Paw during the night. No one ever heard Paw speak in return, but Zeke swore he did. Zeke's personality had changed completely since his Paw died.

The door to the cellar was old and splintered. A metal latch on the outside kept it securely closed. Only Zeke had the key to the lock to keep others from going in. It also kept what was in the cellar from getting out.

Flies buzzed around Ezra's and Zeke's head. The pungent odor of nasty bacteria mingled with the smell of putrid, rotting meat. At the door, Zeke dismissed Ezra and removed the key to the lock from his pocket.

Bloated black flies danced on the door; working their way in the crack and crevices for the prize that lay beyond.

The flies covered him as he twisted the key, and the lock came off in his hand. He pushed the door open slightly and flipped the light switch on, then opened the door all the way.

His Paw was staring at the small window near the cellar's ceiling, used primary for ventilation. Even in death, he could sense that the daylight coming in also meant a way of getting out, a way to freedom, a way to find the living flesh he now craved. But the window was too high up for the animated corpse to reach, and too small to crawl through even if he did.

Paw turned around, his face even more sunken in than the last time Zeke saw him. He was a ghastly sight of a withered and dried out old man wearing blue overalls and a brown cotton shirt. They were the clothes he'd died in when he had a stroke. From a rawhide necklace, the wedding ring of his deceased bride still hung as a reminder of their eternal love.

Flies crawled over his entire body, sometimes so thick it looked like he wore them for clothing. Human bones picked clean of every piece of flesh and gristle was strewn about the room.

"Howdy, Paw, it's me, Zeke. I brought you your supper." Zeke pulled Pauly's body across the floor and left it between him and the zombie.

Zeke took a step back for every step his Paw took forward. Slow determined steps the dead man took, the atrophied muscles struggling to move him forward without falling. Maggots spilled to the floor at each step from crevices in his dead rotting flesh.

Pauly let out a moan. The sound of life motivated the deadwalker to move faster.

Like a turtle snapping at an injured bug on the water, Paw went to his knees and tore into Pauly, just as Pauly returned to consciousness. The screaming didn't stop until a half hour had passed.

Rebecca stood by the sink, washing the dishes after having cleaned up from the evening meal. Even though she was only fifteen, in her mind she saw herself as an adult. She remembered her Maw, and how she would stand at the sink and hand wash the dishes, just like she was doing now.

Children grew up fast on a farm, doing any job they were capable of and adding to the list as soon as another skill was learned. But Rebecca had never imagined life like this. Life without Maw had been bad enough. Now Paw was gone, or at least, changed. Zeke said that even though Paw was a deadwalker now, he was different than all the rest, because he could still talk, and Zeke could hear him. And as the oldest, and more importantly, the strongest, no one had the real power to challenge him.

Rebecca was startled when a hand grabbed the dish she was washing and a towel appeared and started drying it. She was even more surprised to find that it was Zeke helping her.

"Zeke, I didn't hear you come in," Rebecca said.

"I just left Paw. We's had a little after dinner chat."

Rebecca didn't look up from the sink. "There's something just not right about, you know, about feeding him."

"Paw's gotta eat. That city slicker would have ended up as food for some other deadwalker. Better that Paw eats him than another. 'Sides, Paw can think better on a full stomach."

"Zeke, does Paw really talk to you?" Rebecca said what she was thinking almost before she realized it. The ensuing silence made her regret she had.

"Yes, Paw does talk to me," Zeke said, his voice taking a different tone. "It's different than the way he used to talk. Paw used to talk *at* us, telling us what to do. He was distant, just working and running the farm. But now he talks to me with feelings. It's like I'm inside his head and he's inside of mine. He'll tell me he's been thinking and I can tell him what he's been thinking before he tells me. If it weren't for Paw, I could never have kept this place running."

Rebecca was washing dishes faster. They piled up next to the sink as Zeke slowed his job of drying while he continued.

"You know, Rebecca, Paw told me something special."

The words ran cold down her spine. She didn't know why, but she could sense something ominous was coming.

Zeke moved his body behind hers and slipped his right arm around her waist. She went to spin around to her left, but Zeke pushed his chest against her left shoulder blade in a tight embrace.

"Paw says that this place needs a man and a woman's touch if it's going to make it," he whispered in her ear.

Before she could protest, she felt something long and hard rub against her left hip, as he pressed his groin against her.

"Paw tells me that you and me are going to get married. We's going to have children. Not just us, but eventually all the children must marry. 'Cept Ezra. We don't need more like him anyways."

Rebecca was paralyzed with fear. The more she resisted his advances the tighter he made his embrace. Her right ribs were starting to ache with pain, and her left hip felt like it was going to be bruised. She wanted to scream, but was afraid it would only make matters worse.

"I need some water." Jeremiah's unexpected presence shattered the moment.

"Boy, I thought I told you to go to bed," Zeke said.

Jeremiah walked to within arms length of Zeke. "I needed some water." He had witnessed Zeke's unwanted advances on his sister.

Rebecca left the kitchen and headed up to her room as the two brothers locked eye to eye.

"I needed some water, what?" Zeke turned his head and cupped his hand behind his ear.

"King Zeke. I needed some water, King Zeke. Now, are you happy?" Jeremiah offered.

"Happier than a pig in shit," Zeke said, repeating one of his Paw's favorite sayings.

"A-Rod steps up to the bag," Ezra said, swinging the baseball bat slowly through empty air, warming up his muscles before connecting with his target. He set the bat to rest on his right shoulder, waiting for Jeremiah to call the pitch. Impatiently, he repeated, "A-Rod steps up to the bag."

Jeremiah rolled his eyes. "Roger Clemens stands on the mound. He shakes his head once, he shakes his head twice, and now he gives the catcher a nod."

A fresh looking walking cadaver was pressed against the fence, its arms gouged by the three strands of barbed wire at the top that kept it a bay, its fingers inches away from Ezra.

"Clemens goes up in the windup and...turns around and scratches his nuts," Jeremiah teased.

"Come on, Jeremiah, call the pitch." Ezra eyed his target intently; the zombie's teeth clacked together unnervingly in empty air toward him.

"Clemens spits...winds up...it's a fastball!" Jeremiah threw a mock pitch toward Ezra.

Ezra closed his eyes and reared back with the bat, then swung it across, slamming into the zombie's head just above its left ear.

The bat smashed into the skull with such an impact that the top of the skull dislodged completely and now hung down on the right side of the head, attached only by the scalp. The brain was exposed and was squished like gray Play-Doh to the right side. The zombie's body shook violently but the gruesome creature was undeterred from its insatiable hunger for living flesh.

"Strike one!" Jeremiah called.

Ezra shot Jeremiah a look of disapproval, and brought the bat down with both hands on top of the zombie's open skull. The putrid gray mass exploded in small bits mixed with blood and vile body fluids, showering an area six feet wide.

Ezra smiled as the zombie's knees gave up its animation and fell limp, the body still held upright by the barbed wire. He turned and gave Jeremiah a smirk of victory.

"Ezra, you got zombie goo all over you," Jeremiah said.

Ezra looked down at the splatter that had painted his chest and arms. He couldn't see his face peppered with the gore, but the smell worked its way into his nostrils causing him to heave, and finally give back his breakfast.

Jeremiah sensed an unusual tension during lunch, though the other children were oblivious to it. Zeke was more animated in his actions, as if he was *pretending* to act normal. Rebecca was quiet during the meal, rarely looking up from her plate.

When lunch was over, Rebecca cleared the dishes from the table and was busy washing them. Zeke had all the other children outside on the porch, assigning them chores for the afternoon.

Zeke stood silently before the crowd of his siblings, with his right finger waving in the air. "Paw said it's time to get the seed potatoes in the ground. I want all of you but Jeremiah to get out there in the field and work together. Ezra, you and Solomon start busting up the ground. Beth and Sarah, remember when you wash the seed potatoes to scrape off the extra eyes, but make sure you leave three of them. You girls, you too Esther, start planting as fast as the boys get the dirt ready."

The children stood looking down at the peeling paint on the porch or staring off in the distance. The weight of lunch was making them all a little sleepy.

"What are you waiting for? Get!" Zeke snapped, pointing to the field.

"What about me?" Jeremiah asked, again sensing Zeke was hiding something.

"Well, before you get to the field, I want you to walk the fence again."

"We just did that. Why not wait to this afternoon?" Jeremiah asked.

"Two reasons. One, that stranger may have had someone following him. I don't want anyone to surprise us. Two, you said you and Ezra left that deadwalker tangled in the fence. I want you to get it off before the dead weight hanging on it pulls that section of fence down. Three..."

"You said two reasons."

Zeke frowned and his face flushed red. "Three, Paw said to do it."

Their eyes met. Zeke waited for Jeremiah to make one move toward him. He was going to make sure Jeremiah would never challenge him again. Jeremiah's vision clouded with anger. His breathing became more intense.

He grinded his back teeth together, and his knuckles turned white as his clenched his fist.

"Well?" Zeke taunted.

Jeremiah let out all the bad air he was holding in, turned around, and stood with shoulders slumped, looking at his feet.

"That's better. Now get," Zeke said, turned, and opened the front door into the house.

Jeremiah heard the door close, but before he took a step to leave, he heard the lock on the door click. Zeke was up to something and he knew it wasn't good.

Jeremiah stepped lightly on the porch back to the door. He tried the knob and confirmed that it was indeed locked.

As he ran to the side of the house by his room, he tried to open the window. It wouldn't budge, and then he remembered that Paw told Zeke to nail the windows closed now that the dead walked.

He ran to the other side of the house. Through a window, he saw Zeke and Rebecca in the pantry. Zeke had her pinned against the wall, forcing his face and puckered lips towards hers, as she struggled in his grasp.

Jeremiah's insides shook with fear, and he thought he was going to crap his pants. He didn't want Zeke to hurt his sister.

In desperation, he ran as fast as he could to the rear door of the house. He grabbed the knob and twisted, but the door was locked.

His heart sank to his knees.

"Zeke, stop it! Get off me!" Rebecca yelled. She pushed against him with all her might, to no avail. She turned her head away from him, Zeke's hot stinking breath assaulting her.

"Paw said we's to be married. You better do as Paw says."

Tears rolled down her face as images of what he was going to do to her flooded her mind.

"Paw said if you gave me any trouble, I was to bring you down to the cellar. How would you like that? How would you like me to lock you in the cellar with Paw for a spell?"

A sound came from the cellar, up the stairs, and into the panty. It was a voice, faint, but it made the hairs stand up on the back of Zeke's head.

Zeke froze and loosened his grip on Rebecca. She jerked away from him, not knowing why he let her go, and not caring.

"*Zeke...*" The voice was clear now, this time stronger.

Rebecca spoke first. "Paw?"

Zeke shot her a questioning look. "You heard it, too?"

Rebecca shook her head yes.

"*Zeke, come here, boy,*" the voice said.

"You better go down there and see him," Rebecca said, planning her escape.

Zeke looked puzzled. "Paw talks to me. He talks to me in my head. He ain't never talked to me this way before."

"You better go down there and see him," Rebecca repeated.

"*Zeke, come down here now, boy. Now,*" the voice said.

Zeke grabbed Rebecca by her wrist and pulled her reluctantly along with him down the stairs, to the cellar door.

The black flies buzzed her head and she waved her hand in the air to brush them away. Zeke didn't seem to mind them.

The voice continued from behind the door. "*Zeke, what are you doing to Rebecca? I heard her scream.*"

"She won't listen to you, Paw. She don't want to marry me. I told her what you said, and she still won't do it. You want me to send her in there with you?" Zeke was sure his Paw could talk some sense into her.

"Come on in here by yourself, boy. Come get your Maw's wedding ring from around my neck. Give it to Rebecca and she'll do anything you ask," the voice said.

"I'm coming, Paw." Zeke let go of Rebecca and opened the lock with the key. He opened the door and turned on the light.

The emaciated figure of his Paw stood in the middle of the room; flies covered more than half his body. The leather necklace around his neck still had the wedding ring that his wife had worn for the twenty-five years they were married.

"Come get the ring, boy. It's what your Maw would have wanted."

Rebecca was frozen in horror at the shock of seeing her wasted Paw as a member of the living dead. Cracked bones were strewn about the room and human skulls crawling with maggots looked up at her, as if crying for mercy. She gagged at the sight and smell of the waste and decay concentrated in the cellar.

Zeke took three steps towards his Paw before he heard the door slam closed behind him. Rebecca quickly put the latch on the door and snapped the lock shut, sealing Zeke in.

Jeremiah watched through the window at the top of the cellar, relieved his deception had worked and his sister was safe.

This time, he didn't disguise his voice. "All hail King Zeke."

Zeke turned his head and looked up at Jeremiah, who was waving at him from the opened ventilation window above. Zeke's eyes went wide in surprise.

An evil grin crossed Jeremiah's face as he watched his Paw tear hungrily into his panic-stricken brother.

He wouldn't have to worry about Zeke ever again.

But he did have a decision to make.

Would this be the last time his Paw spoke? Or would he now continue to bring *Paw's orders* to the family in Zeke's place?

His newfound power was awfully tempting.

A BOY AND HIS FATHER

ANTHONY GIANGREGORIO

Little Timmy Miller was almost six and a half, and though death wasn't something he really understood, he knew enough to know he might not ever see his seventh birthday.

The reason for this was simple.

Sooner or later, the zombies were going to get into the house and kill and eat him and his entire family.

His dad told him not to worry, that he would protect them, and Timmy idolized his father like no other person on Earth. Timmy's dad was tall, strong and courageous, and so far he'd managed to keep the walking dead from getting him and his mom. But though young, even Timmy knew it was a bad time for him and his parents.

Timmy was playing in his bedroom, the matchbox cars spread out before him. He was pretending he was the mayor of a city and the cars were lined up for a parade. It was a parade for his dad, because he was a hero. Because he was a great man who protected his wife and son from the monsters that wanted to eat them.

While Timmy played, he ignored the sounds of hammering coming from the first floor as his dad reinforced the house's windows and doors. He barely heard the sounds of the dead as they moaned and banged on the outside of the house. To Timmy, the zombies were just another part of life. He was a child, he adapted. And if his dad said it would be all right, that they were safe from the monsters, then that was good enough for him.

"Timmy, can you come here, son!" his father called up to his bedroom.

Timmy didn't hesitate, he knew not to. He dropped the toy police car in his hand and dashed out of his room. He took the stairs two at a time, and seconds later, was in the living room with his mom and dad.

His parents were by the far window that faced the street. His mom was holding a large piece of plywood in place with his father. Timmy saw the arm flailing around the plywood, then his dad used his shoulder and pushed in the wood and the arm retreated. Glass littered the floor near his feet where the zombies had broken it.

When Timmy entered the room, his dad pointed to a can of nails and a hammer on the small coffee table a few feet from him.

"Ah, Timmy, thanks for coming so fast. Can you hand me that can of nails and the hammer, please? We put this up and then I realized I didn't have them near me."

"Sure, Daddy," Timmy said and ran to the table. He scooped them up into his arms and then rushed across the room. When he was halfway there, he tripped on his own feet and began to fall, the nails and hammer going flying. The nails landed and the can tipped over, different sizes of nails spreading across the hardwood floor. The hammer fell heavily, left a dent in the floor, and fell over.

"Oh no, are you okay, honey?" his mom asked. Her face was filled with worry at seeing her son fall.

"I'm fine, Mom, sorry, Daddy, I tripped."

"It's fine, son, as long as you're not hurt. Here, give me the hammer and a handful of nails."

Timmy nodded, surprised he wasn't getting yelled at. Normally, his father would have been at least a little mad at his clumsiness, but now, his dad didn't seem to care.

And then something banged on the plywood his mom and dad were holding against the window and his mom let out a small squeak of fear.

"Hurry up, son, I need that stuff now, please," his dad said, his voice seeming to be forcing calm. Timmy looked up at his dad and saw beads of sweat on his forehead. His dad was scared about something, Timmy just didn't know what.

His father began hammering more nails into the plywood, his banging overriding the noise of the monsters outside that were also pounding on the wood.

When his dad finished hammering on his mom's side, Timmy saw his father sigh with relief. "Okay, Helen, you can let go now," he told her.

She nodded and did as he said, then turned and went to Timmy, hugging him tightly.

"Are you okay, Mom?" Timmy asked. She squeezed him tightly. He could smell her hair, the shampoo she used. It smelled like apricots. He loved that smell, to him it meant 'safe' and 'love.'

"Yes, dear, I'm fine, you were very brave just now," she said.

His dad was breathing hard from the exertion of pounding in the nails. "There, that should hold those bastards...for a while anyway."

"Are you sure, John?" his mom asked. "But if they got in once, they'll get in again, won't they?"

"No they won't, not this time. I sank enough nails into the window frame to stop anything," his dad said.

"But they just..." his mom began.

She was cut off when his dad said, "I said it's fine, Helen, now stop it before you scare the boy." He glared at her and she lowered her gaze, still hugging Timmy.

"Good, now that that's settled, come and help me with the kitchen door, I want to add some more wood to it." Without waiting for her to answer, he grabbed a handful of nails scattered on the floor and headed off.

Timmy's mom hugged him for another few seconds and then let go. "Okay, dear, now you pick up the nails for Daddy and then go back to your room and play. We're fine now, we're safe. You're father will protect us from those nasty monsters."

If Timmy was older, he might have seen through his mother's lies, he might have seen the way her eyes looked away from him, as if she knew the lies she spun were doing more harm than good; but he didn't. He was only six and he trusted his mom implicitly. After all, she was his mother, she was there to protect him, to keep him from harm and make sure nothing bad ever happened to him.

So like any boy who loves his mother would do, he simply nodded and gave her a kiss on the cheek. "Okay, Mommy, I'll do that for Daddy."

"Helen, let's go, I need your help in here!" his dad called from the kitchen.

"I'm coming, John." She stood up, patted and brushed Timmy's hair so it wasn't in his eyes, then walked off, her head low, as if she were crying.

Timmy didn't see this as he had already turned around and was picking up the nails. He hummed a song as he worked, his world really not that different from before the dead began to walk. All Timmy knew that was different in his world was that he couldn't go to kindergarten for some reason or the park. He knew about the monsters but it didn't really sink in to his young mind. And why should it? His dad had said they would all be fine and that was good enough for Timmy.

He finished picking up the nails and placed the can on an end table. He was about to leave and go back to his bedroom when the plywood began to shake, something pounding on it from the other side.

Timmy knew it was the monsters.

Though he was scared, he wanted to see what was going on outside, so he walked carefully over to the boarded-up window and bent over where there was a knot hole at the bottom of the plywood. He looked through the small, dime-sized hole and when he did, he gasped in fear and amazement.

The entire street and front yard was filled with zombies. There had to be two hundred of them easy. Timmy tried to count them, but the shifting heads made it all but impossible. He liked to count and had learned his multiplication tables fast but this was something he never thought he would use them for.

A dark cloud of flies hovered over the heads of the crowd, bobbing and weaving as they fed on the spilled blood covering the animated corpses. Huge horseflies, bloated to the point of bursting, jumped from matted head to matted head as they struggled to stay in flight.

Timmy gasped again when he saw how many were missing eyes, limbs or other body parts. He saw a zombie with a gaping chest cavity, every single organ torn out. The monster looked like a fish that his dad gutted one time when they went camping together. As he looked to the far left and right, he saw that the six foot picket fence surrounding his backyard on both sides of the house was stopping the monsters from getting into it.

Others were eating something Timmy couldn't describe. He saw it was red and runny and glistened in the sun, but other than that he didn't know. He guessed it was meat, but *what kind* of meat wasn't much of an issue to his six-year-old brain.

It should have been.

Large rats ran between the feet of the undead crowd, taking bits and pieces of exposed flesh, and a few dogs darted between the legs, barking and growling. Timmy saw that the zombies didn't seem to care about the dogs, and if he was older he would have understood that the monsters only wanted *human* meat.

"Timmy, get away from that window!" his mom yelled as she ran into the living room and pulled him away from the plywood.

"Mommy, why are there so many monsters out there?" he asked.

She scooped him into her arms, grunting slightly; he was heavier now than when he was younger. "Don't worry about it, honey. Just keep away from the windows, please." She set him down and patted his head, then rubbed his cheek with her hand, caressing his face. "Why don't you go to your room like I asked, dear."

She reached over and picked up the can of nails—the reason she came back into the room—and cradled it in her arms as if it was a newborn baby.

"But what about all the monst…" he began but she cut him off.

"Timmy, please just do as I ask." She was ready to begin crying and was doing her best not to. She wanted to be strong for her son.

Timmy let out a huff and sighed. "Fine," he said and trudged away from her, dragging his feet on the carpet. Normally, she would have yelled at him for this, but this time she didn't. She was quickly learning that when death was imminent and could come in a dozen different ways, either from being torn apart or eaten, little things like her son dragging his feet on the carpet seemed absolutely trivial.

Timmy was upstairs playing in his room and had been for hours, when his mom and dad began to yell and scream and the sound of crashing wood came to his ears.

Jumping up, Timmy kicked his matchbox cars and action figures with his feet as he ran out of the room. He practically flew down the stairs, following his parents' voices, and charged into the kitchen to see his mom and dad at the back door, the monsters trying to get inside again.

The back door was open about a foot and his dad was pushing on it with his right shoulder. In the doorway was a monster and behind it were many more, all trying to force their way into the kitchen.

The boards that had been on the door were now splintered and broken, scattered by his dad's feet.

"Helen! Get me the hammer! The hammer, damn it!" his dad yelled as he struggled to keep the zombies from gaining entry. The moaning was loud and Timmy stared in shock. Flies had entered the house, too, filling the kitchen like small black storm clouds. They crawled on every surface.

His mom picked up the hammer from where it had fallen on the floor and quickly handed it to his father, who then began pounding the tip into the forehead of the monster in the doorway. Black ichor sprayed across the room, spraying his mom in the face. It went in her mouth and she gagged, spitting it out before vomiting violently.

The monster's head began to crack and cave in with each blow of the hammer, and as gray brains splattered onto the floor, the body slumped in the doorway, now blocking it from being closed. Another was right behind it and his dad did the same to this one, but each one down was one more in the doorway, making a barricade that made closing and locking the door all but impossible.

"Timmy, get your mom and get her out of here!" his dad yelled. "Get her upstairs to my bedroom."

"Are you coming, too?" he asked, feeling scared at the violence before him.

"Yes, but I need to give you two a head start. Go, son, get her out of here before they get in!"

Timmy went to his mom, his legs feeling weak from fear. His mom was finishing her bout of vomiting and Timmy wrinkled his nose, the remnants of her last meal smelly and sticky; it made him want to throw up, too.

He helped her to a kneeling position and then to her feet. With her hunched over and leaning on him, Timmy struggled to get his mom out of the kitchen.

As he left the room, he heard his dad yell out and swing the hammer again. Timmy helped his mom upstairs and into his parents' bedroom. She immediately fell on the bed, pulling him with her. She cried large tears as she hugged him for all she was worth. Timmy had tears in his eyes now, too, his mother's terror contagious.

He heard stomping coming up the stairs and moans filled the house. A second later, his father burst into the bedroom and slammed the door closed behind him. He quickly pushed the large credenza to the right of the door in front of it, blocking it.

"Timmy, how's your mom?" his dad asked as he began pushing a small end table across the room. When he was near the door, he picked it up and placed it on the credenza. Just as he finished, the door rattled in its frame as something on the other side tried to get in. The pounding was loud, and it filled the room and made it hard to hear anyone speak.

"I don't know, Daddy, she's crying," Timmy said through sniffles of his own. "But I don't think she's hurt." That was when he saw his dad's right arm and the blood dripping down it. "Daddy, you're bleeding."

His dad looked down at his arm and waived it off as unimportant. "It's nothing, a scratch. One of them bit me, but I yanked my arm away before it could get a good hold on me." He pointed to the master bathroom off the bedroom. "Could you go get me a towel, son?"

"Sure Dad, I can do that," Timmy said, glad to have something to do. He returned a few moments later and handed it to his father. His dad patted the wound and winced in pain. "Ouch, that sucker got me better than I thought," he said as he wrapped his arm in the towel. He pointed to Timmy. "Go sit with your mother, will you, Timmy? We're safe for now." He tossed him the towel he'd used to wipe his arm. "And here, use this to wipe the blood from your mom's face."

"Are those the monsters outside in the hallway, Daddy?"

His dad nodded. "Yes, son, I'm afraid they are. Just got sit with your mom, I'll keep you both safe."

"You promise?"

"You betcha, sport, I promise."

The hours passed, and despite the pounding, exhaustion set in and all three of them became tired to the point they couldn't stay awake. Timmy's Mom and Dad were stretched out on the queen size bed and Timmy slept between them, but after a while he couldn't stand them pressing in on him and he climbed out and went to the small daybed in the corner.

The pounding had stopped sometime in the night, but the incessant moaning and groaning still continued. It was haunting and sad at the same time.

At first Timmy hid under his blanket, but slowly, as time passed, he relaxed some more. It was easy to be brave when his mom and dad were right there in the room with him, only a few feet away. Besides, his dad said he would protect them and that was good enough for Timmy, who trusted his dad whole-heartedly.

With the moans of the monsters lulling him, Timmy drifted off to sleep.

Timmy woke up to screaming.

It was dark in the room and at first he didn't know if he was awake or dreaming, but then something hit the shade on the window and pale moonlight flooded the room as the shade fell to the floor.

Timmy blinked sleep from his eyes to see his dad was on top of his mom. She was beating at his arms and chest, but he acted like he didn't feel it.

Timmy saw his dad's arm where he was bitten and saw it was now a massive, weeping wound of pus and dark ichor. Timmy had no way of understanding that the zombies were infectious and his dad had died sometime in the night to wake up hungry.

He could only watch in horror when his father sank his teeth into his mom's throat, tearing out a large chunk of meat. As he chewed merrily and his mom shrieked in agony and terror, blood shot out of her neck to bathe the closest wall red. In the gloom of the room, it resembled a Rorschach painting, only this one was done in blood.

With her last breath, his mom reached out a bloody hand to Timmy and yelled, "Run, Timmy, run! Get away!" Then she lost consciousness from blood loss. His dad continued feeding on her, tearing off her ears with his teeth, then going in for more. His teeth clacked around her upper lip and pulled at it like a feral animal feeding on its kill. His mom's lips stretched like elastics, then snapped off, hanging from his dad's teeth like Gummy worms. Then Timmy couldn't take anymore analogies and he jumped off the daybed and prepared to run.

His dad caught the movement and snapped his head to face him. Timmy was paralyzed with fear. This was his dad, but at the same time it wasn't. The man before him was more like a wild animal than a human being.

His dad growled and crawled off the bed, and Timmy wet himself in fright. He was frozen by his father's dead eyes as the man crept closer to him.

Something inside Timmy told him that if his dad caught him, the man would be doing the same thing to Timmy that he did to his mom.

At the last possible second, Timmy snapped out of it, and with a yell to rival any before, he dashed to the master bathroom, slamming the door as he entered. As he fell near the tub, his dad began pounding on the door, his fists heavy and powerful. The door wasn't made for security and was in fact quite thin and cheap. Already cracks were showing in the painted veneer and Timmy huddled in the corner, too scared to move. It had taken all his courage just to run into the bathroom.

As he huddled in the corner, his eyes were glued to the bathroom door. With each blow from his father, more wood splintered to fall to the ceramic tiles.

"Stop it, Daddy, leave me alone!" Timmy yelled, but his father ignored his pleas. Timmy could barely see, the tears running fast and thick from his eyes. He was sobbing uncontrollably and he felt like he had to go to the bathroom, but he knew he couldn't even if he tried.

The door shattered near the top and a head-sized hole appeared. His dad shoved his head into the hole and shook it back and forth. His face was slathered in blood—his mother's blood—and it fell to the floor in small red droplets, a stark contrast to the white of the tiles.

Timmy screamed again at his father to stop and go away, but his dad only renewed his machinations, his hands tearing at the wood and making the hole bigger. Soon, his father's entire chest could be seen.

Then a bloody hand reached into the hole and began to pull the door apart. Timmy whimpered, trying not to think what would happen when his dad broke down the door.

Timmy began to look around the bathroom desperately, hoping to find some form of escape, and his eyes settled on the small window over the tub. It was more than large enough for him to shimmy through.

Over his dad's growling and moaning, he heard the door collapse and fall apart, and he knew it was now or never.

Jumping up, he turned and reached up for the window. It was unlocked and he pushed it open. The screen was down and it took precious seconds for him to open it, and by the time he did, his father was entering the bathroom.

Timmy jumped up and began to crawl through the window, and was halfway through when he felt his dad's hands on his legs. Then he was being pulled back into the bathroom.

Timmy yelled in absolute terror and reached out with his hands to the sides of the window, halting his backwards momentum, but an instant later and he was tugged back yet again.

He began to kick with his feet, not knowing why but his fear taking over.

With his dad covered from head to toe in his mother's blood, he slipped in the tub because of it, his feet slick. At the same time, Timmy's right leg kicked out to connect with his father's nose. The nose caved in and it was flattened by Timmy's foot, and Timmy found he was free of his father's grasp.

Using the kick to push off and through the window, Timmy found himself falling to the grass below from twenty feet up. The lawn in the backyard was overgrown and the added softness saved Timmy from being seriously harmed, and it didn't hurt that he was small and didn't weigh much. Still, he had the wind knocked out of him when he landed on his back after spinning in the air.

Trying to suck in a breath of air, he stared up at the night sky, dazed.

And then he heard the loud voices, all of them moaning and groaning. He turned his head to the left to see the tall fence bordering the yard now had monsters behind it. He turned to the right and saw that the undead crowd had gathered there as well.

Timmy didn't understand that his yelling had called attention to him and that the zombies out front had moved around to the sides of the house in search of prey.

Hands and arms slapped the tall fence, the posts already groaning under the combined weight of the zombies.

Timmy looked up at the bathroom window to see his father was halfway through it. He squirmed like a worm, and with one mighty heave, popped out to fall to the grass below. Timmy rolled out of the way and his dad landed right where he'd been. Timmy heard the loud crack of his dad's right leg as it snapped in half.

When he looked at his dad's face, he saw his father made no sign that he felt the pain.

His dad began to crawl across the lawn, his dead eyes focused on Timmy, his mouth hanging open as bloody saliva poured out the sides. Timmy could see a bit of flesh stuck in his father's front teeth and he knew that meat came from his mom. His dad couldn't move that fast thanks to his broken leg, which he dragged behind him, the limb limp and crooked, some white of bone protruding through the material of his pants.

Timmy spotted movement above and he looked back up to the bathroom window and there, gazing down at him, was his mother. But she wasn't really her anymore. Now she was one of them...a monster.

The sound of breaking wood came to Timmy's ears and he looked over his shoulder to see that the fence was giving way under the onslaught of walking corpses. It would only be a matter of minutes before the fence collapsed and the dead swarmed into the backyard.

His dad let out a hungry moan, pulling Timmy's attention back to his father.

"Please, Daddy, don't kill me, please," he begged, crying again. "I'll be a good boy, I promise. I'm scared. Daddy, I'm really scared. The monsters are gonna get in the yard! You said you'd protect me and Mommy, you promised!" Tears slid down his cheeks to splatter in the high grass and choking sobs filled Timmy with dread. Though he was only six, something deep down inside him told him his life was over. That not all young boys lived forever, and that sometimes, they died...horribly.

Timmy crawled into the corner of the yard, and with his back to the eight foot stone wall bordering the neighbor's house behind his, he waited for his father to reach him.

Two things happened simultaneously. The first was that Timmy's dad reached him and the man loomed up and over

Timmy like a wild animal about to pounce on the trapped prey. The second thing was that the fence gave way on the right side of the yard, falling over and letting dozens of zombies tumble in to fall onto one another. But while the ones on the bottom were trapped, the ones behind them climbed over their fallen brethren and made their way to Timmy, hands reaching in preparation of tearing his small body to pieces.

Timmy closed his eyes, waiting for the end. "I love you, Daddy. Go 'head if you're gonna do it." He held out his arms to hug his father.

Timmy hoped that at least when it was over, he could still be with his father after he died. And maybe his mom would join him and his dad and they could still be a family, albeit a walking dead one.

As his father leaned over and prepared to sink his teeth into his son's exposed throat, Timmy actually smiled as he hugged his father tightly. At least once he was dead he wouldn't feel pain anymore, or worry, or anger. At least he would be free.

And best of all, he would still be with his dad.

THE ZOMBIE IN THE YARD

ALAN SPENCER

The pounding fists against the front door meant the thing in the yard was hungry again. Recognizing the threat, Todd Wendell clung to his mother's legs as his father bolted from the living room to heed the rude summons, shouting as he stared out the bay window, "We'll feed you, for God's sake!"

His mother stroked Todd's hair, soothing him, the words she spoke as much a benefit to her as to him. "The monster will go away, baby. It only wants real food. Not us, honey. Don't listen to what it says out there. Once it's eaten, it'll go away. I promise it'll never harm you. Mommy is here to keep you safe."

His father furiously tromped into the kitchen, threw open the refrigerator, and searched inside it for food. Coming up empty, he said, "Monster thinks he can control us. I'll give him what he wants with a side order of a gun shoved up his a..."

"Just do it then," she insisted, knowing her son became scared when his father went on a tirade. "If you're not going to kill him, he might overhear us and get ideas. So do what he says and feed him. Do what we keep doing, please, Layne. It's kept us alive this long."

"I don't care anymore," he groveled, blowing out a hot breath, and then sitting down at the nearby table and rubbing his tired eyes. "We've boarded up the house and so has everyone else in Michigan—the United States! They'll find a way inside, Gloria. If I shoot one, ten more will hear the shot and come after us. I can't shoot him, so I'm stuck. What I'm more worried about is there won't be any food left for us to eat one of these days. Then what'll we do?"

"Not when Todd's listening," his mother said, covering her son's ears. "We'll talk about it later when he's asleep."

"Ah, you always say that, and then we don't talk about it." His father rooted through the fridge again, the end result no different than last time. "It looks like I'll have to dig in the basement freezer because there's nothing left here." He rushed to the basement, stomping down each stair, channeling his anger into each step. "You two stay put."

Todd tugged on his mother's evening gown. "I'm hungry. When's breakfast?"

She gazed out the window with a forlorn look to her eyes. She didn't hear what he'd said, and it wasn't the first time.

His mother plopped onto the couch, and began weeping. Todd went to her, wiping at her tears, a reaction he didn't understand, yet he felt compelled to do so. He was brushed aside when his father charged into the room clutching a frozen turkey.

"Open the goddamn window," he demanded, awkwardly carrying the meat with two hands, like an oversized bowling ball. He went to the second floor and yelled from upstairs, "Hurry up, Gloria! That monster's about to claw open the door. He'll get in and eat us all if you don't move it now!"

Todd followed his parents to their bedroom, and his mother opened the second story window. His father dropped the frozen meat out the opening. Todd ran to his bedroom to get a better view outside.

The turkey landed and bounced three times before wobbling in place and then remained still on the front lawn. Seconds later, he recognized the man who charged after it, the same figure who arrived three weeks ago when this ordeal first started. The man—what used to be a man—was named Howard Hughley. He was Todd's elementary school principal. The man was adorned in a gray business suit, ragged and dirty with past meals, the caked on colors a medley of rusts, cranberries, and grenadines. His face was greasy, dripping in tracks of congealed waxy globules.

Mr. Hughley's left bottom eyelid hung half an inch lower than the other, the eyes themselves black and silver marbles in pools of yellow egg white pus. Drool spooled from the corner of his lips, the act of mastication on full-blast even after death.

Mr. Hughley dug into the frozen meat with his hooked fingers, moaning nonsense, the sound like the grinding of a garbage disposal. The man couldn't procure anything to eat with his teeth, the meat frozen on the inside. Giving up, the man removed an ice pick and boning knife from his suit pockets and chiseled at the meat and reaffirmed the obvious: the meat wasn't edible yet. The walking dead man glared up at them, throwing his head back, and screamed: "*Hraaaaaaaaaaaaaaatch!*"

The zombie collected the turkey and trudged to the shack at the bottom of the hill.

His father shouted, while shaking his fists through the window at the contemptible marauder, "Take it! Eat it up! I hope you choke on it!"

While Todd's parents checked for Mr. Hughley's possible return, staying at the window for many minutes, the child took this opportunity to crawl under their bed. That's where his dad hid the candy bars. He'd been hungry for three days, and his thoughts kept returning to those colorful wrappers and the tasty chocolates inside of them. He hadn't eaten a solid meal in three day's due to his dead principal's efforts.

He thumbed through the selection of Snickers, Butterfinger, Baby Ruth, Chunky, Mounds, Oh Henry!, and Milky Way, enticed by the crinkle of the packages alone. The noises alarmed his mother, and he was yanked out by his legs. She picked him up under the arms and shook him. "*No, no, no!* You can't eat these. I told you. Why don't you listen? Why do you cause so much mischief, Todd, especially right now with everything that's happening? We have to ration our food, including the sweets."

"Hey, Gloria, we're all panicked and out-of-sorts. Calm down. Todd's being a kid. He's hungry, just like you and me."

"And he could die a kid," she spat, shoving him aside. "I'm going to the kitchen for a drink before *that* runs out, too. And don't follow me. You watch Todd."

He waited to be scolded by his father, shielding his head with his hands. The man's eyes were wet like his mother's were moments ago, but he rubbed them with the backs of his hands to dry them. "Put the candy away, buddy. I have something important to show you. I know you're only eight years old, but it's time to become a man. It's too soon in normal circumstances." He sighed. "But it's not *normal circumstances.*"

Down in the basement, his father opened the tall freezer. Inside, the contents were barren. Two racks of ribs and five pounds of ground beef and a honey glazed ham were all that remained of what once used to be a plentiful supply, the items practically falling out when the door was opened. "We had enough food stocked to last a month. Now it's down to nothing. We have enough for a few days, maybe, depending on that thing out there. This is why I have to go out and kill it. I don't care if another one comes along; that one will have to die, too. Help isn't coming. The radios aren't broadcasting news. A chopper hasn't flown overhead for over nine days. The police are dead on their asses. Maybe the National Guard or military will arrive, but right now, it's up to us, little guy. Otherwise, it'll be us who starves, and I won't allow it. Not my family."

He lifted a gun from his belt loop, showing it to Todd. "This is a Ruger, big guy." He pointed to a small lever on the side of the gun. "This is the safety. When the safety's on, it means the gun can't fire. When you take it off, it can fire. You line up the barrel with the target and pull the trigger. It has a soft kick, but the recoil isn't too bad." He placed the weapon carefully in his son's hand, still unsure if he should be doing this with him. "Here, hold it. See how it feels."

The gun was heavier than it looked, the cold steel quickly turning warm in his grip. Todd wasn't sure what to think. He was hungry for breakfast; they didn't eat dinner last night either, and his belly was constantly growling. His parents seemed to have completely disregarded meals the past twenty-four hours.

"What do you think? Are you a big boy?—no, you're a man." His father reached to the gun rack for the 12-gauge. He loaded two shells into it, his face stiffening into something Todd didn't recognize. "I'm going to go out while it's still light outside and see if I can find help. You lock the door behind me. Only open it for me, you got it? If Mr. Hughley or anybody like him tries to enter or does enter, you shoot them. Don't be afraid. I give you permission. Protect Mommy, okay? You're a big boy. A man, Todd." He whispered, "If you do it, I'll sneak you one of those candy bars."

Todd clutched the gun with fervor, imagining a Snickers unwrapping itself. "Okay, Dad."

His father tucked another handful of shells into his shirt pocket, then worked his way to the back basement door. "Tell Mommy where I'm at after I go. Mr. Hughley's head will be a trophy over the mantle by the time I'm through with him. Tell Mom I love her, and I'm sorry. I can't let this keep happening. I've waited too long to take action." He patted Todd's head, though it was a half-assed effort of affection, his mind now elsewhere. "Be a good boy, Todd, and lock the door behind me."

He did as he was told, and after his father exited, he parted the window curtain, watching the man creep behind his AT&T van—his dad was a full-time installer and line repairman—and continue on down into the yard to the property line and the next yard after it. Another quick run, and he was out of sight.

Two hands seized his shoulders, and Todd yipped in fright. "*Ah!*"

"Where the hell does that idiot think he's going?" His mother clutched the doorknob, but she froze. She couldn't walk outside, too afraid of what she'd encounter. She slid to the floor weeping, clutching Todd like a stuffed animal, and squeezed and squeezed him, wringing every ounce of comfort he could shed. "He's going to shoot your principal, isn't he? That crazy man—he's crazy, your father."

She gasped when he showed her the Ruger. "Dad gave me this. I'm going to protect you, Mommy. I'm a man!"

He was about to tell her about the candy bar he'd receive in exchange for protecting her, but he quickly thought against it.

His father didn't return that night, and mother and son sat on the living room couch awaiting his return. His mother had slept on and off, though Todd couldn't rest, being held firmly in her lap. He feared waking her, knowing she'd scold him again for having the Ruger, though it was sitting on the coffee table just inches from him now.

Sunlight filtered through the front windows, it being morning.

With the light, came the creaking on the front porch and footsteps approaching the door. Then at the curtained window, the shadow of a standing figure.

"It's Dad!" He slid out of his mother's grip, and dashed to the door, throwing it open, only to be met by the gangly principal.

The man shoved past him and entered the house, his stench something worse than the trash bag of dog poop Todd had collected last summer for extra money after it had baked in the sun for an afternoon. Shambling towards his mother, Mr. Hughley grabbed her and forced her to the floor.

"Meat!" he shouted, the word garbled, his face literally flicking tobacco spit globules onto her screaming face. He clutched his hands over her throat and began to choke her. "Meat! Meat! Meat!" he screamed.

Todd watched his mother reach out to him as she was losing consciousness, her face turning a dark red cherry. Waving and thrashing her arms, it was a full minute before he realized she was pointing at the Ruger on the coffee table.

Are you a big boy?

No, you're a man.

Crawling on all fours, terrified to rouse the zombie's attention, Todd cleared the distance between himself and the weapon. Reaching out, he lifted the gun that was ten times as heavy as it really was, and in his shaky grip, he pointed and aimed, though he closed his eyes, fearing he'd let his mother down.

Boom, the shot sounded, deafeningly loud, and his principal was thrown off his mother, a spurt of black liquid blasting off his shoulder, and that's when he fled the house, limping as fast as he could, before Todd could get off another shot.

Todd kept the gun with him now, his mother's orders. She went to shower after Mr. Hughley's mess literally covered her upper half in chocolate syrup-like blobs. When she returned in her bathrobe with scalded red skin from a hot shower, she sat down with him at the dining room table. She eyed the gun in his hand, her look both reproachful and grateful. "I can't believe your father gave his son a loaded gun."

"But I'm a man now," he said.

"You're eight," she scoffed at him, and then muttered, "You're hardly a man, and what makes you a man you can't use anyway."

He was starving, but he feared mentioning it to her. Food was a sour topic. Food was what had caused Mr. Hughley to become the way he was, he thought. He stayed up late three Tuesday nights ago when the official report hit the airwaves: *"A new strain of Eccoli has been reported in forty million pounds of beef. Strange side effects include hysteria, death, and intense hunger in those who've died from the poisoning."*

They didn't suffer from the bacteria, his mother had said during many conversations with his father. She also relayed the fact the FDA and the meat packing industries had no way of recalling the tainted product because it had already been consumed by millions, and they'd all turned into what Mr. Hughley had become, a walking dead man.

His mother changed into new clothes and disappeared to her room. After sitting bored downstairs for three hours, Todd entered her bedroom and picked up the bottle hanging loosely in her hands. He opened and smelled it, the whiff burning his eyes and nose. "Gross," he whispered.

Leaving her asleep, he edged towards the bedroom window and saw that nobody was outside for what seemed like miles, and probably was. The residential houses were boarded up and silent. Cars didn't drive by. Not a sound. He snuck under his parents' bed and opened a Snickers bar.

Sneaking back to his room to enjoy his spoils, he found a face peeking in his window.

Mr. Hughley.

He eyed the boy, his purple tongue slavering across his lips. He was poised on the stoop, having had to crawl up the side of the house, somehow still agile in death.

His principal started talking, the words like blockage shifting in a drain pipe. "Why don't you let me in, huh, Todd? We can get along, you know. I'll be nice. Your father's out here and he said I could come in. But he told me he doesn't have any keys, and you and your mom locked every door in the house." Mr. Hughley pressed his open palm against the window, covering the glass in a greasy smudge. "I'd hate to have to break this window. It would make such a mess. And it would wake up your mother, and she's sleeping so peacefully. Liquor will do that." He smiled.

"Or will I have to tell her about what you did at school? You stole Billy Nelson's cupcake from his lunchbox. You also called Mrs. White some awful names in class last quarter. You made the poor woman cry, saying those awful things. You used curse words, Todd. But it's between you and me, pal. If you'd just let me in, I can take what's left in your kitchen, and I'd leave. Just leave, no harm to anyone. I'll move on. I promise. How about it, Todd? I only want what's in your fridge."

The words didn't sink in for Todd. He kept staring at how the man's gums were pure black, the teeth gritty and broken into jagged edges, as if he'd chewed through bone and had shattered them. The voice wasn't Mr. Hughley, the familiar tone he'd heard every day during morning announcements at school, this voice had demurred into a demon's, his vocal cords full of bile and fluids.

"Just let me in, and I'll take what I want and go. So what's it going to be, Todd?"

Standing there, candy bar in hand, Todd's body unable to shift, barely able to breathe, caught by the zombie, his father's voice once again entered his head.

Are you a big boy?

No, you're a man.

Mr. Hughley tapped his finger against the window. His fingernail came off and stuck against the glass under a dollop of caramel skin. "What's...it...going...to...be, Todd?"

The image of a gun going off raced through his mind. Todd pounded down the steps to the first floor, swiped the gun from the dining room table, and ran back to his bedroom. When he returned, he aimed it at the window, but Mr. Hughley was already gone.

"What were you doing in my room earlier, young man?"

He wanted to say, *I saved your life, Mom. He scared me, but I didn't let him get in the house. He wanted to hurt you. I'll protect you. I'm like Dad. I'm not afraid of Mr. Hughley*, but instead he stayed silent. He was scolded for stealing a Snickers and he took his punishment stoically.

"I didn't raise a thief, Todd. I raised a descent boy, and now you decide to misbehave? Of all the times to start acting up." She held the Snickers bar he had taken earlier.

She was swaying with each word, and she suddenly tipped over and fell, landing heavily on the bedroom floor, losing the bottle clutched in her hand. She gasped, reaching for it, fearing the cap was off, but once she checked it was in fact still on, she whooped in joy. With tears in her eyes for no reason, these not being angry tears, she tossed Todd the Snickers bar she'd previously confiscated.

"Go 'head, eat up." She winked at him, the act freeing a fat tear. "I'll have mine…" She raised the bottle and brought it to her mouth. "And you'll have yours."

Todd clutched the candy bar and ravaged it, he was so hungry, the sugar that much sweeter, the nougat, caramel and peanuts an ecstasy in his mouth. He ate it so hungrily that he was sad to realize he'd devoured it in mere seconds. He wanted another one and another one and another one. He pictured the box under the bed, full of at least twelve more of the delectable treats.

His mother sensed this, and regarded him with doughy eyes. Her back was up against the bed, and she waved him to sit beside her. "Sit down, Todd, next to Mommy."

What he didn't notice was that the box of candy bars was sitting out on the other side of her. She selected a Milky Way and handed it to him. He enjoyed one bite and stopped when he took in that sharp tang coming off her words, the same tang that came from the bottle in her hands. "You acted like a man today, and you saved me. I'm sorry I yelled at you. I was scared. That monster had his hands all over me. He would've killed me, and I'm not ready to die. You should never be ready to die either, Todd. Death is the end of everything you see and feel and hear and know. It's the scariest thing you can ever imagine. It's nothing you want to happen to you. I'm too young, and you…you shouldn't even be in death's crosshairs, but we are, all of us. Your father could already be dead."

She raised the bottle to her lips, and when she noticed he wasn't eating his candy bar, she raised it to his lips for him.

The candy suddenly tasted bitter to him.

"Eat it before I change my mind," she said.

He forced it down, though he was beginning to feel sick.

In the following days, Mr. Hughley made various appearances, either putting on a show outside to threaten them or demanding more food. The first time he demanded more food, Todd threw down a rack of ribs out the second floor window. Instead of skirting to the shack for privacy, Mr. Hughley stayed in the road in front of their house where he'd created a fire pit out of human skulls and a spit from a steel rod propped on two sawhorses. The fires burned, and he cooked the ribs, using a hunting knife to cut off the meat sliver by sliver. After eating the meat, he boiled them in a giant pot and sucked the marrow from the bones.

Todd felt his mother shiver as they watched the dead man enjoy his feast, especially when he used a phalange—what she described to him as a finger bone—to floss his teeth.

The last meat in their stock—though she set aside a honey glazed ham that they'd later eat after the hunger pangs were so intense they had no choice but to eat something— was five pounds of raw beef. The dead man used that beef to stuff into a human torso without a head or limbs. Hanging the torso from their maple tree, he smoked the body with the fire burning beneath it. Todd and his mom watched in horror as Mr. Hughley ate the body, randomly using a meat cleaver to render his cuts, so violently, so passionately, the demented dead man was having a romp cannibalizing the torso.

Todd didn't blink once during the show, and he withheld the urge to wet himself, to break down and cry, but he kept thinking how he had to be a man, more than a big boy, because a big boy was a defect, a belittled ranking against a true-to-life, honest-to-God man.

With no more meat to give the undead man, Mr. Hughley kept the fires burning, and he cooked five more human bodies he found on his own during the next few days, before he too ran out of meat.

He would be coming after Todd and his mom for his next meal.

In the middle of the night, sleeping next to his mother in bed, she stirred him awake by a friendly nudge to the shoulder. "Todd...Todd...Todd," she kept whispering, so as not to frighten him. "Wake up, honey. Do you want something to eat?"

This time he didn't smell the sharp tang of liquor on her breath, but instead he smelled chocolate.

She brought him to the floor again, the carpet covered in empty candy wrappers. Desperate to give him one, to alleviate her guilt for hogging the candy, she crinkled the wrappers, unable to find a candy bar. "Oh know, oh know, I thought there was one left. Todd, I didn't mean to. Can you forgive me? I...I didn't meant to, I swear to you, I'd do nothing to hurt you, I love you more than anything, more than my husband, more than my own life, I'd never do anything to hurt you, please believe me. I love you with all of my heart. Do you believe me? Todd, tell me you believe me. You're my big boy. No, you're my big man. You'll protect me. I love you."

And that's when she found the Baby Ruth and she was so relieved that she burst out crying, while handing him the last candy bar.

At four that morning, gunshots rang out, scattered and erratic. Todd's mother woke with a start in bed. "What the hell was that?" she asked.

Before she managed to peer out the window, the front door opened. Todd's father returned. Running down to meet his dad, he saw his father was out of breath, covered in sweat, and bleeding from his neck and left forearm. He was so pale, so gaunt and weak looking that Todd was suddenly afraid to approach him. His mother caught her struggling husband as he was about to fall to the floor, his legs going out from under him. She helped him to the bathroom, and then she pushed the door closed and locked it. By the time Todd turned around and realized this, his mother insisted from behind the closed door, "Go away, Todd, this isn't for you to see!"

His stomach went tight as he stood awkwardly in the hall, waiting for something to happen. The bloody streaks on the wood floor seemed ultraviolet bright.

He thought that he'd earned the privilege to be included in adult matters because he was an adult now, because he'd fired a gun, saved his mother's life, kept the doors locked and Mr. Hughley out of the house. This wasn't fair, being a man this whole time, and only crying a few times, but he didn't have to mention it, because Mom didn't see it, and if he didn't say anything, nobody would have to know.

"Those things are everywhere," his father's voice blasted through the bathroom door, going in and out of high and low volumes, as if he was raising his head above the surface of water to talk while drowning. "They're hiding out at Price Savers, at least three dozen of them. There's nobody out there, not a soul. The police station's been ransacked, and every house is empty. We're it. It's because we still have food. But when there's no more food…when there's no more food…he'll still eat…he'll still…eat…"

Then suddenly the man lost his gusto to speak, saying lamely, "*Let me rest, Gloria… then we'll drive out of here to find somewhere safe… We'll drive…somewhere…safe…*"

Todd knocked on the bathroom door after everything was quiet for a while. His mother snarled at him from the other side of the door. "Todd, not right now!"

Giving up, he stayed in the living room, waiting and waiting for her to open the door, but she wouldn't, not for many hours. So he sat on the couch, his arms tight around his stomach, so hungry, but concerned for his parents and what would happen when that bathroom door finally opened.

Then the tapping on the bay window disturbed him.

He turned his head to see Mr. Hughley was looking in, his eyes like glowing marbles. "*Shhhh.*" He pressed his skinless finger up to his lips, the bone white against his mouth. "Todd, you know me, right? I'm your principal. You know I wouldn't hurt you. I only want the food in your house."

Todd didn't mean for it to slip out, but it did. "There's no food left, not even for us to eat."

Mr. Hughley's face wasn't enraged, but instead seemed enticed, his lips slobbering, his eyes doubling in size. "No food left, is that true, Todd? Now be honest. I'm your principal."

Todd hung his head down, knowing he'd done something wrong. He couldn't lie, not when an adult was looking him in the face. "N...no food left."

With the glint of a hunting knife in each hand, Mr. Hughley was about to break through the glass and attack him, but Todd saw it coming. Remembering the bodies the man had cooked outside, and smartening up, becoming a man, he acted like a man, and pulled out the Ruger tucked behind his back. He fired two rounds into the dead man's face, and the ordeal was finished with the roll of gun smoke, the shattering of glass, and Mr. Hughley thrown into the shadows of the evening darkness without another word escaping his rotten lips.

The broken window stared back at Todd like a gaping wound, and in that darkness he watched for Mr. Hughley to return. Minutes passed slowly, then an hour, and nothing else happened.

The silence was a constant until a new threat lurked behind him, a set of hands reaching for his throat. His mother screamed in the background, and that's all he knew of her in that incredible moment, as another dead man shambled towards him. All he could do was point the gun and squeeze the trigger, failing to recognize the person who used to be his father...

Todd's mother patted his head on the way out the front door. It was the following morning. "Everything's going to be okay. We've got each other, Todd. Dad said we'd find help eventually if we keep on driving. Someone's out there with food and shelter. All that matters is that I still have you by my side."

Together, they piled into his dad's work van. Driving from the house, the 12-gauge was propped between the seats.

Later, turning onto the major highway, his mom broke the silence, saying, "You've really grown up these past few weeks. You've become a man, Todd. Your dad would be real proud of you if he was still with us."

Acknowledging the compliment, Todd kept the Ruger tight in his grip, as they rolled on deeper into the bleak landscape.

ABOUT THE WRITERS

Jim Bronyaur lives in Pennsylvania, and sits at a desk in a corner and writes lots of horror. He's been published over forty times, all of which can be found at his site: www.JimBronyaur.com. For those who dare to speak to him, he's on Twitter: www.twitter.com/jimbronyaur.

Billy Burgess is the author of over a dozen short stories. He won a 2008 Granny Award for his short story, Full Moon. His recent work has appeared in the anthologies, Flash, Howl: Dark Tales of the Feral and Infernal, and Passionate Hearts. Visit his website at http://billyburgess.webs.com.

Anthony Giangregorio is the author of 35 novels, almost all of them about zombies and has edited over 20 anthologies.

His work has appeared in Dead Science by Coscomentertainment, Dead Worlds: Undead Stories Volumes 1-7, and Wolves of War by Library of the Living Dead Press. He also has stories in End of Days: An Apocalyptic Anthology Vol. 1-5, the Book of the Dead series Vol. 1-6 by LDP, Zombie Zoology by Severed Press, and two anthologies with Pill Hill Press.

He is also the creator of the popular action/zombie series titled Deadwater and his action/ horror novel Dead Rage is being optioned for a movie.

Check out his website at www.undeadpress.com.

Dane T. Hatchell grew up in Baton Rouge Louisiana and has lived there all his life. In his youth he was a fan of old school horror movies, and a collector of magazines such as Creepy and Eerie. Now in his early fifty's, he is devoting his free time to writing to satisfy a lifelong passion. You can contact Dane at Enadious@gmail.com. Special thanks to Sarah Graves for her contributions as my copy editor.

Kelly M. Hudson was born in Kentucky and currently resides in California. He loves horror and has over a dozen stories published in various anthologies, as well as a novel called The Turning published by Living Dead Press and available on Amazon.com and other places. If you wish to know more about Kelly, please visit his website www.kellymhudson.com for links to other stories and news.

Lindsay Kupsco is a graduate of Columbia College Chicago. She has her degree in Fiction Writing, which gives her a lot of free time to wait tables. This is the first time she's ever been published. She has an unhealthy obsession with all things horror and anxiously awaits the dawning of the Zombie Apocalypse.

Jesus Morales is known as "Dark Riddle" in the business. A true Chicagoan, he metamorphosed from a popular graffiti artist to a horror writer and illustrator. The creator of odd and stylized books such as Knight Syndrome and Dark Love, he also writes science articles and science fiction. In occult circles he hails from the mysterious Chicago region of Gothicane and is known as the 7th Dark from BTB and the Synoptic Knight Templars.

William Todd Rose is a dark fiction author residing in Parkerburg, WV. His short works have appeared in a variety of magazines and anthologies, as well as being featured on several podcasts. To date, his novels include Shadow of the Woodpile and Cry Havoc, with a second edition of The 7 Habits of Highly Infective People being released by Permuted Press in 2011. To learn more about the author, to download the free e-book Sex in the Time of Zombies, please visit him online at www.williamtoddrose.com

Marc Shemmans is from Birmingham, England. He has had several short stories and novellas published in numerous anthologies and magazines. He's also a screenplay writer who writes original scripts based on the dark nature of life and the apocalypse which he knows is destined to happen at any moment. He has also written screenplays which are based on novels by Graham Masteron, Tim Lebbon and Guy N Smith.

Alan Spencer has published the novels "The Body Cartel" (Damnation Books) and "Inside the Perimeter: Scavengers of the Dead" (Living Dead Press). In January 2011, "Ashes In Her Eyes," his third novel, will be released by Panic Press. He was recently nominated for the "Pushcart" Prize for the short story, "Suffering Begins in the Mouth and Ends in the Belly." Keep an eye out for his fiction in numerous Living Dead Press anthologies and the upcoming "Morpheus Tales Urban Horror" special issue.

Gary Wedlund escaped high school hell, only to become an Army slave for three years. He slipped the chains, soon working as a roofer, transferring funds to the Columbus College of Art and Design, where he graduated to the unemployment rolls. A teaching certificate, obtained at Otterbein College put Gary back into middle school purgatory. Almost incidentally, a major in math and an MBA at Ohio State qualified Gary to play guitar in several forgettable rock and roll bands. In the meantime, he fed his family on road-kill and Kroger food purchased by chits procured through employment as a radio system's specialist. He is blessed with a wife, four daughters, and one bathroom. Gary has several short stories to his credit, a shelf full of unpublished novels, and is the author of Living Dead Press's Zombies in Our Hometown.

PLAYING GOD: A ZOMBIE NOVEL
by Jeffery Dye

It was supposed to be a regeneration virus to help soldiers on the battlefield—regrowing limbs and healing wounds— but a simple act of carelessness unleashed it on an unsuspecting world.

For the virus was not perfected, and once exposed, the host quickly dies, only to rise again as one of the undead.

As countries are quickly overrun, scientists and military teams battle to contain the outbreak.

There is no other option.

If the infection continues to spread, soon the entire globe will be consumed. And perhaps that will be a just punishment for a mankind that dared to try to play God.

DEAD HOUSE: A ZOMBIE GHOST STORY
by Keith Adam Luethke

The old mansion on the edge of town, aptly named Dead House, has a history of blood, pain, and death, but what Victor Leeds knows of this past only scratches the surface of the true horrors within.

But when his girlfriend is attacked by a shadowy figure one rainy night, he soon finds himself caught up in a world where the dead walk and ghostly wraiths abound. And to make matters worse, a pair of serial killers are fulfilling carefully made plans, and when they are done, the small town of Stormville, New York will run red. The last ingredient to open the gates of Hell, and plunge this small upstate town into madness, is rain.

And in Stormville, it pours by the gallons.

The Lazarus Culture
by Pasquale J. Morrone

Secret Service Agent Christopher Kearns had no idea what he was up against. Assigned on a temporary basis to the Center for Disease Control, he only knew that somehow it was connected to the lives of those the agency protected...namely, the President of the United States. If there were possible terrorist activities in the making, he could only guess it was at a red alert basis.

When Kearns meets and befriends Doctor Marlene Peterson of the Breezy Point Medical Center in Maryland, he soon finds that science fiction can indeed become a reality. In a solitary room walked a man with no vital signs: dead. The explanation he received came from Doctor Lee Fret, a man assigned to the case from the CDC. Something was attached to the brain stem. Something alive that was quickly spreading rapidly through Maryland and other states.

Kearns and his ragtag army of agents and medical personnel soon find themselves in a world of meaningless slaughter and mayhem. The armies of the walking dead were far more than mere zombies. Some began to change into whatever it was they ate. The government had found a way to reanimate the dead by implanting a parasite found on the tongue of the Red Snapper to the human brain. It looked good on paper, but it was a project straight from Hell. The dead now walked, but it wasn't a mystery. It was The Lazarus Culture.

BOOK OF THE DEAD
A ZOMBIE ANTHOLOGY VOL 1
ISBN 978-1-935458-25-8

Edited by Anthony Giangregorio

This is the most faithful, truest zombie anthology ever written, and we invite you along for the ride. Every single story in this book is filled with slack-jawed, eyes glazed, slow moving, shambling zombies set in a world where the dead have risen and only want to eat the flesh of the living. In these pages, the rules are sacrosanct. There is no deviation from what a zombie should be or how they came about. The Dead Walk.

There is no reason, though rumors and suppositions fill the radio and television stations. But the only thing that is fact is that the walking dead are here and they will not go away. So prepare yourself for the ultimate homage to the master of zombie legend. And remember... Aim for the head!

REVOLUTION OF THE DEAD
by Anthony Giangregorio
THE DEAD SHALL RISE AGAIN!

Five years ago, a deadly plague wiped out 97% of the world's population, America suffering tragically. Bodies were everywhere, far too many to bury or burn. But then, through a miracle of medical science, a way is found to reanimate the dead.

With the manpower of the United States depleted, and the remaining survivors not wanting to give up their internet and fast food restaurants, the undead are conscripted as slave labor.   Now they cut the grass, pick up the trash, and walk the dogs of the surviving humans.   But whether alive or dead, no race wants to be controlled, and sooner or later the dead will fight back, wanting the freedom they enjoyed in life.

The revolution has begun!

And when it's over, the dead will rule the land, and the remaining humans will become the slaves...or worse.

KINGDOM OF THE DEAD
by Anthony Giangregorio
THE DEAD HAVE RISEN!

In the dead city of Pittsburgh, two small enclaves struggle to survive, eking out an existence of hand to mouth.

But instead of working together, both groups battle for the last remaining fuel and supplies of a city filled with the living dead.

Six months after the initial outbreak, a lone helicopter arrives bearing two more survivors and a newborn baby. One enclave welcomes them, while the other schemes to steal their helicopter and escape the decaying city.

With no police, fire, or social services existing, the two will battle for dominance in the steel city of the walking dead. But when the dust settles, the question is: will the remaining humans be the winners, or the losers?

When the dead walk, the line between Heaven and Hell is so twisted and bent there is no line at all.

RISE OF THE DEAD
by Anthony Giangregorio

DEATH IS ONLY THE BEGINNING!

In less than forty-eight hours, more than half the globe was infected.

In another forty-eight, the rest would be enveloped.

The reason?

A science experiment gone horribly wrong which enabled the dead to walk, their flesh rotting on their bones even as they seek human prey.

Jeremy was an ordinary nineteen year old slacker. He partied too much and had done poorly in high school. After a night of drinking and drugs, he awoke to find the world a very different place from the one he'd left the night before.

The dead were walking and feeding on the living, and as Jeremy stepped out into a world gone mad, the dead spotting him alone and unarmed in the middle of the street,

he had to wonder if he would live long enough to see his twentieth birthday.

THE CHRONICLES OF JACK PRIMUS
BOOK ONE
by Michael D. Griffiths

Beneath the world of normalcy we all live in lies another world, one where supernatural beings exist.

These creatures of the night hunt us; want to feed on our very souls, though only a few know of their existence.

One such man is Jack Primus, who accidentally pierces the veil between this world and the next. With no other choice if he wants to live, he finds himself on the run, hunted by beings called the Xemmoni, an ancient race that sees humans as nothing but cattle. They want his soul, to feed on his very essence, and they will kill all who stand in their way. But if they thought Jack would just lie down and accept his fate, they were sorely mistaken.   He didn't ask for this battle, but he knew he would fight them with everything at his disposal, for to lose is a fate worse than death.

He would win this war, and he would take down anyone who got in his way.

MONSTER PARTY
Edited by Anthony Giangregorio

Zombies, vampires, werewolves and ghosts are just a few of the monsters in this anthology.

But this isn't any anthology, you see, this is a party.

Or to be more to the point…a *Monster Party*.

Ever wonder what would happen if a werewolf and a zombie squared off? Or perhaps a vampire and a Frankenstein monster? Or better yet, how about a world where every conceivable monster is real and humans are their prey?

If those burning questions have been driving you mad, then look no further than this book.

So go on over to the buffet table, grab yourself a plate (the shrimp looks good) and get yourself a drink, and enjoy the fun ride that is the *Monster Party*.

THE WAR AGAINST THEM: A ZOMBIE NOVEL
by Jose Alfredo Vazquez

Mankind wasn't prepared for the onslaught.

An ancient organism is reanimating the dead bodies of its victims, creating worldwide chaos and panic as the disease spreads to every corner of the globe. As governments struggle to contain the disease, courageous individuals across the planet learn what it truly means to make choices as they struggle to survive.

Geopolitics meet technology in a race to save mankind from the worst threat it has ever faced. Doctors, military and soldiers from all walks of life battle to find a cure. For the dead walk, and if not stopped, they will wipe out all life on Earth. Humanity is fighting a war they cannot win, for who can overcome Death itself? Man versus the walking dead with the winner ruling the planet. Welcome to *The War Against Them*.

DEADTOWN: A DEADWATER STORY
B OOK 8

by Anthony Giangregorio

The world is a very different place now. The dead walk the land and humans hide in small towns with walls of stone and debris for protection, constantly keeping the living dead at bay.

Social law is gone and right and wrong is defined by the size of your gun.

UNWELCOME VISITORS

Henry Watson and his band of warrior survivalists become guests in a fortified town in Michigan. But when the kidnapping of one of the companions goes bad and men die, the group finds themselves on the wrong side of the law, and a town out for blood.

Trapped in a hotel, surrounded on all sides, it will be up to Henry to save the day with a gamble that may not only take his life, but that of his friends as well.

In a dead world, when justice is not enough, there is always vengeance.

END OF DAYS: AN APOCALYPTIC ANTHOLOGY
VOLUMES 1-3

Edited by Anthony Giangregorio

Our world is a fragile place.

Meteors, famine, floods, nuclear war, solar flares, and hundreds of other calamities can plunge our small blue planet into turmoil in an instant.

What would you do if tomorrow the sun went super nova or the world was swallowed by water, submerging the world into the cold darkness of the ocean? This anthology explores some of those scenarios and plunges you into total annihilation.

But remember, it's only a book, and tomorrow will come as it always does.

Or will it?

ETERNAL NIGHT: A VAMPIRE ANTHOLOGY
Edited by Anthony Giangregorio

Blood, fangs, darkness and terror...these are the calling cards of the vampire mythos.
Inside this tome are stories that embrace vampire history but seek to introduce a new literary spin on this longstanding fictional monster. Follow a dark journey through cigarette-smoking creatures hunted by rogue angels, vampires that feed off of thoughts instead of blood, immortals presenting the fantastic in a local rock band, to a legendary monster on the far reaches of town.

Forget what you know about vampires; this anthology will destroy historical mythos and embrace incredible new twists on this celebrated, fictional character.

Welcome to a world of the undead, welcome to the world of *Eternal Night*.

DEAD HISTORY 2
A Zombie Anthology

Edited by Anthony Giangregorio
From the dawn of mankind, the walking dead have been with us.

The greatest moments in history are not what they appear.

Through the ages, the undead have been there, only the proof has been erased, documents destroyed, and witnesses silenced.

The living dead is man's greatest secret.

In this tome, are a few of the stories of what really happened all those years ago.

History isn't alive, it's dead!

INSIDE THE PERIMETER: SCAVENGERS OF THE DEAD
by Alan Spencer

In the middle of nowhere, the vestiges of an abandoned town are surrounded by inescapably high concrete barriers, permitting no trespass or escape. The town is dormant of human life, but rampant with the living dead, who choose not to eat flesh, but to instead continue their survival by cruder means.

Boyd Broman, a detective arrested and falsely imprisoned, has been transferred into the secret town. He is given an ultimatum: recapture Hayden Grubaugh, the cannibal serial killer, who has been banished to the town, in exchange for his freedom.

During Boyd's search, he discovers why the psychotic cannibal must really be captured and the sinister secrets the dead town holds.

With no chance of escape, Broman finds himself trapped among the ravenous, violent dead. With the cannibal feeding on the animated cadavers and the undead searching for Boyd, he must fulfill his end of the deal before the rotting corpses turn him into an unwilling organ donor.

But Boyd wasn't told that no one gets out alive, that the town is a death sentence.

For there is no escape from *Inside the Perimeter*.

THE BOOK OF CANNIBALS
ISBN 13: 978-1-935458-52-4   ISBN 10: 1-935458-52-3
ARE YOU HUNGRY YET?

THE PLACE TO GO FOR ZOMBIE AND APOCALYPTIC FICTION

LIVING DEAD PRESS

WHERE THE DEAD WALK

www.livingdeadpress.com

www.ingramcontent.com/pod-product-compliance
Lightning Source LLC
Chambersburg PA
CBHW070951180726
48291CB00004B/1245